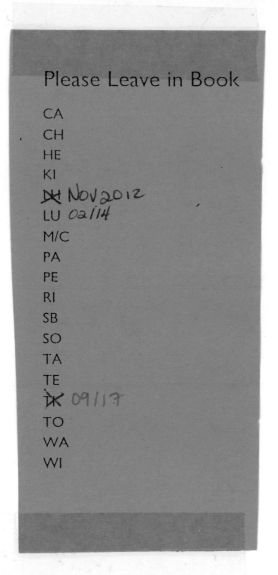

TEXAS BLOOD

**Center Point
Large Print**

**This Large Print Book carries the
Seal of Approval of N.A.V.H.**

HASCAL GILES

❖━❀━❖

TEXAS BLOOD

❖━❀━❖

CENTER POINT PUBLISHING
THORNDIKE, MAINE

This Center Point Large Print edition
is published in the year 2003 by arrangement with
Golden West Literary Agency.

The text of this Large Print edition is unabridged. In other
aspects, this book may vary from the original edition. Printed in
Thailand. Set in 16-point Times New Roman type by
Bill Coskrey and Gary Socquet.

ISBN 1-58547-334-0

Library of Congress Cataloging-in-Publication Data

Giles, Hascal.
    Texas blood / Hascal Giles.--Center Point large print ed.
        p. cm.
    ISBN 1-58547-334-0 (lib. bdg. : alk. paper)
      1. Texas--Fiction. 2. Large type books. I. Title.

PS3557.I3443T49 2003
813'.54--dc21

                                                    2003046041

CHAPTER ONE

◂═◉═▸

WATCHING THE ROCKS AND SAGE sweep by the open window of the stagecoach, Scott Rawley began to pick out landmarks that told him they were approaching the town of Blackwood, nearing home and a time when he would have to talk about things he had kept to himself for years.

His face was turned away from the interior of the coach and his gray Stetson was pulled low over his eyes to shield them from the dust. Even without looking, he could sense his father's anxiety. Frank Rawley, sitting stiffly erect a yard away, kept crossing and uncrossing his legs and drumming his fingers on the wood strip that ran along the back of the seat. Along the way, Scott had seen Frank take his gold watch from his pocket several times, glance at it, then rub his thumb over the embossed star on the leather fob before putting it away.

The coach rattled around a curve to bypass an upthrust cluster of sandstone and splashed through a break in the brush along Halfway Creek. Scott saw the town ahead of them. Blackwood's Main Street was comprised of a double line of buildings, mostly of wood that had been sun-baked to varying hues of grays and browns. Its drab appearance was enhanced here and there by a structure of white adobe or red brick.

A few minutes later, at half past two in the afternoon, the one o'clock stage came within sight of the Wells Fargo office in Blackwood. The passengers inside the Concord raised their voices in a halfhearted cheer. They were needling the driver, who had seen a man checking the clock at the last stop and bluntly informed him that he could count on reaching his destination two hours later than the posted arrival time.

Scott Rawley was less vocal than the others about the stage driver's indifference to time. Trickles of perspiration seeped from the tufts of crow-black hair that poked from his hatband and left damp trails on his sun-browned face. Sweat came easily on a day like this, but it was more profuse when a man's nerves were on edge.

He drew a deep breath and glanced obliquely at his father. Frank Rawley had moved to the end of the seat so he could look out the open window nearest the street. This was a day of triumph for Frank, the day he would reach a goal he had worked for years to attain. Scott had also looked forward to this day. He had plans of his own, and it would be easier for his father to accept them while his spirits were buoyed by a feeling of success.

During the many times he had thought about it, Scott had felt it would be easy on a day like this to break his ties with the Crowfoot Ranch, but now he was unsure. The words he had rehearsed in his mind a hundred times were going to sound offensive and ungrateful, and no matter how he expressed himself, Frank was going to be hurt and angry.

Scott sleeved the sweat from his forehead. There was no good time, he realized, to tell your father that you had no interest in the heritage he had expected to remain in the family for generations, and that you planned to ride away from it.

Frank Rawley's voice cut across his thoughts. "Got

here before anybody was expectin' us," he said. "Caught 'em by surprise."

The coach careened around the corner at Arlie's Blacksmith Shop and turned into Main Street as Frank spoke. Looking past his father, Scott saw people stop along the boardwalk and wheel about to rush toward the Wells Fargo office. He recognized most of them as the same townsfolk who made a ritual of meeting the weekly westbound stage to satisfy their curiosity about who was coming and going.

Frank had his arm thrust through the window, waving and smiling at old acquaintances. The driver, who had been pushing his double span of horses at breakneck speed for the last hour, slowed the teams to a walk. Frank drew his arm inside and leaned back with a sigh.

"Damn good to be home, son," he said.

Scott nodded, welcoming any distraction that would let him put aside his worrisome thoughts. He said, "Sure is. I think the driver lied to us. He told us we'd be two hours late so we'd be happy that it turned out to be only an hour and a half."

Frank Rawley laughed at Scott's suspicion. He shifted his rangy, thick-chested frame to a more comfortable position and Scott could see the relief in the ruddy, square-jawed face. Despite years of struggling to survive the unpredictable hazards of the Texas frontier, Frank had retained his cheerful nature. His laughter came from deep in that big chest and brought a sparkle to his pale blue eyes—eyes like Scott's, which could lose their mild expression in an instant and turn to frosted ice when faced with a challenge.

"Nah," Frank said. "That's old Gabe Walker up there on the catbird seat. He's so cantankerous he runs late most of the time just for the hell of it. I know his weakness, though. If you want to get the best of a man, work on his weaknesses. Gabe's a hard-drinkin' man. After I heard him tell the prospector how late we'd be, I promised him that quart of bourbon we brought back from Red Butte Junction if he'd get me to Blackwood before the bank closes."

Frank leaned closer to Scott. He tightened his grip on the small canvas bag that he had held on his lap or close by his side throughout the trip. Lowering his voice, he said, "Truth is, I'm a little skittish about packin' this bag of money twenty miles along the trail to the Crowfoot. I want to get it to the bank as soon as I can."

The serious expression in Frank's eyes faded. Chuckling, he nudged his son's shoulder. "Don't worry about losin' our good liquor. I'm goin' to keep your tongue dry until we get the new calf crop checked out."

Scott nodded and looked away, unable to share his father's good humor. He wanted to blurt out that he would not be around to hunt for calves, but decided against it. There would be time to talk on their way home.

Only two other men had bought tickets to Blackwood. They were on the forward seat opposite Scott and his father. As the coach neared its final stop, they began to stir and stretch their arms.

One of them was a long-haired old man whose face and body were trail-worn. The hawkish face beneath his broken-brimmed black hat was creased by time and

8

weather, but his eyes shone with energy. His name was Zeke Bowman, and he had talked almost without pause during the journey. Most of his conversation had been directed at the man next to him, who responded with bored grunts and an occasional nod. From listening to them, Scott learned that Bowman was a prospector who was working his way toward the Arizona goldfields. He had paid little attention to Bowman, but his interest was aroused when the prospector voiced doubts about his companion's identity.

Studying the face of the man beside him, the prospector said skeptically, "Say your name's George Pratt, eh? Well, maybe you are and maybe you ain't, and it don't make no never-mind to me. I'd bet a full poke, though, that you ain't no whiskey drummer like you say. I've seen them buggers. Pale as milk gravy, they are, paunchy mostly, with hands like a woman. It don't strike me that a man with a face burnt by sun and wind, hard and closemouthed like you, has spent much time sittin' around saloons makin' trade talk. No, by gum, that don't fit. But it don't make no never-mind to nobody but you, now, does it?"

George Pratt tugged at his narrow-brimmed townsman's hat, squared wide shoulders inside his salt-and-pepper suit, and turned his dark eyes on the prospector's face. Anger deepened the color of Pratt's face for a moment. He managed a thin grin and tapped the heel of one high-topped shoe against the hard leather case, which he had been using as a footrest. "I could show you some of my samples, old-timer, but you'd probably want to taste them. Instead, I'll make you a bargain: You mind your business and I'll mind mine."

Zeke Bowman cackled loudly, slapped dust from the knees of his Levi's, and said, "That's tellin' me, I reckon. Yessir, that's tellin' me."

Scott smiled, relieved that a potentially tense moment had ended without rancor. George Pratt's occupation was of no concern to Scott, but he shared the prospector's suspicions.

There had been other passengers along the way, some departing and some boarding at each stop. Pratt and Bowman had boarded the stage at Sagemore this morning, and after introducing themselves, Scott and his father had spoken only a few words to the two men.

Aside from a mild curiosity about the whiskey drummer, Scott had no interest in them, and they offered no farewells as the trip ended. George Pratt stepped out of the coach first. He paused to lend a hand to the prospector as the old man stumbled to the ground, then went to the back of the coach and lifted a valise from the boot. He carried the two bags down the street toward the Denver House Hotel.

Frank Rawley appeared to be in no hurry to leave. Scott leaned back beside him, determined not to think about the confrontation that was sure to come before the day ended. He smiled and yanked at the tail of his father's hide vest. "I thought you gave our bourbon to that schoolmarm you had in your room the last two nights. I sure hope she tells her students to do as she says and not as she does."

"By damn!" Frank Rawley groaned. "I must've plumb forgot to leave that bottle. Hell, I figured I'd never see her again, so I decided I'd just keep my liquor."

His face sobered. "I never once fooled around with another woman while your mother was alive. I want you to know that. In my young days I was a rounder, but not lately. I guess I had to prove that this old cow nurse still has some fire left in his boiler after forty-seven long years. Aw, hell, son, you're old enough to know a man has these urges, and when they come on him he's—"

"Don't start explaining," Scott cut in. "I know you loved Ma, but she died five years ago. It's time you started living like a bachelor again. You've treated me better than I deserve, and you've worked your butt off to make the Crowfoot grow. I wish I was the kind of son who—"

"Oh, Lord," Frank Rawley growled. "If you're goin' to get mushy on me, I'm bound to throw up."

He sank against the back seat cushion with the calmness of a man who had put a bad time behind him. Despite Frank's apparent happiness, fatigue had deepened the lines across his forehead and around his eyes. It had taken them fifteen days to drive their herd to the railhead at Red Butte Junction. After selling the cattle, they remained there four days to rest and enjoy the pleasures of the town's saloons, poker palaces, and dance halls. The last two had been spent bouncing over the rough stage trails that brought them back to Blackwood.

Heat waves danced above the trampled dust of the street like transparent fingers waving at the blistering sun, and the air inside the coach was oppressive. Frank Rawley mopped his face with a bandanna and stuffed it back in his pocket. He might have wanted to sit quietly

11

and savor this moment with his son, but there was no time for that. The Pioneer Bank would close in less than half an hour.

"I've got to get movin'," Frank said presently. "It's a good thing we sold our horses along with the herd, 'cause I don't think I'd be able to walk if I'd been sittin' a saddle this long. I've got calluses on my rear from pushin' them cattle seventy miles through brush and dust. Just think how it'd be if the Missouri Pacific hadn't run a branch line into Red Butte. We'd be drivin' to Ellsworth or Kansas City, and grow old before we got there."

He tucked the money bag under one arm and reached for his Stetson, which hung on a peg beside the window. Frank shook the money bag proudly. "One hundred thirty-seven head at thirty bucks apiece. After the broker's fee, we kept over thirty-seven hundred. That's not bad for two hardscrabble ranchers like us."

He ducked his head to disembark, then looked back at Scott. "I'll take care of that note at the bank first, pay for the hay we had to buy from Huff's Livery last winter, and settle our bill at Grange's. Maybe we can spare enough to buy us a couple pairs of Levi's apiece before we head home. We'll talk about it when I get back. If I don't quit jawin', Otis Potter will draw the blinds and lock the door on me."

Scott stepped down on the boardwalk behind his father, grinning as a small knot of people surged out from the wooden awning that sheltered the front of the Wells Fargo office. Men were calling out Frank Rawley's name, shaking his hand and slapping his shoulders. Someone said, "It's good to have you home, friend," and another yelled, "I hope you got rich in Red Butte, Frank. You owe me at least a dozen drinks!"

Scott heard his father's booming laugh above the din of voices as Frank moved through the crowd. Gabe Walker, the burly watery-eyed driver, was leaning against a wheel of the coach. He stepped forward and grabbed Scott's sleeve.

"Everybody likes old Frank, don't they?" he said, rubbing a thick palm across his lips.

"Not everybody," Scott said softly.

At the rear of the crowd he had spotted John Tripp standing beside the station's doorway, his curl-brimmed black hat pushed back to reveal the glimmer of his iron-gray hair. Close by his side, as always, was Cal Baylor, ramrod of Tripp's Bar 40 Ranch. They were watching the activity around Frank Rawley, but they were not taking part in it, and Scott wondered why they were there.

This could not be a happy day for John Tripp. The land Frank Rawley expected to gain title to today lay between Tripp's Bar 40 and Frank Rawley's Crowfoot. Like many Texas ranchers, John Tripp had used the public lands to graze Bar 40 cattle for years. He regarded the stretch of open range that lay between the two ranches as his own. He was infuriated when he learned Frank had bought it, and Scott remembered well the day Tripp rode to the Crowfoot and vowed to turn Frank's ambitions into failure.

For a brief interval, Tripp's eyes met Scott's glance. The Bar 40 owner drew his chin in close to his brocaded vest, smiled blandly, then nudged Cal Baylor with his elbow, and the two of them walked away.

"No," Scott said, frowning. "Not everybody likes old Frank."

Gabe Walker looked puzzled by Scott's grim tone, but his mind was on something else. He said, "Frank looks like he's pretty busy. I was wonderin' if you know about that little somethin' we talked about this mornin'?"

Scott pointed to the railed baggage rack atop the stagecoach. "Yeah, I know. We've got saddles, bridles, and two bedrolls up there. You can leave them inside the station. We'll pick them up later. Pa's bedroll is the one with the yellow slicker on the outside. If you'll dig into it, you'll find a bottle rolled up in his blankets. You can help yourself if you'll put everything back the way it was."

"Sure, sure," Gabe Walker said. "I'll do that, and I'm obliged to you."

As Scott turned to look for his father, someone grabbed him from behind with such force that he stumbled and almost lost his balance. Before he looked around, he caught a faint odor of jasmine and knew the soft hands grasping his shoulders belonged to Della Grange.

"Scott Rawley!" she squealed, pulling him around to face her. "It's a good thing you're back. There's a dance at Staley's tomorrow night, and you've got to take me. You know he has it every spring, but I was sure I'd end up going with some ugly old man when you left on that trail drive."

Scott started to reply, but Della stepped aside as she caught sight of Frank Rawley, who was trying to slip away from the crowd. Frank saw her at the same time and rushed toward her. He opened his arms, the money bag dangling from one hand, and Della rushed into them. He gave her a hug, kissed her on the forehead, and held her close for a moment.

They came back toward Scott, Della's violet eyes sparkling as she gazed at Frank and began asking questions about the trail drive. She looked like a feisty, talkative schoolgirl at the side of the husky rancher.

Bob Grange's General Store, where Della helped her father with his paperwork, was next door to the Wells Fargo office. Scott guessed that Della had been watching through the window for the arrival of the stagecoach. He saw her father, a chubby, round-faced man with a glistening bald head, standing in the store's doorway, laughing at Della's antics.

"Now here's the handsomest man on the Blackwood range," Della said while she clung to Frank Rawley's arm and led him toward Scott. Tossing her hair, she said, "If you don't start paying more attention to me, Scott, I'm going to marry Frank and become your evil stepmother."

Frank winked at Scott. He cupped his hand under Della's chin and said, "Now don't you start makin' promises you're not ready to back up, 'cause I might take you up on 'em."

Touching Della's elbow and guiding her closer to Scott, Frank glanced over his shoulder toward the Pioneer Bank at the far end of the street. He said, "Scott, why don't you take Della down to the Denver House and treat her to some coffee and apple pie. I'll meet you there as soon as I've finished my business. I want to hear some more about how Della's goin' to throw you over and take up with me."

"Now don't you go grabbing Miss Emma in places you're not supposed to touch," Della teased.

Miss Emma Doss was the bank's seventy-year-old book-keeper, a thin, pinch-faced spinster with a sour disposition. Frank lifted his chin and said, "Miss Emma would pay me to grab her where I ain't supposed to grab."

Those were the last words Scott Rawley ever heard his father speak.

Frank showed Della a devilish smile and headed down the street, pausing to shout a greeting to a passing horseman.

As they started walking in the opposite direction, toward the dining room at the Denver House Hotel, Della twisted her head for another look at Frank. "Your pa is some kind of a special man! You look enough like him to be his twin, but you don't have his ways."

"I know," Scott said. "I've got better manners, and I don't snore as loud. And we sure do resemble. He's six feet, I'm six four. He's two hundred pounds, I'm two twenty. His hair is gray and mine's black. He's—"

Della jabbed him with her elbow. "Oh, shut up! You know what I mean. Your eyes, the shape of your face . . . things like that."

Scott looked down at her and laughed, admiring the creamy tan of her skin and the tantalizing curve of her lips.

Della was the prettiest girl in town, and she liked to be

seen in the company of men. Her striking figure, clad in a close-fitting yellow blouse and smooth blue denim skirt, was a refreshing splash of color against the weathered storefronts along Main Street. She had a way of holding on to Scott so that some part of her body was always touching him, and he felt the rhythmic bobbing of her breast as she slipped her arm beneath his and hugged it close to her.

Scott was too busy listening to Della to talk much. She pranced along at his side, talking excitedly about the dress she was going to wear to the dance at Staley's, and waving now and then to passersby. Finally, Scott slowed his steps. He chewed at the edge of his lower lip, feeling again the knot of dread in his stomach. He said, "I won't be here for the dance. First thing in the morning I'm pulling out for—"

He was not sure Della heard him. The roar of gunfire reverberated above the street noises, startling him. Scott stopped talking. Close behind the echo of the shot he heard the sound of glass breaking somewhere.

Surprised voices rose in a hum of excitement around him, and Scott was aware of hurried feet moving along the street. The few people in town were leaving the boardwalks, scurrying to the middle of the dusty thoroughfare, shouting and pointing. Scott whirled to look back the way they had come. Fear grabbed at his lungs, tightening his breath. Something bad was happening at the Pioneer Bank and Frank Rawley was in the middle of it.

His mind did not want to accept the horror of the sight that unfolded before him. The bank was a hundred yards away, a two-story brick building with an arched entrance and two barred windows facing Main Street. Eyes squinted, his heart pounding, Scott watched the activity up the street. He watched and did not move. Shock stunned him, numbed his mind, and he froze in his tracks.

He saw two masked men come out of the bank and run into the sunlit street. Almost at the same instant, a rider pounded into sight from the weed-grown alley which separated the bank from the small adobe building that housed Doc Eversole's office and living quarters. The rider was leading two saddled horses.

Frank had crossed over from the other boardwalk and was only about twenty feet from the bank. His path brought him almost face-to-face with the masked men. Frank knew instantly what was happening. The money bag that had been tucked under his arm fell to the ground as he stopped abruptly. His hand slapped at his right thigh, but the holster that carried his Peacemaker Colt was not there. It was in his bedroll at the Wells Fargo office.

The man nearest Frank was lean and long-legged, with solid shoulders and narrow hips. He wore a flat-crowned pearl-gray Stetson and a black wool vest over a checked shirt. A yellow bandanna covered most of his face, but Scott could see a straight, pointed nose and a blocky chin below the mask.

Sunlight flashed on a mop of silvery hair at the back of his head as the man swung his glance from side to side. He was the one who gave the orders. When the rider with the spare horses slowed to allow the others to grab for their saddles, the man in the pearl-gray hat yelled, "Hold it! I think we've got a depositor here."

The rider who held the spare horses was tall and lithe, handling his spirited mustang with ease and grace. He appeared upset and annoyed by the delay in getting away. He clutched all the reins in one hand and waved the other frantically. The mask ballooned over his mouth, and he appeared to be yelling objections. Behind him, the other robber stood spread-legged in front of the bank door, holding his gun against his hip while he swiveled his head to watch the street. He was not as tall as the other two, but his body looked more compact and muscular.

The man in the pearl-gray hat swung his gun toward the figure in the street. He took deliberate aim with the six-gun and fired. Frank's blue shirt rippled against his chest, and he rocked back on his heels. Blood gushed from his mouth and splattered on the street. He stayed on his feet, swaying, his hand still searching for his gun.

Fire and smoke flashed from the masked man's weapon as it exploded again. Frank Rawley pitched forward on his face. His legs twitched in the dust. His outstretched fingers clawed the ground near the money bag, then he rolled over on his back and lay still.

CHAPTER TWO

THE GUNMAN ran to Frank Rawley's side. He bent over the still form briefly, then scooped the money bag from the ground and scurried back to the horse one of the men was holding for him. He leaped into the saddle, shouted a command to the others, and the three of them sent their horses galloping toward the open prairie.

Scott did not realize he was so near the town jail until Sheriff Wade Bandy charged onto the boardwalk twenty feet away, grasping a Winchester in his hands. The sheriff cursed and shouted, "Hell's bells! They've robbed the bank!"

A thousand feet beyond the last of Blackwood's sun-dried buildings a cloud of dust marked the flight of the robbers. The distance was too great for an accurate shot, but Wade Bandy tried. He fired once, saw it was useless, and dropped the rifle on the boardwalk. He swore under his breath and ran up the street toward the Pioneer Bank.

The episode at the bank had lasted less than five minutes. Scott Rawley remained motionless. The warmth of Della Grange's body revived his senses. She buried her face in his chest and wept uncontrollably. Between sobs she screamed, "They've killed him! They've killed Frank. . . ."

Scott shuddered. He pushed Della's hands away and looked around for a horse. He saw three or four at the hitching rail in front of the Texas Star Saloon across the street. He took a step toward the saloon, then turned and looked toward the prairie. The robbers were out of sight, blocked from view by the fringe of cottonwoods that marked the meandering course of Halfway Creek.

His shoulders sagged. By the time he could find a horse and get started, the robbers would be too far away to be overtaken. Della Grange put her hand on his arm and said, "Let's hurry. Maybe we can still help Frank."

A lump swelled in Scott's throat. "I think he's dead, Della. He fell like a dead man."

Scott started up the street with Della at his side. He tried to hurry, but grief deadened his muscles and his boot heels dragged in the dust as he moved toward the spot where Frank Rawley had fallen. Della's father came up beside them, mumbled words of sympathy, then grasped his daughter's shoulders and led her away. Scott barely noticed Bob Grange. Tears stung his eyes, and he blinked to clear his vision.

The sheriff was already near the front of the bank. Scott saw Wade Bandy take a handkerchief from his pocket and kneel beside Frank's body. He could tell by the lawman's movements that he was wiping the blood from Frank's face and closing his eyelids. The sheriff retrieved Frank's hat, placed it over the rancher's face, then went inside the bank.

People began to stream out of the saloons and small shops along the street. Farther on, Scott saw three women and a flock of children hurrying toward the bank, coming from the intersection of Oxbow Street, which was Blackwood's principal residential area.

Ignoring the crowd, he quickened his pace. Some of them recognized Scott and slowed to allow him to go ahead of them.

Shoulders bent, his sky-blue eyes moist, he stared at his father's lifeless body. Dropping to his knees, he lifted the hat from Frank's face, hesitated a few seconds, and replaced it. The front of his father's shirt was wet with blood. Two holes about three inches apart marked the path of the slugs that had penetrated Frank's chest.

When he stood up, the muscles in his arms and legs quivered, and he stiffened his back in an attempt to steady his nerves. Instinctively, he ran his hand over the bone-handled Colt .45 on his thigh, longing for a chance to use it. Before they boarded the stagecoach in Red Butte Junction, Frank had said, "One gun between us ought to be enough, since Texas is gettin' so damned civilized. I don't want that heavy old Peacemaker chafin' me, so I'm packin' it away with my gear."

Frank had spent six years with the Texas Rangers, earning a reputation with his gun. Even with the odds against him, he might have been able to kill the outlaws, or at least drive them away, if his Peacemaker had been with him.

Raising his glance, Scott saw Wade Bandy come out of the bank and walk toward him. The sheriff stopped beside him and said, "That hellion could see Frank didn't have a gun, and he didn't even ask him to raise his hands . . . just shot him down. That's cold-blooded murder!"

Scott looked again at his father's body, sensing that something was amiss. He saw what it was and swore softly. "The killer took Pa's watch."

"Damned greedy bastard!" Wade Bandy rubbed his hand across his forehead. "I'm sorry as hell about this. That bag Frank was carryin' . . . Did he have money in it?"

Scott nodded. "It was our cattle money . . . over three thousand dollars. I tried to get him to take a bank draft, but Frank wanted the money in his hand, wanted greenbacks so he'd know it was good."

"Damn shame," Bandy grunted. "One of 'em was sure a kill-crazy sonofabitch."

Wagon wheels crunched in the dirt behind them. Scott looked around and saw the black-curtained hearse from Grove's Mortuary coming to a stop a few feet away, the matched team of horses pawing the dust and blowing through their nostrils.

Asa Grove, fat, sweaty, and wheezing as he breathed, climbed down from the seat of the glistening boxlike wagon. He stood with his legs spread apart, a white linen duster flapping around his pear-shaped stomach while he surveyed the crowd that had formed a hushed circle around Scott. The undertaker raised his hand to be sure they saw him, then leaned against the side of the hearse. Looking past him, Scott noticed the jagged hole in one of the bank's windows and recalled hearing the sound of falling glass.

He motioned for the undertaker to join him and the sheriff, then turned to look at his father again. His hands shaking, he reached into the hip pocket of his Levi's for the notebook he had used for tally sheets when they counted the Crowfoot cattle for the broker in Red Butte Junction. He squatted beside Frank Rawley's body and ran his forefinger over the streaks on the flannel shirt. Grimacing, he wiped his finger across one of the white pages in the tally book and stared at the rusty red stain left on the paper.

Wade Bandy tapped him on the shoulder. "What're you up to? What's the idee of smearin' Frank's blood on things?"

"Just a reminder," Scott said. "Something to remind

me of what I've got to do. When I've settled with Pa's killer, I'll burn the paper."

The sheriff's lips tightened. He read the fury in Scott's face, started to say something, then changed his mind. He looked back at the Pioneer Bank and swung his gaze over the people milling in the street.

"A lot of folks are goin' to fret about this . . . wonder how safe their money is from now on," he said. "Nobody inside got hurt, but Otis Potter is sittin' in there with his mouth hangin' open like a frog catchin' flies. He's still too shook up to make sense, but Miss Emma says it looks like the robbers got a little over eight hundred dollars. One of them fired a shot at her when she threw an inkwell at them as they was leavin'. The slug missed her and broke the window."

"Eight hundred," Scott mused bitterly. "We're the big losers . . . two or three years of work and all the money we had. I've got to find those men. I want them dead and I want our money back."

The sheriff put his hand on Scott's arm. The firmness of his grasp indicated both sympathy and disapproval. "Now, look here, son. I know you're good with a gun. I recall that run-in at the livery stable a while back, but word of this mess will spread all over the county. Folks elected me to uphold the law. They'll be lookin' to me to find the robbers. I won't have you takin' over my job. You look after your pa's ranch, and I'll look after the scum who killed him."

"Maybe you will, maybe you won't," Scott said. His sky-blue eyes were like frosted ice as anger began to overcome his shock. He put his face close to Wade

Bandy's hat brim and said grimly, "If you find him, you can kill him. If I find him, I'll kill him."

The sheriff lifted a hand to protest further, but Scott turned away to talk with Asa Grove.

The undertaker had his hands shoved into the pockets of his duster. His face wore a sober, sad expression. He said, "We've lost a good man. Me 'n Frank go back a ways. Sometimes when he was in town he'd come by my place just to pass the time of day . . . ask about my family and things like that. Not many people visit with undertakers, you know. Folks don't feel at ease. Makes 'em think of death. Frank didn't care. He'd tell stories and laugh and go on, but, hell, Frank liked everybody."

"I don't," Scott said. He did not mean to prolong the conversation, but he was too angry to care about hiding his feelings. "There's a lot about this place I don't like."

Asa Grove rocked on his heels, his breath wheezing. He gave Scott a solemn stare and said, "Frank knew that about you, and it worried him. He told me you was restless and moody, looking for something better than range country can offer. You'll learn there ain't anything better. You're Texas born, got Frank's Texas blood in your veins, and it'll tie you to the land one day. Like my pa always told me—and I'll bet Frank's told you the same: You get back from your roots what you put in. Maybe you ain't put enough in. You ought—"

"Let's get Pa out of the dirt," Scott cut in impatiently. "I'll go with you to your place and talk about the funeral."

The undertaker shook his head. "Maybe it'd be best if

you drop by in the morning. I'll handle everything. I know what Frank wanted. We talked about it."

Scott looked at the ground and breathed a nervous sigh. "I guess that's all right, but I want a lined coffin— not one of those twenty-dollar pine boxes. Frank held back a hundred and twenty-five dollars for expenses— our hotel bill, stage fare, and something to eat on. He gave me twenty and put what was left in his money belt. There's probably sixty-five . . . seventy dollars on him. Take that for the funeral."

Asa Grove put his hands in the duster's pockets and flapped it indignantly. "Nobody's ever treated me like Frank, and I won't take money for anything I can do for him now."

"If you knew Frank so well," Scott said, "you'd know he wouldn't want a free funeral."

The undertaker dropped his chin to his chest, his eyes half closed. "I guess I'll take the money," he murmured. "Come by in the morning. We ought to get Frank buried early. It's powerful hot for this time of year."

Scott nodded and started up the street. Wade Bandy came up beside him and said, "If you're stayin' in town, we ought to get together later."

"I need to ride on to the Crowfoot and tell our hired hand about Pa. Hobe Calder's going to be hard to handle. He and Pa were mighty close."

Wade Bandy studied the grim expression on Scott's face and appeared unsure of what he wanted to say. He ran his tongue along the bristles of his brush mustache. "I'll want to talk with you after the funeral, then."

"I figured," Scott said, and he walked slowly down the

street toward the livery stable.

The sun was a pale yellow ball hovering on the brink of the western horizon when Scott Rawley came within sight of the Crowfoot Ranch. He stopped his horse on the crest of a bald knoll, where he had a panoramic view of the rolling grasslands that provided graze for Crowfoot cattle.

From this point he could look down on the gabled roof of the ranch house, built of post-oak logs that Frank had scoured the countryside to locate, in a land where cottonwood and cedar were more plentiful. Beyond the barn, spaced an acre apart, were other outbuildings—a hip-roofed barn, tool house, harness room, wagon shed, and bunkhouse. Planning for future growth, Frank had built the bunkhouse to accommodate a crew of six, but its only occupant was Hobe Calder.

In one of the corrals, Scott saw his bay and Frank's line-backed dun romping around the enclosure. They had taken a six-horse remuda on the cattle drive but had left their personal mounts at home. It made little difference now, Scott thought sadly, because Frank would never ride the dun again.

The Crowfoot lay in rolling country, dotted here and there by low mesas and buttes. It was a good place to raise cattle. Rock-ribbed ridges and mound-shaped hills ringed numerous expanses of flat grazing land in the valleys and sheltered basins.

The area to the south, where shadows were beginning to draw grotesque patterns along the scars of a landscape chopped apart by wriggling arroyos and dry washes, held little interest for him. He looked westward, centering his attention on the line of trees that marked the course of Grizzly Creek as it cut a swath across an undulating plain. Before Frank had contracted to buy the new acreage, the creek had marked the boundary of the Crowfoot graze. If Frank had lived to complete the transaction at the bank, the Crowfoot would have extended to the far-off line of purple hills that marked the legal boundary line between John Tripp's Bar 40 and the Rawley ranch.

While he rested, Scott's thoughts tracked back to a day four years ago when he had returned home after a long absence. The boy who had ridden away three years earlier came home as a man, back from river country, back from the Big Muddy with stories to tell of his duties on the side-wheeler *Nebraska Queen*, which hauled freight up the Missouri River from St. Louis to Fort Benton and ports in between.

He was home for a visit while the Missouri was blocked by ice and the riverboats were sitting high and dry on their skids. He had found life on the treacherous river far more exciting and challenging than the tedium of range work, and he meant to return to it.

His visit turned into a stay of four years, but his desire to return to the river never left him. Only a sense of loyalty, together with Frank Rawley's need for help in paying his debts, had kept Scott on the Crowfoot. Frank was pleased to have his son with him, and Scott was reluctant to reveal his plans until the time was right, but it had always been his intention to go back to the river.

On that day long ago, he had stopped at this same spot,

riding a rented horse then as now. He had anticipated a joyous reunion with his parents, but it had turned out to be a day as sad as this one. He had learned that his mother was dead, dying with only memories of a seventeen-year-old boy who had ridden away to learn about the world—a boy seeking adventures and triumphs that were unknown in cattle country. Somewhere along the many trails he had ridden, there was a letter still trying to find its way to him with the news of her death.

Scott still felt guilty because he had not been with her when she died. The picture he carried in his mind was of a trim, soft-spoken woman whose gray eyes were filled with tears while she pleaded with him not to leave her.

Frank had tried to comfort her, saying, "Let him go, Dora. I know his feelin's . . . that yen to go over the next hill and see what's there. He'll be all right. He'll sow a few wild oats and be back. He's pretty much a man now, and Billy Clyde'll look after him."

Frank liked Billy Clyde Marcum. Their paths had crossed at Huff's Livery one day, when Billy Clyde was passing through in search of a riding job. Bad weather and a late spring had thrown the Crowfoot behind in its work, and Frank needed an extra hand to get back on schedule. He hired Billy Clyde with the understanding that the job would last only until the roundup was completed.

Within a week Billy Clyde had become Scott's best friend, a friendship he thought would last forever. Scott admired everything about Billy Clyde—his carefully trimmed black beard, flashing white teeth, his loose-limbed cocky walk, and the way he worked. Even Hobe

Calder, a man usually suspicious of strangers, was impressed by the way Billy Clyde sat a horse and threw a rope, working long hours without any complaint. He seemed to be immune to both fatigue and pain. When brush ripped his face or a rope burned his palms, Billy Clyde either laughed or cursed, and stuck to his job.

At the time, Billy Clyde was twenty-one years old, but he had been on his own since he was twelve, and his experience went far beyond his years. In the evenings, he and Scott sat on the bench beside the well, and Billy Clyde talked. Scott drank in every word, fascinated by tales of long cattle drives, time spent in rowdy mining camps, fights with Mexican bandits, and nights with pretty women. In his boyish eyes, Billy Clyde Marcum was a model of the man Scott wanted to be.

"Before I'm old, I'm gonna go everywhere, do everything, and jump every woman I can," Billy Clyde told him. "If I was to tie myself down in the same place for months on end, I'd die before I hit thirty."

Scott said, "I know what you mean. If you've got a ranch, you've got chores and worries, chores and worries. Every day it's the same thing. I feel real tied down. I've been asking Pa to take us on a trip to St. Louis or Denver or someplace like that. He says we can't afford it. Pa wants land. Every cent he gets his hand on goes to pay for land."

The day before Billy Clyde's work at the Crowfoot ended he revealed his next venture. He knew of a basin north of the Trinity River, which was full of wild mustangs. Two men could round up a good-sized herd, Billy Clyde declared, and sell them to the army post at Fort

Clear for a sizeable sum.

"I could be your partner," Scott said, his face flushed with excitement. "I'm good with horses."

"You are that," Billy Clyde agreed. "You're plumb natural at most anything you do, 'specially with a gun. I watched you when Frank was pitching up them rocks for you to draw and shoot at. You're just a young'un, but you'll do fine as a partner. We'll get on well together."

When Billy Clyde left the next day, Scott went with him, carrying the memory of his mother's kiss on his cheek and his father's lingering handshake. His partnership with the carefree cowboy was the worst decision Scott ever made, but some good came from it. Eventually, it led him to St. Louis and an interesting life on the Missouri River.

While he rested on the ridge, thinking about the past and the violent death of his father a few hours ago, Scott saw a horseman come out of a coulee and ride toward the corrals. It was Hobe Calder, coming in from the range after a day's work.

He remained on the knoll a long time, dreading to go farther. He could not put it off forever, so he lifted the reins and started the horse down the slope toward home. The Crowfoot had never seemed the same after his mother died, and now the ranch would hold even less appeal for him. His only companion would be a fatherly hard-nosed hired hand who loved the Crowfoot Ranch as if it were his own.

Scott was afraid his time with Hobe Calder would not be pleasant. When the funeral was over, Hobe would expect him to walk in his father's footsteps, to assume the task of building the Crowfoot into the kind of ranch Frank Rawley had wanted it to be. Hobe's longtime friendship might turn to hate when he learned that Scott intended to find his future on the riverboats of the Missouri—not on the Texas range.

CHAPTER THREE

B Y THE TIME Scott reached the ranch yard, Hobe Calder had freed his horse and draped his saddle across the top rail of the corral. He had seen Scott coming and waited there, a towering hulk of a man in sweat-soaked clothes with a smile on his face.

"Hallelujah! You're home!" Hobe shouted in his rumbling bass voice.

He kept talking as Scott handed him the horse's reins and stepped to the ground. "I've been out there in the manzanita thickets most of the day lookin' for calves. Found an old cow a while ago tryin' to have a calf that got turned around wrong. Took me more'n an hour to help her birth it, tuggin' and twistin' at that little baby 'til my arms wore out. He made it out alive, though."

Hobe was seldom quiet and Scott usually enjoyed his stories, but today only his own grief seemed important.

"Another thing," Hobe said as he unloaded the bedroll that Scott had picked up at the Wells Fargo office before he left town. "I was over past the creek this mornin', and there's Bar 40 cattle runnin' all over the place. I reckon John Tripp ain't goin' to give up until Frank waves the final papers in front of his face. If it was me—"

Leaving the thought unfinished, Hobe looked back

along the trail to the ridge where Scott had rested. "Where's Frank?" he asked. "Is he stayin' over in town?"

"No," Scott said soberly. "Pa's not coming home. He's dead. Three hardcases were in the midst of robbing the bank when Pa got there to pay off his debt. They killed him and took our cattle money."

Hobe Calder stepped away from the horse and dropped his hands to his sides. He cocked his head and searched Scott's face, the hint of a grin still on his lips. "Aw, c'mon. Don't josh me. What's Frank up to?"

"He's dead, Hobe . . . gunned down for no reason. He didn't have his gun on him. We'll have the funeral tomorrow."

Moisture glistened in Hobe Calder's dark eyes. He stared solemnly at Scott for a minute, then said, "I'll take care of your horse."

"I'll do it," Scott said.

Hobe grabbed the horse's bridle. "I said I'd do it." His voice softened and he said, "Why don't you wait for me at the well? I'll bring your bedroll over there."

Scott walked across the yard and sat down on the pole bench near the well. During his childhood he had spent many hours at this spot beneath the shade of their lone pin-oak, whittling shapes from cedar sticks and, later, listening to the tales of Billy Clyde Marcum's wanderings.

A few minutes later Hobe Calder came back with the tarp-covered pack resting on one brawny shoulder. He dumped the bedroll at the end of the bench but did not sit down. He turned half away from Scott and looked toward the Bar 40 boundary. There was no breeze, but

Scott could smell the odor of sweat and cattle droppings from Hobe's clothes.

"Did Frank die easy?"

"I don't know. I was pretty far away. The man who killed him shot him twice. Maybe Pa didn't feel the second one."

"Uh-huh," Hobe grunted, and sat down.

He took off his black Stetson and stared idly at the inside of it. He wore his hat Montana-style, where the cold-weather riders favored a tall crown to conserve body heat. Hobe's scalp was hairless. Years ago, when his hairline retreated to a fringe, Hobe had taken it all off with a straight razor and had kept it that way.

Hobe rested briefly and rose again. "How're we goin' to pay for the new graze?"

Scott's eyes narrowed. He said, "I don't give a damn about that. I'm not staying here."

"What?" Hobe's voice was a surprised growl.

"I'm sick of hearing about land," Scott said. "Maybe I'll sell what we've got to the Bar 40, or leave you here to run the ranch, or whatever. I don't want to talk about it right now, but I'm going back to the river as soon as I can."

"The hell you say!" Without warning, Hobe's meaty right hand cuffed Scott on the side of the jaw. It was a hard blow, powered by two hundred fifty pounds of muscle and sinew. Scott fell over on his side. Bells clanged in his ears and colored lights flashed in his head.

He caught himself on one elbow. His arm wobbled, but he managed to push himself to a sitting position. He shook his head to clear it, then bounced to his feet, fists knotted and poised to strike.

Hobe Calder stared at him, his arms at his sides and his breath hissing through his nose. "Damn ungrateful snivelin' pup, that's what you are!"

With any other man, Scott would have already landed his first blow. His body was as tense as a drawn bowstring while he fought to control his anger. He backed away and sat down on the bench.

He looked at Hobe Calder from the shadow of his hat brim. "Don't ever do that again. You've been like a second father and I'd hate to hurt you, but I will. I won't stand for being manhandled by anybody."

Hobe Calder said nothing. He glared at Scott for a few seconds, spat on the ground, and walked toward the corral. He kept his back to Scott, his arms resting on the top of the fence while he stared into the distance.

Scott stayed on the bench. His anger died, and he felt sick and weak. He leaned forward, braced his elbows on his knees, and sat with his head cupped in his hands. After a while, Hobe Calder came back and stood in front of him.

"I'm sorry I popped my cork," Hobe said, "but it sounds like you don't have much respect for Frank. That rankles me. He's been buildin' this place for you, lookin' to the time he'd be sittin' in a rockin' chair with grandkids playin' around him while you raised good beef cattle. Frank's layin' dead, and you act like all he's done don't amount to more'n a pile of horse manure."

Hobe's deep voice crackled with anger. He turned as if to leave, then faced Scott again, his hands on his hips. "I hope you didn't tell Frank you was leavin' before he died. It would have broke his heart."

"I didn't," Scott said. "I was goin' to tell him on the way home. Pa was goin' to have what he wanted if he'd got to the bank—twenty thousand acres of land. I figured it'd be a good time to leave, and I haven't changed my mind. Cattle and land was Pa's wants, not mine."

"Uh-huh," Hobe grunted. "You're about like one of them deserters from the Army, and they shoot them if they can find a good excuse. In my book, you're not much of a man."

Hobe's tirade was beginning to grate on Scott's nerves. He leaned back, spread his arms along the top edge of the bench, and looked up at the big man. "Pa's not the only one who made sacrifices around here. I used to go to school with my butt hanging out through ragged britches and my feet scooping up snow through the holes in my shoes. The other kids laughed at me or felt sorry for me, and I didn't like it either way. Christmas was as dull as any other day around here, and I never got a birthday gift in my life. I came home from the Missouri with a few good clothes, but now I'm back to patched Levi's and ragged shirts. That's what owning land has got me."

"Tough deal," Hobe said sarcastically. "You need to get your head straight, son. If you're goin' to live in Texas, you've either got land or you've got nothin'. That's what brought the settlers out here to begin with, but gettin' it and holdin' it don't come easy."

"I don't plan to live in Texas," Scott said.

"So you said. Are you figurin' on workin' toward bein' a river pilot when you get back to St. Louis?"

Scott shook his head. "No. I'm just a crewman—

loading freight, firing the boiler sometimes, and keeping a lookout for sandbars and shoals when the water's low. The river's like something alive, changing all the time, daring you to tackle it. It gives me a good feeling to be there, and the work's worth doing. We haul cookstoves, lumber, seed grain, and even horses and mules for new-comers who're starting a new life in places as far north as Dakota Territory. It's fun—not like sitting on a stretch of grass worrying about droughts, hookworms, cattle prices, and debts you can't pay."

Hobe Calder rolled his tongue against his cheeks and cleared his throat as if he had a bad taste in his mouth. The bench creaked under his weight as he sat down beside Scott.

"I didn't figure you was aimin' at a pilot's job," he said dryly. "You'd have the whole load on your back—makin' sure the boat, the crew, and the cargo was in safe waters. Uh-huh, a man couldn't rest real easy thinkin' about that. There was a time when I didn't care about no kind of job that wasn't more fun than work."

He paused, and Scott hoped the man had said his piece and would go away, but Hobe had not finished. "I can tell you what's a joy. When I was a youngster, I spent time up on the Yellowstone trappin' beaver. I didn't have to answer to nobody but me. Sometimes I'd get me a partner or take a Mandan Indian girl along for company and pleasure, and we'd work the rivers. At the end of the season, we'd go to the *rendezvous* and sell our pelts."

Hobe scraped his boot around in the dirt and sighed. "Uh-huh, that was a good life. There'd be a hundred trappers or more at the *rendezvous,* and it would go on for a month. We got drunk, told lies, gambled, and fornicated. When it was over we was broke and tired, but happy all the same. We'd head out and start all over again."

"I reckon you know how I feel," Scott said. "You've had a taste of doing what you want to do. Why'd you give it up?"

"It come to me one day that it wasn't goin' to last," Hobe replied. "Fun is for kids, but a man grows up one day and sees that it ain't something he can hold in his hand or make a life out of. I saw myself endin' up as a dried-up old drifter lookin' for my next meal."

Hobe shifted his position so he could watch Scott's face as he continued. "I got out just in time," he said. "Most of the beaver was goin' across the waters to England, but all of a sudden them British gents took a likin' to silk hats and quit buyin' beaver. There was some around who still liked beaver coats, but there wasn't enough of them, and the fur trade died. The same thing's goin' to happen with riverboats. The railroads are spreadin' out everywhere and they'll put the paddle wheelers out of business."

"I'll wait 'til it happens," Scott said firmly. "I'm going back."

Hobe Calder spat into the grass again and stood up. "What you like is not havin' any responsibility for anything or anybody. That's why you don't want to be a river pilot, and that's why you don't want to keep the Crowfoot. You'll end up as a saddle-bum like that Billy Clyde Marcum you rode away with years ago."

Scott had listened long enough. He said, "Mind your

own business, Hobe."

"I'll do that from now on, but first I want to know one thing: Are you goin' after Frank's killer, or do you figure to let the sheriff run him down?"

A knot of muscle jumped along Scott's jaw. He met Hobe's questioning stare with eyes that were cold and unblinking. "Because I don't think much of range work doesn't mean I didn't love my pa. I'm not going anywhere until I find his killer."

"Good. Frank don't—didn't like Wade Bandy's way of workin'. Soon as one election is over, Wade starts worryin' about how to win the next one. He does the paperwork and lets his deputies do the law work. The deputy we've got in town ain't much to brag about. I hear Pat Logan got that job because the town marshal at Sagemore asked Wade to hire him. The marshal is Logan's cousin, or uncle, or some such. I'm glad you've got enough guts to set things right before you dump the Crowfoot and run."

"I'm not running from anything," Scott snapped, "and I haven't made up my mind about the ranch. If you take it over, you get half the profits. If I sell it, I'll give you a share of the money. You're entitled to it."

"I don't want nothin' from you. Frank didn't leave the Crowfoot to me. He left it to you. I know cows and horses, and I won't have no trouble hookin' up with another outfit. That's what I'll do as soon as we get Frank's killer."

"Soon as *I* get him," Scott corrected. "You'll stay here and look after things. I don't want some nester to take over the house, and I don't want our calves to stray onto

Bar 40 graze and end up with the wrong brand. I want to get the best price I can if I sell the place."

Hobe's chin quivered and his fists clenched and unclenched at his sides. He turned on his heel and strode toward the bunkhouse at the far side of the yard.

Scott stayed where he was, upset by Hobe Calder's attitude. It had been difficult to hold his temper in check while he listened to the man insinuate that he was cowardly and disloyal. He accepted it as Hobe's reaction to the grief he felt as a result of Frank Rawley's death. Deep inside, Scott felt a strange urge himself, a desire to strike out and hurt someone, anyone. Perhaps Hobe felt the same.

Hobe Calder was not gone long. A few minutes after he went to the bunkhouse, he came out with a bundle of clothes under his arm and walked toward the corral. Hobe was on his way to the creek for a bath and a swim. Scott thought about going with him but decided against it. They both needed time alone. He would wait for Hobe to return before he went for his own bath.

Halfway across the yard, Hobe changed directions. He guided his horse to the well, shifted his bundle nervously under his arm, and said, "I'll be back directly to fix us some supper."

"I can do that," said Scott.

"I said I'd do it." Hobe's voice was gruff, but Scott was encouraged by the hint of a grin on the man's broad face when he added, "I want to keep my health as long as I can."

Since Scott had been back home, Hobe and Frank Rawley had shared the cooking duties, both declaring that food prepared by Scott was inedible.

Scott lingered at the well bench, feeling lonely and much less confident than he had wanted Hobe to believe. He wondered if he was capable of tracking down his father's killer, and if he could outgun him if he found him. He needed to be on the trail now, before it grew any colder, and he needed something to occupy his mind besides hate and grief. He would have to wait, however, until his father was buried with the respect and dignity he deserved.

Memories of the past intruded upon Scott's thoughts. He could not come near the well without being reminded of Billy Clyde Marcum. It was where he and Billy Clyde had finalized their plans the night before they rode away to trap wild mustangs. Nearly eight years had passed since then, but Scott had not forgotten that Billy Clyde Marcum had betrayed his trust and deserted him.

When he returned to the Crowfoot, Scott had been willing and eager to talk about his work on the *Nebraska Queen*, but he had let both Frank and Hobe know that he would not discuss his travels with Billy Clyde, and they had respected his wishes.

Billy Clyde had not lied about the mustangs. They found the horses where he had said they would be and began with a stroke of luck. Someone had been there before them and had left a pole corral that needed only minor repairs to put it in shape to confine wild horses.

Despite their skills, they soon learned mustangs were not easy to trap and were even harder to tame. Their dreams of good times and easy money faded. It took them nearly three months to capture and saddle-break six horses, and another ten days to drive them to Fort Clear.

Bold and cocky, confident of his skill as a trader, Billy Clyde insisted on handling the transaction with the Army. He came away with three hundred sixty dollars. It was as much as they could have earned in six months as ranch hands, but Scott shuddered at the thought of repeating the experience.

Billy Clyde knew how to put the memory of hard times behind them. He said, "We'll ride up to Waverly and have us a celebration. I know a bordello there where they've got the prettiest women in Texas and good liquor to go with it. We can get there tomorrow, and I'm going to grow you up fast from a boy to a man."

Scott went to sleep that night with dreams of learning to live the kind of life Billy Clyde Marcum enjoyed so much, but he never saw the bordello at Waverly. When he awoke at sunrise, Billy Clyde was gone. Scott's share of the money was also gone. During the night, Billy Clyde had taken Scott's share of their stake and disappeared into the wilderness.

Anger, disappointment, and fear vied for control of Scott's emotions. He was alone in strange country with his horse, a few days' supply of food, and broke. His first thought was to ride on to Waverly, but he quickly changed his mind. That was what Billy Clyde would expect him to do, and he would not be there.

Scott had not seen Billy Clyde Marcum since that night. He rode away from the camp, vowing silently that some day he would find him and beat him senseless or kill him. His first concern, however, was survival. He drifted north and eastward, hoping to find a riding job, but he saw only two ranches along the way and both had full crews. He kept moving, fighting loneliness and a sense of panic, too proud to go home as a failure and admit that he was incapable of making it on his own.

Finally, after a week of wandering, he came across a trail herd following the old Shawnee Trail to the cattle market at Sedalia. The trail boss was shorthanded and offered Scott a job.

In a Sedalia saloon, Scott met a riverman from St. Louis who was visiting relatives in town. While they drank together, Scott listened to the man's stories about the good life on the Missouri River. The next day he sold his horse, boarded a stagecoach for St. Louis, and experienced a taste at last of the carefree, exciting existence he had thought he would enjoy as Billy Clyde Marcum's partner.

He became known and respected by the captains along the Missouri, and could have his choice of a berth on any boat that sailed the river. Only after he had earned this kind of security did he feel comfortable about going home for a visit—a visit that had become long and troubled and was ending in tragedy.

Scott pushed to his feet, picked up his bedroll, and walked briskly toward the house. He was annoyed at himself for dredging up the past, when he had all the worries he could handle at the present.

The sun had slipped behind the western ridges and the air was cooler, but his face was clammy with sweat. He went inside and stood momentarily in the parlor doorway. Reminders of his parents were all around him—Frank's old buffalo gun resting in a rack above the fireplace, his mother's favorite flower vase standing empty on an end table, familiar pictures and smells of a silent and lonely home. In a frame above the stone fireplace was a faded tin-type of Frank Rawley's Ranger company, some of the men squatting on their heels in the foreground and the others standing stiffly behind them.

Across the bottom of the photograph someone had written: "Texas Born and Texas Proud."

Scott left the parlor and walked down the hallway to his bedroom, brushing moisture from his eyes. He spent the next hour preparing for the next day. After gathering a small supply of food from the kitchen, he searched drawers and closets for clean blankets and fresh clothes to replace those he had taken on the trail drive. He put together a new bedroll, then sat on the bed and stared at the floor, his thoughts wandering back and forth between memories of the pleasant times he and Frank had enjoyed in Red Butte Junction and the bloody scene in front of the Pioneer Bank.

Unless there was another clash between him and Hobe Calder, he planned to retire early and rise early. As soon as his father's funeral was over, he would begin his search for the men who had killed him.

CHAPTER FOUR

A T DAYBREAK Scott Rawley was back at Milam Huff's Livery Stable, riding his own bay gelding and leading the horse he had rented to take him home. Hobe Calder, mounted on a tall buckskin, rode beside him.

Nodding toward the bedroll behind Scott's saddle, Hobe said, "I ought to be goin' with you. I ought to do that much for Frank."

"You've done your part," said Scott. "You were his right hand and his best friend. He didn't make a move without asking your opinion. You've been more like a partner than a hired hand, but finding his killer is my job. You're needed at the Crowfoot."

"Uh-huh," Hobe grunted.

They had settled most of their differences at supper the night before. When Hobe announced that the meal was ready, Scott went to the table with a feeling of tension and discomfort. Hobe quickly put him at ease. He clamped his big hand on Scott's shoulder and said, "Let's forget about that little difficulty a while ago. When you told me about Frank, it hit me so hard my thinkin' went haywire. I thought I ought to stick up for what's his, but the ranch is yours now."

When they dismounted beside the livery barn, Hobe unstrapped the bedroll and began unsaddling their horses. Scott led the rented horse toward the stalls at the rear of the arch-roofed barn, which sprawled among corrals and stacks of hay on a side road a hundred yards from Asa Grove's Mortuary.

Milam Huff, a gaunt, stoop-shouldered man, stepped around the corner of the barn and lifted his hand in greeting. A cotton-haired youth in bibbed overalls and a flop-brimmed black hat came along behind him.

"He'll take that bronc off your hands," Milam Huff said, and the youngster took the horse away.

The liveryman was dressed in his Sunday suit, a shiny blue serge that showed its age. "Sad day, Scott," he said. "Sad day. I dressed for Frank's funeral when I got up. I guess you'll want it done right away."

"I'm going over to Grove's now and tell him to get started," Scott said. He took a silver dollar from the pocket of his Levi's and offered it to Milam Huff for the livery fee.

Huff backed away, lifting his hands in denial. "You can't pay me . . . you know that. Anything I have is yours for free. It's hard to repay a man for your life."

"This has gone on long enough, Milam," Scott said sternly. He slipped the coin back in his pocket and stared absently at the brush-studded hills that scalloped the horizon beyond the town. He stood that way a moment, folding his arms and trying not to appear rude because of his dislike for accepting favors.

Scott had once helped Milam Huff out of a difficult situation, but the man's continuing gratitude had become embarrassing. The incident had occurred almost a year ago, on a Saturday when Scott had come to town for supplies and had stayed until early evening to take Della Grange to dinner at the Denver House. He had stabled his horse so he and Della could walk and talk a while, and it was almost eight o'clock when he returned to the livery.

Even before he entered the barn he heard loud voices from within. He recognized Milam Huff's twangy drawl as the liveryman said, "It's the way I make my living, mister. You owe me two dollars for two nights' board and the grain I fed your horse. I don't aim to be cheated by no down-and-out drifter!"

Scott lengthened his stride. He pushed through the door and saw the two men standing in a circle of light cast by a lantern, which hung on a post near one of the stalls. As he approached them, a slender man in range garb shoved Milam Huff aside and set his foot in the stirrup of a saddled roan. Milam grabbed the man's arm and yanked him back to the ground, cursing.

When the man whirled around, Scott got his first clear view of him. The light washed across a hook-nosed face with a day's growth of dark beard and deep-set eyes shadowed by heavy black eyebrows. His Levi's were dusty, his boots brush-scarred, but the gun on his thigh was clean and shiny.

"I don't pay for nothin' I can take from an old coot like you," the man snarled. "Get out of my way, old man, or I'll knock you on your butt and blow your brains out!"

Stubborn and fearless but too slow on his feet, Milam Huff clung to the arm. The bearded man grasped Huff's shirt collar with his left hand and lifted his other fist to deliver a blow. By that time Scott's long strides had taken him within an arm's length of the two, and he was quicker than the drifter. He smashed his fist against the man's jaw, driving him backward.

The drifter staggered drunkenly for two steps, then regained his balance. Scott waited, his fists ready, expecting to feel a few blows himself before the fight ended.

But a man-to-man brawl was not to the drifter's liking. His hand streaked toward the butt of his Colt. Scott knew a split second of fear and surprise, then his own gun was in his hand. He felt the recoil in his wrist as it exploded. The force of the bullet whirled the man half around, and he fell on his side next to the stall. His hand was on his gun butt, but Scott's shot had stopped him before he could draw the Colt from its holster.

The gunshot brought four or five people running from the street. Among them was Doc Eversole, who looked at the hole in the drifter's shoulder and suggested they go to his office so he could treat the wound.

"Fish around in his pockets, Doc, and find the two dollars he owes Milam," Scott said. "Take his horse with you. He'll want to leave town as soon as you get him patched up."

The doctor found the money, handed it to Milam Huff, and went outside with the drifter leaning on his shoulder for support.

One of the men who came in with the doctor said the drifter had been in Blackwood for the past two days, drinking and playing poker at the Texas Star Saloon, but he had not heard the stranger's name.

When Sheriff Wade Bandy searched his files a few days later, he found an old flyer with a picture of the hooked-nose man's face on it. His name was Les Wagner, and the poster said he was wanted for rustling. After inquiring of other Texas lawmen, the sheriff learned that Wagner had already served three years in Huntsville prison on the rustling charge. He had been released six weeks ago, and there were no reports that he had broken any laws since.

When Wade Bandy passed this information on to Scott, he commented, "While I was diggin' up information on Les Wagner, I found out he's got a rep as a gun-slick. He killed a couple of fast men in fair fights before he took up stealin' cows. I'm surprised you could beat him."

"So am I," Scott had said, and he meant it.

Today was a strange time for visions of the gunfight to flash through his mind, Scott thought. Perhaps it was because he knew his skill with a gun might be tested again soon.

Hobe Calder found a place for the bedroll and saddles, and his steps appeared deliberately slow as he came across the livery lot to rejoin Scott. "You ready to go?" he asked solemnly.

A quiver ran through Scott's stomach and he drew a deep breath. "Yeah. Let's take a final look at Pa."

Their stay at Grove's Mortuary was brief, and afterward they walked behind the horse-drawn hearse along the rocky road that led to the town cemetery. It was less than half a mile to the burial site, located on the slope of a hill north of Blackwood, but the trip seemed to take hours.

Scott covered most of the distance with his head bowed, but as Asa Grove's hearse creaked to a halt a few feet from the newly dug grave, he straightened and looked around him. A crowd of about twenty people had gathered at the cemetery, many of them businessmen who had delayed opening their shops to pay their respects to Frank Rawley. A half dozen men stepped forward to unload the coffin and carry it to the edge of the grave. They put it down gently, then moved aside to allow everyone a clear view of the slender, black-cloaked figure of the Reverend Wesley Boone, pastor of the Blackwood Baptist Church.

Scott's glance lingered momentarily on the wooden cross a few feet away, marking the grave of his mother who had died while he was somewhere on the Missouri River. He closed his eyes as the minister offered a prayer. The Reverend Boone read from the Book of Psalms, told everyone Frank Rawley was a good and honest man, and in less than fifteen minutes the ceremony was over.

The preacher touched Scott's shoulder. He said, "My prayers are with you, son," then melted into the crowd.

As far as Scott was concerned, the funeral was merely a ritual to satisfy tradition. His grief was like a sore inside him and it would stay there, but his thoughts were already turning to the tasks that lay ahead. At last, the time was approaching when he could go after the bank robbers. He was so restless and anxious at the cemetery that he heard only fragments of the minister's comments.

His clearest memory was of Della Grange's soft sobbing, which was audible during pauses by the Reverend Boone. He hardly noticed the faces behind the wide-brimmed Stetsons and gingham bonnets as men and women paused to shake his hand before they left the cemetery. He became quickly alert, however, when John Tripp tapped him on the shoulder and said, "I'm sorry about your pa."

"Sure," Scott said. It was the most civil response he could muster.

A step behind the rancher, Cal Baylor studied Scott with a tortured look in his gray eyes. The Bar 40 foreman appeared embarrassed or ill at ease, and Scott was puzzled by his behavior. He took a half step forward as though he wanted to shake hands, then backed away with a nod, following John Tripp toward a cluster of piñon trees where most of the mourners had left their horses.

During his lifetime, Scott had not exchanged more than a dozen words with John Tripp. All he knew about the Bar 40 owner was what Frank Rawley had told him. Before hard feelings had developed between them over the land purchase, Frank would sometimes share a drink with Tripp when they met in town by chance. Frank had described Tripp as a loner, cold and stuffy—and tough.

From old-timers in Blackwood and his casual conversations with the man, Frank had learned as much as anyone could know about Tripp's background. He was the foster son of old Major Buford Tripp, who had come west in the thirties and had earned his rank while fighting for Texas's independence from Mexico. When the Republic was finally secure, those who fought for it were given generous awards of land scrip in lieu of a bonus for their services.

The Major, as he was still called, had exchanged his scrip for rangeland and that was the beginning of the Bar 40. When he came to Blackwood, the Major brought with him a tow-headed boy of five. Buford Tripp never married, but he raised the youngster to manhood and gave him his name. The Major never told anyone where he had found the boy or why he had adopted him, but he was proud of young John and kept a close rein on him while he was growing up.

Within a few years, the Major had become a wealthy

man, not from his cattle alone, but also from wise invest-
ments in mining ventures and cotton-growing operations
in other parts of the West. He passed on to his son his
own aggressive, ambitious traits, but somewhere along
the way a rift developed between them, and at the age of
nineteen John Tripp left Blackwood.

John Tripp stayed away for more than ten years,
returning to assume ownership of the Bar 40 almost a
month after the Major died of old age. He had been in
Pennsylvania during his absence, he told Frank Rawley,
attending college there and later establishing a prosperous law practice in Philadelphia.

Ironically, when John Tripp arrived in Blackwood, he
was accompanied by a lanky, moody-looking youth of
sixteen. The youngster had been orphaned when his parents, who were close friends of Tripp, had died in a hotel
fire. Tripp had never attempted to assume a father's role,
but he provided a home for Cal Baylor and taught him
the cattle business. Five years later he gave Baylor the
foreman's job at the Bar 40.

"Tryin' to repay a debt, I reckon," Frank Rawley had
said when he learned of Tripp's relationship with Cal
Baylor. "He got took in as an orphan, and now he's
takin' in one."

Throughout the funeral ceremony, Hobe Calder had
stood stoically at Scott's side. His hat was in his hands,
his fingers rolling and unrolling the brim while the sun
drew beads of sweat from his hairless scalp, and Scott
heard him mumbling under his breath.

"Are you talking to me?"

"No," Hobe replied. "I'm talking to God. I'm telling

Him to make a place for Frank and not to do nothing to help the man who killed him, because I want to put a lot of lead in that sonofabitch!"

Scott gave Hobe a warning glance. "I thought we had this settled. You're not going after the killer. You're going back to the ranch when we leave here."

"The hell I am!" The tone of Hobe's voice was mean. "I've changed my mind about the way we settled things. If you're giving up the Crowfoot, I'll just be marking time. I'm my own man, and I'll do as I please!"

Scott was nervous and unsure of himself, but he needed to reach an understanding with Hobe Calder— peacefully or otherwise. He glared at the big man and said, "I need you with me for a while, Hobe, but I don't intend to argue with you and listen to you cut me down. Pa wouldn't have fired you if you'd cut his ear off, but I will if we can't get along."

"Suits me," Hobe said. "You won't have to fire me. I want to even things for Frank. I'll quit my job and do it."

Despite his rebellious manner, Hobe was taken aback by Scott's threat. There was anger in the man's eyes, but his voice carried more bluff than conviction.

"No, you won't," Scott said confidently, hoping his grin would soothe Hobe's anger. "You won't quit. You'll stick to the Crowfoot as long as it's there."

Hobe turned and stomped away a few paces and stood staring at the sky. He scuffed his heels in the dirt, paced around in a circle, then returned to face Scott. With hands on hips, he said, "I reckon you're right. I ain't happy with any of your notions, but I'll stay a while."

Nodding with relief, Scott took a final look around the

cemetery. Two grave-diggers were tossing shovelfuls of dirt atop Frank Rawley's coffin, and nearby Asa Grove leaned against the rear wheel of the hearse and waited for them to finish their work.

Scott was about to leave when he spotted Della Grange and her parents standing among the few mourners who had lingered near the grave. Della was holding a vase of wildflowers clasped against her breast. The Granges caught his glance and came toward him, expressing their condolences.

Martha Grange, a stately, smooth-skinned woman with a soft voice, reached Scott first. She put her arms around his shoulders and gently hugged him, whispering, "We all loved Frank, and I know it's hard for you. I'm so sorry."

Bob Grange shook Scott's hand, then Della came close to him and squeezed his arm. She rose on her tiptoes as though she were going to kiss him, but brushed her fingers across his lips instead. Her eyes were clouded with tears. "I'll stay here until everything's done. I want to leave these flowers for Frank."

Scott swallowed hard. "He'd like that."

She touched his arm again. "Don't go looking for vengeance, Scott. Those men are heartless. They'll kill you, too, if they can. Let the sheriff take care of them."

"I can't do that," Scott said. He patted her shoulder, backed away, and walked down the slope with Hobe Calder.

CHAPTER FIVE

I T WAS STILL EARLY MORNING when the funeral ended, but the sun had soared above the sagebrush and cedars along the eastern horizon and was punishing the earth with its heat. Scott welcomed the cooler air of the livery barn as he and Hobe walked inside the harness room. There was an awkward silence between them, both aware they might never see each other again. A man on the trail of a known killer faced the risk of a bushwhacking or a shoot-out that he might not be fast enough to win.

Scott had left his holstered gun draped over his bedroll. He picked it up and strapped the shell belt around his waist, tying the holster down with a rawhide thong so the Colt would not bounce against his thigh when he walked. Before he had ridden to the Crowfoot the previous day Scott picked up his gear, but his father's belongings were still at the Wells Fargo office. They had discussed it earlier, but Scott wanted to break the silence. He said, "It might be unhandy to carry Pa's saddle and bedroll today. You might want to wait until you bring a wagon to town."

"No problem," Hobe said. "I've got a big horse."

Scott nodded and could think of nothing else to say. He put the bedroll across his shoulder, waited for Hobe to go first, then followed him outside.

Milam Huff had led their horses into the barnyard. They were saddled and standing side by side with their reins trailing. As Scott was anchoring the bedroll behind

55

the bay's saddle, he saw Otis Potter's one-horse rig parked twenty feet away in the shade created by the shadow of the barn.

The banker leaned sideways and called, "I've been waiting for you, Scott. I need a word with you."

Frowning, Scott gave Otis Potter a disinterested glance and continued to work with his pack. He was in no mood to be delayed.

"I can't wait all day," Potter yelled when Scott made no move toward him. His voice was louder, and he sounded nervous. "I'm already late, and Miss Emma is going to raise hob with me."

"We'll talk when I get back," Scott said.

The banker's horse lurched against its collar and Potter snapped the reins to calm it. "What I've got to say is important. You need to hear it before you go anywhere."

"Better see what it is," Hobe Calder suggested. "I'll finish that up for you."

With uneasiness gnawing at him, Scott approached the canvas-topped rig. Otis Potter shifted in the seat and his lips moved silently, as though he were rehearsing a speech. He was a pale-faced man, with owlish eyes and bristling muttonchop whiskers that gave him the appearance of a tired bloodhound.

"You said you were in a hurry," Scott said pointedly.

"Yes . . . yes," Otis Potter said. "I shouldn't be talking business at a time like this, but I have to do it." He leaned closer to Scott and said, "Frank's note is due today."

"I know that. He was trying to pay you a day early. He had the money, and you know what happened to it. I'm going to try to get it back."

"You'll need to do it fast. The bank has to be paid. We couldn't give Frank such a large loan without ample recourse, so we required that he put up the Crowfoot Ranch as security. That's what I wanted to tell you."

Scott frowned. He was not sure he understood what the banker was talking about. His father had kept him informed about most of his business affairs, but Scott did not know all the details regarding the note at the Pioneer Bank.

Frank Rawley had negotiated the loan a few weeks before Scott came home for what was to have been a two-month visit. It was the note that had kept Scott at the Crowfoot, his conscience demanding that he stay with his father until the ranch was out of debt.

Assured by his father that the ranch could produce enough cattle to pay off the loan in the four-year term agreed upon, Scott had not concerned himself with banking rules, interest rates, and pledges of security. He knew the annual payment was thirty-four hundred ninety-eight dollars, and so far they had delivered the money on time. The look on Otis Potter's face told Scott he had overlooked something.

The banker ran his finger around his shirt collar and stretched his neck uncomfortably. "If you're fortunate enough to recover the money," he asked, "will there be enough to make the payment in full?"

"There was enough." Scott's voice was bitter. "According to the sheriff, Pa had more money than you had."

Otis Potter jerked his shoulders. "That's hardly the case. Luckily, the robbers were in a hurry and didn't bother with the safe. They kept moving back and forth, looking at the street every few seconds, and they seemed content with what they took from the teller's window. When they saw your father approaching, they ran outside. The bank has quite adequate funds for a town this size."

He fixed his owlish eyes on Scott's face and cleared his throat. "That's neither here nor there. I'm not sure you realize the seriousness of your situation."

"It's serious, all right. I've got to track down a killer, and I don't know where to start. If I don't find him and our money, I reckon we'll lose the land and everything we've paid on it."

Otis Potter stared at his hands, avoiding Scott's eyes. "You'll lose more than that. You'll lose the whole ranch. That land is wedged in between the Crowfoot and John Tripp's Bar 40. Now that Frank's dead, the only person who'd want it is John Tripp, and he knows he's got me over a barrel. He won't pay enough to satisfy the debt, and the bank's not in the business of owning land. I'll have to foreclose on the Crowfoot and auction it off to get the bank's money back."

Scott rubbed a hand across his forehead. His pulse throbbed and a feeling of panic chilled his blood. There was a tremor in his voice as he said, "Something's bad wrong, Mr. Potter. I'd think Tripp would gloat over the chance to get fifteen thousand dollars worth of land for less than thirty-five hundred. You don't need to auction the Crowfoot to raise that kind of money."

Otis Potter forced a rasping chuckle. "You don't know the Tripps. Rich as he was, the Major never spent a cent he didn't have to, and John's like him. He's already using the land and he'll just go on doing that. He won't pay a dime for what he's already got, but he'll pay something for the Crowfoot—not much, I'd wager, but enough to get the bank off the hook."

"Is that legal?" Scott asked incredulously. "Can you take the Crowfoot away from me and sell it to John Tripp for a little bit of nothing?"

"It's legal," said Otis Potter. "If it wasn't, there wouldn't be a bank in Texas. It's sad, but it's business. You'll get a little something out of it—maybe a thousand or two. Tripp will offer just enough to make it look decent. The Crowfoot's worth ten times what Frank owed, but Tripp has a way of making life hard for those who oppose him. If it comes down to an auction, nobody's going to bid against him."

Through clenched teeth, Scott said, "You're as much of a thief as the gang who took Pa's money!"

The banker's mouth dropped open, and he looked offended. "Don't put the blame on me. Frank borrowed the money with his eyes open. I've got stockholders and a Board of Directors. They tell me what to do and I do it. I hold the deed to the land and I'll hand it over to you if you can pay the note."

Sweat ran from Scott's hatband and dripped off his eyebrows. He wiped it away and shook his head. "How much time do I have?"

"I have authority to allow a two-week grace period when a man's in a bind. I'll go that far with you."

"You're real generous," Scott said bitterly. "It might take me a week to find those killers and it might take a year. Maybe you can stall that auction for a while. You don't have to tell Tripp how bad things are."

"He knows. John Tripp's not the kind to mourn the dead when that man had something he wanted. He was bold enough to ask me how I planned to settle Frank's debt before I left the cemetery. Frank woke Tripp up to the fact that the open range is going to disappear, and now he wants all he can get. He knows what I'll have to do, and he's waiting to get his hands on the Crowfoot."

Fiery lights flared in Scott Rawley's eyes and turned them ice-blue. He yanked at the lapels of Otis Potter's coat, almost tipping him from the buggy. "How does John Tripp know about our private business?"

Cringing, pushing at Scott's hands to free himself, the banker gasped, "We—we've got several stockholders. Your friend Milam Huff's one of them, but Tripp's the nosiest. They know about all the bank's business."

Scott lowered his arms and backed away, resting his right hand on his gun. He wanted to fire a bullet into Otis Potter's mouth, to stop the words that made his search for the robbers even more urgent.

He stroked the bone-handled Colt with his fingers, knowing he would not use it. Otis Potter was not his enemy. His enemies were the outlaws who had killed his father. Somewhere they were riding free—perhaps celebrating with the Crowfoot's money.

Scott's anger would not die. He looked at Otis Potter and said grimly, "Pa put twenty years of his life into the Crowfoot and it's used up a good part of mine. That's too much to give up. Nobody's going to take the Crowfoot away from me. I'll find the robbers if there's a way. If I don't, maybe I'll come back and kill John Tripp."

He sucked in short breaths, fighting to control his frustration and anger. "I need more time than that, Mr. Potter. Hold off on that auction for at least a month."

The banker twisted his hands and rolled his eyes like a man in pain. He said, "I'll try to stretch it to three weeks, but that's the best I can do. I can get Milam Huff and enough of the other directors to outvote John Tripp once, but he won't let them string it along any longer."

Sliding to the edge of the buggy seat, the banker shook Scott's hand. "I saw your father die, and it was horrible. I'm afraid you're up against more than you can handle. I'll pray for you."

"Do that," Scott said flatly, then turned away. Otis Potter clucked to his horse and sent the buggy rolling toward the dirt road that would take him to Main Street.

Hobe Calder had finished outfitting the horses. He stood towering beside his buckskin, his arms folded across his chest. Scott went across the yard to rejoin him. He thumbed a hand toward Otis Potter's back. "Did you hear what he was saying to me?"

"Yeah. I also heard you tell him you was goin' to keep the Crowfoot—come hell or high water."

Scott shrugged. "I don't know what got into me. I was too mad to think about what I was saying. It's one thing if I want to sell the Crowfoot, or walk off and let it rot, but I won't have it stolen by a penny-pinching rich man."

"Uh-huh," Hobe grunted. "It's easy to ride away from home if you know you can come back. It's harder when you know you can't. Bein' drunk and bein' mad works on a man about the same way. Stuff that's been hidin' deep inside comes out in the open. I don't think you'll be goin' back to the river."

"Don't bet on it."

Hobe's face colored. "You think about what Frank's done for you. He knowed the yardstick Texas cowmen live by. In dry years, you need ten acres for every cow. Frank wanted to be able to graze two thousand head when he could grow into it. He figured anybody who wanted land better get it before it's too late. He said Texas is so dirt poor the land office will have to start sellin' every acre the state owns. When the open range is gone, land prices will go sky high."

"I don't want to talk about it," Scott said. "I'm losing time, and I've got to stop by the sheriff's office before I can leave town."

Raising his hands apologetically, Hobe swung aboard his horse and lifted the reins. "Get Frank's killers. I'll look after the ranch, and I'll shoot anybody who tries to sell the Crowfoot out from under us."

"Just keep the calves alive," Scott said.

Hobe Calder's face grew solemn, but he would not risk displaying any farewell sentiment. He swung the buckskin around and sent it trotting away from the livery yard.

Scott rode out behind him. Milam Huff stepped from his small lean-to office at the front of the barn. He waited there as though he wanted to talk, but Scott waved to him and continued toward the center of town.

Blackwood's Main Street was beginning to come alive. It was seldom a busy place on weekdays, but those who had come to pay their respects to Frank Rawley took advantage of the trip to buy supplies or visit with friends. As he rode along the street Scott passed a couple of wagons, a few horsemen, and groups of people loitering along the boardwalk. The men were clustered in twos and threes, whittling and chatting while they stood under the wooden awnings of the false-fronted buildings to escape the sun. Most of the women appeared to be entering or leaving Helen Morton's Dress Shop.

Scott did not want to be delayed by well-wishers. He rode with his head down, his eyes shadowed by his hat brim, and barely nodded to those who waved or called a greeting.

As he dismounted in front of the sheriff's office and looped the bay's reins over the hitching rail, he saw John Tripp and Cal Baylor farther down the street. They were walking leisurely in his direction. He studied them the way a cautious man might watch a wolf slinking around his herd.

John Tripp was the best-dressed man in town, but Cal Baylor did not look as if he belonged in the company of someone such as the prosperous rancher. Since coming to Texas, Baylor had gone to extremes to shed his eastern image. He spoke with an exaggerated drawl, and his clothes looked as if they should belong to a grub-line rider rather than the foreman of a prosperous ranch.

His Levi's were clean, but they were worn thin and faded at the knees and around the pockets. The brim of his brown Stetson was frayed and discolored. The heels of his scuffed boots were worn to a backward slant, but Cal Baylor still walked with an easy catlike grace. The holstered Colt that rested midway along his long thigh was plain, crafted of ordinary blued steel and hardwood butt-plates. The Bar 40 foreman had mastered a cowboy's work, and Scott was sure he had become just as skilled with a gun.

Scott wanted to avoid another face-to-face meeting with John Tripp. He pretended to adjust his stirrup strap, waiting for the men to pass. They were still on the edge of his vision when they stepped off the boardwalk and crossed to the other side of the street. Cal Baylor headed for the door of the Texas Star Saloon, and John Tripp continued along the street toward the Pioneer Bank. Otis Potter's Board of Directors would meet sometime today to discuss the robbery and Frank Rawley's unpaid note. It was a meeting John Tripp would not want to miss.

Just inside the doorway, where he could watch the street through the front window, Sheriff Wade Bandy stood with one booted foot propped in a wooden chair, leaning forward so he could rest his folded arms on his leg. Behind him, seated at the corner of a scarred desk, was Pat Logan, the deputy chosen by Wade Bandy as his assistant in Blackwood.

"Got a proposition for you," Bandy said bluntly, barely turning his head as Scott stepped inside. "It's one that'll keep me 'n you from buttin' heads."

"That why you asked me to come by?"

"It is."

The sheriff dropped his foot to the floor and stood with his thumbs hooked in the pockets of his striped moleskin pants. "Pat was over at Caprock yesterday to testify in a court case, and he missed the robbery. He got back soon enough for us to check the trail and see if we could figure out which way them owlhooters went, but we lost their tracks at the creek."

"If I'd been here," Pat Logan said, "I'd have took after them as soon as they fired their last shot, instead of standing around looking at a dead man who nobody could help."

The deputy's chair was tilted back on two legs, and his booted feet were propped against the desk for balance. Pat Logan was only a few inches over five feet tall, but he could not be considered small. Powerful muscles compensated for his lack of height, rippling over his wide shoulders and thick thighs in corded sinews that tightened the seams of his clothes.

Scott whirled, angered by Logan's sneering remark. He said, "That dead man was my pa!"

A quick stride took Scott closer. He lashed out with his foot and kicked the tilted chair over backward.

Pat Logan crashed to the floor. He slid against the rear wall, crushing the crown of his hat flat against his skull. Cursing, a stunned look in his golden brown eyes, the deputy sprang to his feet like a cornered catamount. Swearing loudly, Pat Logan dipped his hand toward his ivory-handled Colt.

"Don't touch it!" Scott warned. The moment the deputy's fingers twitched, Scott's palm fanned his side and his gun came up in one swift, fluid motion. Before Logan could grip his gun butt, the sight of Scott's Colt was at the tip of his nose.

Sheriff Wade Bandy stepped between them, his seamed face flushed. "Hell's bells, Pat, have you gone loco? I could've told you not to draw against him. He couldn't grow up in Frank Rawley's house without learnin' how to handle a gun. That hot head of your'n is goin' to get you killed."

"He had no call to dump my chair," Logan muttered.

"I'd say he had reason enough," Wade Bandy growled, and walked to the other side of the room.

Turning his back on Pat Logan, Scott holstered his gun and went to stand beside the sheriff. Bandy lifted a cardboard carton from the floor and set it on a wooden storage cabinet, where Scott could see its contents. It was filled with papers of varying sizes and colors—"wanted" flyers, handwritten notes, letters and wire dispatches from other lawmen. Some of the posters carried pictures, but most of them bore only brief descriptions of the suspects.

Wade Bandy picked up a handful of papers and let them flutter back into the box. "I've been through these things three or four times. They tell me there's plenty of robbin', killin', and fightin' goin' on in Texas, but I couldn't find anything that would give me a line on them hombres who passed through here. You can take a look if you'd like."

Scott shook his head. "I'll take your word for it. If that's all you want with me, Sheriff, I'll be going."

"That's not all." Wade Bandy's voice assumed an authoritative tone. "You're hell-bent on killin' somebody, and that worries me. I want them robbers brought in by the law . . . brought in to stand trial so we'll know we've got the right ones."

"Are you trying to tell me I don't have a right to look for the man who killed my father?"

66

"No." Wade Bandy said. "I'm tellin' you it ought to be done legal. It's up to us lawmen to make Texas civilized. We need to stop the bushwhackin', hangin' sprees, and vigilante law. We need more people out here, and we can't get 'em if decent folks are afraid for their lives. My proposition is that I want to make you a special deputy . . . let you ride out with a badge. I'll do my best to find the thieves, but I'll do it right. I want you to do it right, too. The man who shot Frank deserves killin', but he ought to be brought into court so a judge can order him killed by hangin'."

The sheriff's interest in new settlers might be sincere, but he was also influenced by other motives. Wade Bandy had been in office for twenty years. He was sixty years old, and he lived in fear that he would lose his job to a younger man. Word of the bank robbery would spread fast, and residents of the county would be watching to see what the sheriff did about it. The next election was six months away, and Bandy needed to look good to the voters. If the robbers were caught, he wanted the credit to go to his office—to himself or one of his deputies.

It took Scott only a minute to consider the sheriff's proposal and decline it. He said, "I don't want a badge. You don't have any jurisdiction outside the county, and I don't know how far I'll have to go. Once you deputize me, you'll give me a lot of rules to go by. If I take time to warn a locoed killer he's under arrest, he'll fill me full of lead while I'm talking. When I find the men I want, I'll take care of them my own way."

Wade Bandy's lips tightened. "You'd better listen to

me or you'll—"

Scott headed for the door. Pat Logan rushed across the floor and grabbed his arm. "Don't walk away from the boss when he's talking to you."

Shaking off the deputy's hand, Scott whirled to face Pat Logan. He drew back a clenched fist, held it there an instant, then relaxed. He took a deep breath and said, "I'm sorry I knocked you on the floor a while ago. I'm too upset to mind my manners, but I'm leaving now."

The startled look on Pat Logan's face brought a thin smile to Scott's face as he went outside. Once before, he had challenged the deputy's authority, and he did not want to push him or Wade Bandy too far. Before he solved all of his problems, he might need their help.

He freed the bay's reins and stepped into the saddle. The sheriff came to the doorway, still talking. "You'd better watch your step, Scott. If you do any bush-whackin' or kill a man without givin' him a fair chance, I'll bring you in for murder! Do you understand that?"

"I won't shoot anybody in the back," Scott said. He sent his horse cantering toward the open prairie, his eyes fixed on the brush along Halfway Creek where he had last seen Frank Rawley's killer.

CHAPTER SIX

TWO EMPTY CARTRIDGE CASINGS caught a shaft of sunlight and sent brassy reflections spearing up from the ground. Scott spotted them on a patch of hardpan fifty feet beyond the brush and trees that lined the banks of Halfway Creek a mile north of the ford on the stage road.

They lay a foot apart, where they had bounced after being thrown to the ground. The shells could have been discarded by anyone, but Scott guessed this was the spot where the killer had halted his horse and replaced the two bullets he had fired into Frank Rawley's chest.

Dismounting, he picked up the shells and rolled them in his palm, inspecting them at length. They were ordinary 45's, like those in Scott's shell belt. He put the shells in his pocket and went back to his horse. Apparently, the outlaws had not crossed the creek immediately after fleeing town. They had stayed in the water, following the creek's course until they could leave it on this bare stretch of ground where the sun had baked the yellow clay to an unyielding surface that would leave no tracks.

After leaving the sheriff's office, Scott had spent two hours riding along the banks of Halfway Creek, down one side and up the other. The trail was cold, but he was looking for anything that might give him a hint as to which direction the robbers had taken—a broken branch, a scarred rock, or a scrap of torn clothing. Finding the empty shells helped. From their location, it appeared the trio had headed south, in the general direction of the town of Bluestem.

Scott was glad to be away from the town—away from the questions, delays, and formalities that had followed his father's death. He had to find the robbers and recover the cattle money in three weeks if he was to keep the Crowfoot out of John Tripp's hands, and much of the morning was already gone.

Leaving the hardpan, he headed his bay southward. The prairie that surrounded Blackwood was almost level and Scott made good time for the first five miles. His pace slowed as the land changed to a series of swales and mounds, which rose gradually toward a ridge of blue-tinted hills. With nothing to guide him, tracking down the outlaws would be a slow and tedious job. He would have to scour the countryside, ask questions about three men riding together, check with law enforcement officers who might know of other recent holdups or killings, and keep riding until he learned something that would give him a trail to pursue.

While he rode, he tried to put himself in the place of a wanted man. He wondered if he would seek refuge at some remote spot on the sparsely settled prairie, or if he would choose the more lively surroundings of a town where he could mingle with others and act like a law-abiding citizen who belonged among them. The bank robbers had shown themselves in Blackwood for only a few minutes, their faces masked, and they probably had little fear of being identified. With money to spend and appetites to satisfy, Scott guessed the outlaws would lie low for a while in or near a town.

Shortly after noon, he crossed the ridge and descended into a valley that had good grass and was well watered. Longhorn cattle grazed in scattered bunches, and he saw that they wore the Anchor brand. Farther down the valley cottonwoods and tall weeds marked the course of a stream. Scott turned toward the trees, saying aloud to his horse, "I guess we'll wet our whistle and take a breather."

Weeds and vines had grown into a stirrup-high tangle that made it difficult to reach the water. He kept riding until the underbrush looked less forbidding, finally spotting a place where animals or people had flattened the undergrowth to open a narrow aisle to the stream. As he reined the bay toward the opening, the horse balked, lifting its head and lowering its rear.

Puzzled, Scott stroked the bay's neck and spoke softly, trying to coax it forward. The horse grew more agitated and rebellious, bracing its feet and fighting the reins. Obviously, the bay had seen or smelled something that frightened it. Scott swung from the saddle, led the horse to a grassy area, and stroked its neck until the bay was calm. He took a set of hobbles from his saddlebags and secured the horse's forelegs to make sure it would not bolt and leave him stranded.

The fine hairs on the back of his neck crinkled with apprehension as he walked to the edge of the creek. It was a small stream, ten or twelve feet across and boot-deep. He had to bend low to get through the overhanging foliage, and at first he saw nothing unusual. As he swung his glance from side to side, however, he noticed the white scars on the tree trunks where a sharp knife had sliced branches from a dozen cottonwoods. He edged his way along the bank and saw that the trimmings were heaped in a pile where the shoreline broadened to a bare strip of sandy, pebble-strewn land fifty feet upstream.

He had to force a path through saplings and tangled vines to get to the brush pile. Squatting, he peered through the wilted leaves. The soles of a man's boots, worn and cracked by age, were visible beneath the crisscrossed branches. Scott stood up, his heart racing. He clawed the brush away and looked down at the range-clad figure of a dead man.

The man lay facedown. His dusty black Stetson was jammed on the back of his head. At one time, his flannel shirt might have been red, but it was faded almost colorless. There was a small frayed hole in the shirt beneath the man's left shoulder blade, where a bullet had burrowed its way to his heart.

Kneeling, Scott rolled the man over. His breath hung in his throat and he drew his hands away. It had been four years since he had seen that face, but it had not changed much. The fine black beard had been carefully trimmed, and the skin that showed around it was still clear and unblemished. The dead man was Billy Clyde Marcum—the carefree partner who had tamed wild horses with Scott, then stolen his money and disappeared.

For a while Scott sat on the ground and stared in disbelief at the dead man. Rigor mortis had locked the muscles and joints, but the cooling effect of the creek and the covering of brush had slowed the body's deterioration and kept the buzzards away.

Billy Clyde's right arm lay across his waist and the other one was stretched stiffly along his side. The bullet had flattened after it entered his back, leaving an egg-sized hole in the blood-soaked shirt where it blasted away flesh when it exited Billy Clyde's chest.

Shuddering, Scott turned away from the dead man. Despite his old grudge against Billy Clyde, he felt a sense of loss. Whatever Billy Clyde had done, he did not deserve to die from a bullet in the back. But what was he doing here, and who had killed him?

The answers to these questions might never be known. Billy Clyde Marcum had always been somewhat of a mystery to Scott, and he probably would remain one. But Scott did not want to leave him here. With the brush removed, the body was exposed to view from the sky. If a single soaring buzzard spotted it, scores of others would soon congregate at the site. Within a few hours, the carrion birds would pick the flesh from Billy Clyde's bones.

Scott rubbed sweat from his brow, looked around helplessly, and went back to his horse. He had nothing in his bedroll that was suitable for digging a grave. The closest thing to a scoop in his possession was the small skillet that he had packed along with a coffeepot and some canned goods.

He needed help. Cattle were grazing in the valley, and somewhere they had to have an owner. Scott unhobbled his horse and rode farther south. After a while, he saw a series of cattle paths converging on a gap in the trees where the creek was wider and deeper. When he reached the clearing, Scott felt a sense of relief.

A quarter of a mile beyond the stream, a split-rail fence enclosed a square of land and a ranch house built of stone and hewn logs. Water sloshed around his boot heels as Scott sent the bay splashing across the creek. The fence gate was open, and a sign above it said: "Anchor Ranch, Matt Latham, Prop."

There were two hitching posts near the sandstone porch that ran along the front of the house. As Scott dismounted and tied the bay's reins around one of them, Matt Latham stepped through the door to greet him.

"Howdy," the rancher said. He ran appraising eyes over Scott's long frame and the bedroll behind his saddle. "Riding through, or looking for work?"

"Riding through, but I need your help. There's a dead man by the creek, and I don't have anything to dig a grave with. I was hoping you could lend a hand."

From somewhere within the house, Scott heard the rattling of pots and pans. A woman's voice called, "Have we got company, Matt?"

Latham turned his head toward the doorway. "Just a stranger riding through, Clara. I don't know if he'll stay for supper." Looking again at Scott, he said, "You're welcome to take a meal with us."

Scott shook his head. "Thanks, but I'll be going on. I'd like to get the man buried before the buzzards find him."

Surprise and caution were evident in the narrowing of Matt Latham's eyes and the stiffening of his stocky frame, but apparently he did not want to alarm his wife. He appeared to be in his mid-fifties, strong and healthy, but he moved his left leg stiffly and had come to the porch with the aid of a cane.

Latham kept his voice low as he asked flatly, "What's a dead man doing on my land? Did you kill him?"

"No," said Scott. "Somebody shot him in the back and covered him with brush. If my horse hadn't shied away from the water, I never would've found him. I hadn't seen him in a long time, but he's sort of—sort of a friend of mine named Billy Clyde Marcum."

"I see." The rancher frowned. "Most of my sort-of

friends are people I have a bone to pick with. Maybe—"

Latham broke off the thought as a teenage boy stepped through the doorway. He was the same height as the rancher, with ash-brown hair and a muscular chest that strained the buttons of his black-and-white checked shirt.

"My boy Jeff," Latham said.

"I'm forgetting my manners." Scott introduced himself and shook hands with both Jeff and Matt Latham.

"Pleased to meet you, sir," Jeff said politely. "I heard what you were saying to Pa. I'll get some tools from the barn."

"Do that," Latham said, and the boy strode away. The rancher rubbed the shaft of his cane along the seam of his wool pants. "I might not be much use to you, but I can help some. I tried to pull a steer out of a bog one day last week and the bugger gored my leg. We'll get the feller buried, though. Jeff just turned sixteen, but he can outwork the both of us. Strong as a mule!"

"Looks it," Scott agreed. He glanced back toward the creek, searching the sky for circling birds, but there were none in sight. "I guess I ought to tell you why I was riding across your spread."

"That's up to you."

"I'm looking for three men who robbed the Blackwood bank. They killed my Pa. I don't have much to go on, but I believe they headed for Bluestem. I was wondering if you'd seen three men passing this way together."

Latham shook his head. "I ain't been out much lately,

but Jeff might've seen somebody. He's full of vinegar, on the go all the time—hunting, fishing, or checking on cattle."

Presently, Jeff Latham returned with picks, a digging fork, and two shovels. He also had a gunbelt around his waist, which held a holstered Colt on his right hip.

As the youth approached the porch, Matt Latham excused himself and went into the house to explain to his wife the purpose of Scott's visit. While he was gone, Scott told Jeff about the bank robbery and the killing of Frank Rawley, asking him if he had seen three strange horsemen.

"Yes, sir, I saw some men I didn't know." Jeff's gray eyes brightened, pleased that he was able to provide some useful information. "I was hunting rabbits down in a coulee and I saw three men ride up the valley in the direction of Blackwood."

"Can you describe them?"

"I was pretty far away. Two of them were about the same size, built something like you but not quite as tall. I could see that one of them had real light hair, maybe like mine, but it could've been gray. The other man was a head shorter, and that's all I remember. One of them hung back, riding about twenty feet behind."

Scott's breath quickened. "Was one of them wearing a pearl-gray Stetson?"

"I don't know." Jeff frowned and stared thoughtfully at the ground. "You'd think I'd remember hats, especially since I saw them twice. They came back right at dark yesterday. I was down the valley a ways, looking for strays. I was in thick brush and something told me to stay there until they were out of sight."

"Are you sure they were the same men?"

"Yes, sir, but there was only two of them this time. One of the tall men wasn't with them."

Scott thanked Jeff Latham for his help, his spirits rising. It appeared that his hunch was right: The robbers had passed this way. Busy with his own thoughts, he let the conversation die, and Jeff Latham crossed the porch and sat down in a cane-bottom rocking chair.

Matt Latham returned, coming around the side of the house with two saddled horses, and the three of them rode toward the creek in silence.

Scott felt pressed for time. He had told the Lathams only enough to explain his reason for crossing their land, saying nothing of the deadline he had to meet to save the Crowfoot ranch. At last, he had picked up signs that he was on the right trail, and he was eager to pursue it.

Jeff Latham's sketchy descriptions could fit a host of people, but Scott was sure the youngster had seen the outlaws. Three men had ridden across the valley toward Blackwood, however, and only two had come back. What had happened to the third man? When they reached the creek, that question was soon answered.

Billy Clyde Marcum's corpse lay as Scott had left it, but the body's appearance had changed. The skin was mottled and discolored, and there was an unpleasant stench in the air.

It was Jeff Latham's first look at a dead man. As they broke through the brush and weeds, the youngster approached the site reluctantly. He walked in a half circle, his face turning pale when he finally crept closer and looked down at the still form. For a moment he was motionless, then he looked at Scott and his father, the veins in his throat pulsing while he tried to find his voice.

"He's—he's one of the men I saw!" Jeff exclaimed. "I remember now that one rider had a beard. That's him!"

Scott's arms dropped limply to his sides. "Damn," he muttered.

Limping to Scott's side, Matt Latham put a hand on his shoulder and said, "I'm sorry. Looks like he's been dead a day or more."

"Probably since a few hours after the robbery," Scott murmured. "He was shot from up close, so it must've been somebody he knew or trusted. I'd guess one of the men he was riding with killed him."

Death came often to the western range, where men who sought to carve out pockets of civilization were always at risk from those who dared to kill and loot, confident that the handful of law officers scattered across a vast land stood little chance of capturing them. Matt Latham was aware of these dangers. Even the death of a stranger aroused his sympathy, reminding him that he could die as quickly and unexpectedly. He looked at the dead man for a long time, then said, "We ought to go through his pockets and see if he has anything that will tell us who to notify."

"I doubt it, but we can look," Scott said. "You do it."

Latham rummaged through the pockets of Billy Clyde's Levi's, turning the body gently to reach them all.

He rose, a puzzled expression on his face. "Nothing," he said. "I've never seen a man who didn't have a coin, good luck piece, a spare cinch ring, or something in his pockets, but this feller ain't got nothing. I've been wondering about what happened to his horse, too. Maybe whoever killed him also robbed him."

"I don't think so." Scott pointed at Billy Clyde's Colt, which was still in its holster. "If they'd robbed him, they'd have taken his gun. A saddled horse standing around here would have been a sign something was wrong, so they must have taken it with them."

Matt Latham frowned. "Well, I don't know much about your sort-of friend, but I know we need to get him buried. You want his gun?"

Scott shook his head. "He was real partial to his gun. Let's bury it with him."

As an afterthought, Latham leaned over the body again and unbuttoned the flap of Billy Clyde's shirt pocket. He ran his fingers inside and withdrew a scrap of paper, which had been folded into a small square. He spread it open, glanced at it, then handed it to Scott. It was a note written in pencil: *I.O.U. 2 dollars and your pay this week will come to 6 dollars instead of 4 this time only.*

The note was signed "Whit Kirby, Bluestem Livery."

"Not much help, is it?" Latham sounded disappointed.

"It's a place to start," Scott said. "Maybe Billy Clyde is going to be worth something to me after all."

Scott put the note in his own shirt pocket. His hand touched another piece of paper—the tally sheet with a smear of his father's blood on it. He had not forgotten why it was there, and he was not ready to destroy it.

Latham had brought with him a square of bleached canvas to cover the body. They rolled Billy Clyde Marcum onto it and wrapped it around him, lashing it close around the head and feet with ropes. Jeff Latham had walked off to the side to avoid touching the dead man, but after the body was covered he was ready to help.

They carried Billy Clyde to higher ground, where the grave would not be disturbed if the creek overflowed its banks during a flood. It took them nearly three hours to dig the grave. They buried Billy Clyde Marcum under a lone cedar tree that would serve as a landmark for anyone who might want to locate his grave.

As soon as the last shovelful of dirt was tamped down, Scott and Matt Latham had to rest. They sank to the ground, their chests heaving while they mopped sweat from their arms and faces. Matt Latham had put his cane aside to help with the work, and the exercise seemed to loosen the muscles of his injured leg. Young Jeff did not appear tired, but his shirt was sweat-soaked and his face was flushed.

"You want to talk over him?" Matt Latham asked.

Scott shook his head.

Jeff Latham said, "I'll do it. It wouldn't be right to leave him here without saying something. I remember a piece of scripture Ma read me from the Bible."

He went to the head of Billy Clyde's grave, removed his hat, and bowed his head. Scott and Matt Latham stood beside him while he intoned, "The Lord gave and the Lord hath taken away. Blessed be the name of the Lord."

Scott let a few seconds of stillness drift by, then said, "Thanks. I'm glad you did that."

"You're welcome, sir," Jeff replied, and began to collect the tools they had brought from the Anchor Ranch. Scott walked with Matt Latham to his horse and extended his hand in gratitude.

The rancher glanced at the sun. "I know you've got a manhunt on your mind, but a good part of this day's gone. We'd be pleased to have you spend the night at Anchor."

"Appreciate it," Scott said, "but the days get long this time of year. I'll feel better if I ride on."

Matt Latham raised his hand in a farewell salute. Jeff called, "Luck to you, mister," and the two of them put their horses in a gallop toward the Anchor Ranch house.

Scott rode quickly away from Billy Clyde Marcum's grave, eager to reach Bluestem and talk with a liveryman named Whit Kirby.

CHAPTER SEVEN

EAST OF THE ANCHOR RANCH, the hills that bordered the valley were shaped by gentle slopes with rounded crests and were easier to negotiate than the western ridge. By sundown, Scott had crossed the highest of the hills. He stopped his horse atop a knoll and looked down on a horseshoe-shaped basin that opened southward on a rolling prairie.

From hillside to hillside, the basin was about three miles wide. The floor was rocky, clogged by greasewood and stunted pines. Scott had not seen much of this part of the country, but he knew the general lay of the land. His father had seen to that. When Scott was a boy, Frank Rawley had devoted many Saturdays and Sundays to long rides with his son.

Frank had said, "When folks talk about where they've been, I don't want you to be ignorant about a place no more'n a day's ride from home."

They had traveled at least once to the region's four other towns—Sagemore, Caprock, Bluestem, and Hub. Frank had also familiarized him with the crossroads stores and saloons off the main stage roads, insisting that they camp overnight on each trip so Scott would learn how to live in the open.

Scott turned his eyes in the direction of Bluestem, wishing he could reach the town sooner. He was eager to learn from Whit Kirby what the liveryman knew about Billy Clyde Marcum's association with the bank robbers, but it was late and he was too tired to go on. It was thirty miles from Blackwood to Bluestem. Scott had covered half the distance, and the rest of the trip would be easier.

From his vantage point above the basin, Scott looked around for a place to camp for the night. Behind him, the dying sun was splintering the sky with shafts of yellow and red. To his left, he saw the colors shining back from moving water, and he remembered that a creek followed the contours of the basin, sweeping around the upper end before it curved back to flow across the prairie. That would be Medicine Creek, Scott recalled, the same stream that twisted its way past Bluestem on its way to a junction with the Salt Fork.

Scott nudged his horse toward the basin floor, eager to get out of the saddle and stretch his legs. The lowland was not as hospitable as it had looked from afar. It rose and fell between dry washes and arroyos carved by flash floods. Surrounded by rough ground and brush, Scott lost sight of the creek, but the bay smelled water and quickened its pace.

Presently, he topped a rise and saw the creek ahead of him. He also saw signs that he was not alone in the basin. Parked on a grass strip between clumps of brush and the willows that flanked Medicine Creek was a wagon. It was a weather-beaten buckboard fitted with arched staves that held a ragged canvas cover.

Scott wanted to talk with anyone who might have seen two strange riders passing through the country. The wagon's owner might have spotted the bank robbers and be able to verify that Scott was on the right trail. He almost changed his mind about going to it, however, because there was no sign of life around the vehicle.

The wagon appeared deserted. There were no horses in harness or anywhere in sight. Singletrees for a two-horse team were still linked to the wagon's undercarriage on each side of the hewn tongue, which lay with its point on the ground. Scott could think of reasons why the vehicle might appear abandoned. It was possible that the buckboard's owner had been waylaid and robbed. A team of draught horses could be sold for more than a hundred dollars, and Scott had heard of men being killed for less.

Halting his horse, he studied the wagon and debated the wisdom of going closer to investigate. He thought he saw the bed sway, as though someone were moving inside, but he was not sure. His logic told him he could find no help at an abandoned wagon, but he could not leave without making sure no one lay wounded in the buckboard, needing help to survive. He walked the bay forward, scanning the area warily. It was customary in range country to call out before entering another's camp, but Scott decided to forego such courtesy. If there were outlaws or killers nearby, he did not want to risk walking into an ambush by alerting them.

Twenty feet from the buckboard he dismounted, dropped the reins to the ground, and continued on foot. He drew his gun and approached from an angle that would give him a view of the other side. He saw nothing unusual. The rear flaps of the wagon sheet were drawn together over the tailgate. Walking on tiptoes, he held his breath until he was at the rear of the wagon. He grabbed one edge of the closed cover and flung the flap aside.

His breath escaped in an audible gush. Standing near the front of the vehicle was a beautiful girl of about nineteen or twenty. She was completely nude. The sun was behind the hills, but enough light filtered through the wagon sheet to reveal high, rounded breasts that rippled with her vigorous movements. Her stomach was flat, framed by flaring hips and tapering thighs, and the soft light put an olive hue on her satiny skin.

She had a towel in her hands. When Scott first saw her, she had her arms upraised and was rubbing the cloth through the golden hair that fell in damp ringlets on her shoulders.

Her expression was frozen by fear. Her green eyes grew large and round, and her red lips parted as she gasped in fright. She was as still as a statue. Scott was no less surprised. He stood rooted in his tracks, his face flushed with embarrassment. He searched his mind for something to say, but he was too flustered to utter a sound.

After a few seconds, the girl instinctively pulled the towel over her breasts, then lowered it to cover her mid-section. Her hands fluttered up and down, trying to stretch the small towel so it would cover more of her body.

Finally, Scott reacted. He backed away and murmured, "I—I'm sorry, ma'am. I didn't mean to . . . I mean, I thought somebody might need help, and that's why—"

He did not finish the stammering apology. He choked off the words as he heard the hiss of footsteps moving on the grass behind him. Fear shook the nerves along his spine. An angry voice said, "If you move an inch, stranger, you're dead! Drop that gun and turn around slow."

A few inches in front of his face the canvas flaps swished shut as the girl darted forward and grabbed them with both hands. The sudden movement caused Scott to flinch. He dropped the bone-handled Colt and turned around.

Near a patch of greasewood, which had hidden them from view while they sneaked close to him, were two men with drawn guns. The one who had spoken was tall and thin. His black woolen shirt was pinched in pleats around his skinny waist by a loaded shell belt, which slanted across the front of his Levi's to hold a tied-down holster on his right leg. His face, sharp-chinned with bony cheeks and deep-set blue eyes, appeared more cautious than angry.

The other man was of medium height, compact and

muscular. He stood with his legs wide apart, the hand that held his gun braced against his belt while he stared at Scott through dark eyes shaded under the brim of his black Stetson. He was clean-shaven, but points of beard as black as his hair showed under the tanned skin. He was calmer, his thick shoulders squared with confidence, and Scott appraised him as the more dangerous of the two.

"He saw me naked, Jake!" the girl yelled from the wagon.

The thin man's lips quivered and his shoulders jerked back and forth. "You—you were fixing to rape my sister! I'm going to kill you!"

Jake's knuckles were white as he squeezed the gun butt, but Scott saw doubt and indecision in the man's eyes. He held up a restraining hand and cautioned, "Whoa, Jake! I didn't come here to hurt your sister. I saw your wagon, no horses, and I thought you might have been robbed and left for dead. I was just looking to see if anybody needed help."

"You was looking, all right," the other man said, his voice brittle with sarcasm.

"Let me handle it, Lew," Jake said, his eyes boring into Scott's face. There was a quaver in his voice when he spoke again. "I ain't going to listen to any lies. Lew and me was decent enough to go down and move the picket lines for our horses while Lily was bathing in the creek, but I know what you were doing. You were out there peeping through the brush and getting yourself worked up while you watched her. If we hadn't showed up when we did, you'd be in the wagon beating her up and pleasuring yourself with her. I've seen your kind, and I'm going to kill you. I'll leave you dead with a gun in your hand and tell the law I beat you when you tried to draw on me. That's the way—"

"You going to kill him or talk him to death?" the other man cut in. "If you don't have the guts for it, I'll do it for you."

Scott glanced at Lew. The man had shifted his gun away from his body, a precaution against powder burns if it had to be fired. Lew grinned defiantly as their eyes met.

"Shut up!" Jake said. His voice rose to a nervous pitch. "Us Vernoys never have amounted to much, but we stand up for our women. I'll kill him myself."

"No you won't!" It was the girl's voice, throaty and commanding.

She parted the wagon flaps and hopped to the ground. She was dressed in Levi's and a pink shirt, but she had not taken time to put on her shoes. A rifle butt nestled against her cheek and she was looking down the barrel at her brother.

Scott drew a sigh of relief. He stepped sideways to get closer to Lily Vernoy. She gave him a warning glance and he stayed where he was, but her beauty was so unusual he could not take his eyes off her. Her emerald eyes, soft skin, and sensuous lips were even more distinctive under the open sky. She looked almost childlike with her toes curling away from the bite of the stiff grass, but there was a firm set to her chin as she glared at Lew and Jake.

"Why don't you leave us alone?" Lew snapped. "Hell,

you ain't going to kill me and Jake to save this hombre."

"I wouldn't do that," said Lily Vernoy. The look she gave Lew was far from friendly. "You'll be missing a couple of fingers or a few toes, though, if you try to kill him. He got an eyeful, but he said he thought someone might need help. I don't think he meant any harm."

Waving his gun, her brother stepped forward to argue. "You might know he'd lie after he's caught up with. He was spying on you while you was naked. Ain't that enough?"

"I never saw you naked," Lew growled.

Without looking at him, Lily said coolly, "It's not because you haven't tried, Lew Bender. I've heard you prowling around my wagon at night when I'm getting ready for bed. When Jake's not around, you're always trying to brush against me or get me to go for a ride out in the brush with you. Your bad luck's not a good reason to take it out on somebody else."

"Something's got to happen to him before he leaves," Jake said stubbornly. "He'll be going around talking about seeing Lily Vernoy naked and maybe bragging that he did it with you, unless we hurt him enough to learn him better."

"I don't care what strangers say about me," she said. "We're not exactly famous enough for anybody to know who he's talking about."

Jake's expression remained grim. He holstered his gun and said, "I care. If I can't shoot him, I'll whup him with my fists so's he'll know better than to spy on you again."

The lines around Lily's mouth softened as her fear and anger waned. She said to her brother, "Let it go, Jake,"

and then to Scott, "Pick up your gun and go on to wher-
ever you were going."

Scott's gun lay on the ground where he had dropped it,
near the rear wagon wheels. To reach it, he had to pass
Jake Vernoy, and Scott made a mistake by not keeping
his eyes on the man. As he came abreast of him, Jake
drew back his arm and slammed a knotted fist against
Scott's jaw. The force of the punch echoed with a
grinding roar in Scott's head. He staggered sideways,
catching his balance by dropping to one knee.

Jake rushed at him, his foot upraised to kick him in the
face. Scott rolled aside, and the boot found nothing but
air. He rose, blinking to clear his vision. Jake whirled
and came toward him again. From the corner of his eye,
Scott saw Lew Bender lift his gun. Lily Vernoy shouted,
"Put it away, Lew, or I'll blow your arm off."

He forgot about Lew Bender and braced for Jake's
charge. Scott did not step aside this time. He bunched his
shoulder muscles, lowered his chin against his chest, and
waited. He hit Jake while the man was in mid stride. He
aimed the blow to go beneath the bony chin and smash
into the soft tissue of Jake's neck. It found its mark on
the man's Adam's apple, a torturing maneuver Scott had
learned the hard way in dockside brawls along the Missouri.

Jake's head flew back and he flopped to the ground,
retching, gagging, and clutching his neck while he struggled for breath. But despite his frail appearance, Jake
Vernoy was strong and stubborn. He pushed himself up
on all fours, facing the ground while he rocked back and
forth on his hands and knees. He looked over his

shoulder at Scott, his face pale and slack. His mouth was bloody, and strings of brown hair hung over his eyes.

"Give it up, Jake," Scott said quietly. "It's a foolish fight, and I don't want to hurt you anymore."

Jake's response was a muffled "Yeah," as he got slowly to his feet. His fists were clenched but hanging at his sides, and Scott thought the fight was over. An instant later, he knew better.

The limp arms were deceptive. Before rising, Jake had filled his hands with loose dirt. Catching Scott off guard, he flung it in his face. Half blinded, Scott backed away. When he raised his hands to wipe at his eyes, Jake hit him in the mouth, crushing his lips against his teeth. The taste of blood was on his tongue and his mouth burned, but Scott was not stunned. He had wanted to stop fighting, but Jake was too stubborn to agree. Scott was hurt and angry, and he was determined to use all his strength and skills.

Jake tried to follow his blow to Scott's mouth with a looping left hand. Scott blocked Jake's swing, ramming his right fist into the man's stomach. Jake grunted. He sucked in his waist, bending in the middle and hunching forward. Scott grabbed a handful of Jake's hair and lifted the man's head. He cocked his arm and punched Jake squarely in the face. Blood spurted from the man's nose and streamed over his mouth.

Scott lost any desire for compromise and began to enjoy the fight. The anger and grief inside him poured out through his fists. Jabbing, slashing, punishing blows rained on Jake's face and belly. He gave ground, his arms flailing as he tried to defend himself. If there was any sting left in Jake's fists, Scott did not feel it. Sweating, cursing, ducking, and weaving, Scott ignored Jake's feeble efforts and kept hitting him.

Jake lasted another ten minutes before he fell to the ground in a bleeding, exhausted heap. Scott was like an animal driven by fear and a need to survive. He straddled Jake's motionless form. He grabbed the man's shirtfront, lifted him a foot off the ground, and drove his fist into Jake's battered face. He started to hit him again, but Lily's voice stopped him.

"Hold it!" she shouted. "You're going to kill him!"

Scott felt as if he were awakening from a dream. He stared at the bruised hand that gripped Jake Vernoy's shirt, then relaxed his fingers and let the man fall to the ground. He stood still, his chest heaving, and waited for his nerves to become calm. Ignoring Lily and Lew, he picked up his gun, wiped the barrel clean on his pants leg, and slid it into the holster. He retrieved his hat, brushed his tousled hair away from his forehead, and put it on.

When he turned around, he saw that Jake Vernoy had managed to sit up and was staring listlessly into space. Scott walked to his side and extended his hand. Jake grasped it, and Scott helped him to his feet. He felt a grudging respect for the skinny man.

"Looks like you'll live," Scott said.

Jake did not try to talk. He took a bandanna from his pocket and started wiping the blood from his face, eyeing his sister and Lew Bender sheepishly.

"I guess you feel like a real snake-stomper now," Lew Bender sneered.

"I feel tired and my mouth hurts," Scott replied. "I can't say that it's been a pleasure meeting you folks, so I'll be riding on."

Lew Bender's voice stopped him. "Not so fast, cowboy. Maybe I'll have something to say about that."

"You don't," Lily Vernoy said. She was still beside the wagon, with the rifle cradled loosely in her arms. She turned so that the barrel pointed in Bender's direction. "Jake started this when he tried a sneak punch. You were talking so tough about fighting for my good name, I should have let you take the beating."

The stocky man said arrogantly, "He wouldn't have beat me."

"We'll never know, will we?" Scott said.

"Maybe we will," Bender murmured. "Maybe we'll meet again."

Scott shrugged and headed for his horse. Lily Vernoy hurried away from the wagon to overtake him. She touched his arm as he picked up the bay's reins. "I'm sorry about this whole thing. I really believe you thought we might be in trouble or in need of help. You've got a better heart than we have. I'm sorry things got out of hand."

"Don't mention it. It wasn't your fault."

"Oh, it was my fault," she said. "I should've had sense enough to put on some clothes before I dried my hair." She smiled and her face colored. "I'm a nosy woman, so you'll have to ignore me if I pry into something that's none of my business. We're out here in the middle of nowhere and hadn't seen anybody for days until you came along. I've been wondering what brought you here."

Scott was glad to tell her. He wanted as many people as possible to know he was trailing the bank robbers, hoping someone might have seen them. Sensing that Lily had forgiven him for his inadvertent intrusion on her privacy, Scott felt at ease with her. He introduced himself for the first time and told her about his father's death. He meant to say little more, but they talked so long that Lily seemed like a friend, and Scott described his shock at finding Billy Clyde Marcum's body and recounted the story told him by young Jeff Latham.

"I feel even worse now because we slowed you down and added to your troubles," Lily said quietly. "Do you think you'll find those men?"

Scott nodded. "Someday I will, but I've got to do it fast. I need the money they stole. I'm on my way to Bluestem to talk to a man who might give me a lead, but I can't make it tonight. I was looking for a place to camp when I saw your wagon. You can pass along what I've told you to your friends if they're curious."

Lily Vernoy looked over her shoulder toward her brother and Lew Bender. "A brother's not the same as a friend, and Lew certainly doesn't qualify. He's a cowhand who worked on a spread near our place. When Jake decided to go to New Mexico Territory and homestead some land, Lew tagged along."

Her eyes were soft and sympathetic as she shook her head and added, "You don't ever know about other people's troubles. I'm sorry about your father. I wish I hadn't gotten so excited and told Jake that you saw me— saw me—"

She avoided being more explicit and Scott laughed at her embarrassment, feeling pain from the cut on his lip. He said, "That was worth a punch in the mouth, so don't apologize."

Lily's cheeks turned crimson, and Scott continued smiling as he climbed into the bay's saddle. He looked down at her and said, "Good luck in New Mexico."

"You'll have more luck chasing a killer than I'll have in New Mexico. I don't want to go, but I don't have a choice. I'm not going to have a choice about a lot of things."

She appeared sorry to see him leave, and Scott noticed a tremor in her voice. She had concealed her feelings until now, but Lily was tense and worried. Scott considered staying nearby until he learned the reason for the fear in her eyes. He pushed the thought aside, however, telling himself it was a bad time to become involved in the affairs of a girl who was a stranger to him. Jake Vernoy would carry a grudge because of the fight, and Scott did not trust Lew Bender. He could not risk being delayed by new problems.

With a farewell wave, he rode back the way he had come. When he was far enough into the brush to be out of sight of the buckboard, he chose a path that would take him across the neck of land that was enclosed by the circling creek, planning to spend the night near the mouth of the basin. His diagonal course would take him at least three miles from the Vernoys' camp and that much closer to the town of Bluestem—perhaps closer to a clue that would lead him to his father's killer and the money the robbers had taken from him.

CHAPTER EIGHT

DUSK LAY ACROSS THE LAND, draining all color from the sage and trees. Scott rode for another hour but covered little distance. He sat straight in the saddle, looking over his shoulder often, watching for any movement and listening for unusual sounds. He felt uneasy and threatened, without knowing why.

He leaned forward with one hand on the saddlehorn and tried to relax. While he rode, his thoughts tracked back over the events of the day, and he blamed these reflections for his apprehension. He could not forget that someone had killed Billy Clyde Marcum and left his body under a canopy of brush not many miles away. A bushwhacker's bullet could kill him just as easily. If he died without recovering his money, what would happen to Hobe Calder and the Crowfoot Ranch?

His concern for Hobe surprised him, striking him as ironic. He had already offended the man who had served his father faithfully through the years and considered the Crowfoot his home. His promise to share the proceeds with Hobe when he sold the ranch had been met with more disdain than gratitude. Hobe had lost his respect and affection for Scott at that moment. The big cowboy regarded him as a wanderer who was afraid of responsibility, a man too weak to assume his father's role among those who believed that only good land, good grass, and cattle could guarantee a stable life.

Hobe's words kept echoing in Scott's mind, and he

wondered if the vagabond ways of the rivermen would remain satisfying into his old age. At the moment, he was not sure about anything. He drew himself erect and turned his attention to his horse's progress. He did not have the time nor the energy to worry about things that might or might not happen. If he failed to track down the bank robbers, he would not have to make any decisions about the Crowfoot. The bank would make them for him.

He chose the best place he could find for his night camp, but it was not to his liking. There was too much brush. Only a narrow strip of grassland separated the trees along Medicine Creek from the chaparral that covered most of the basin, but Scott was too tired to look for a better location. He had slept only four hours before riding to Blackwood for his father's funeral, and he had been in the saddle since early morning. The excitement generated by his discovery of Billy Clyde's body and his fight with Jake Vernoy subsided, leaving in its wake nothing but fatigue.

Night camps had been a part of Scott's life throughout his twenty-four years, and he followed the routine he had practiced scores of times. He watered his horse, picketed it where it could graze through the night, then took care of his own needs.

He opened the bedroll, spread his blankets atop the tarp, and set out the utensils and food he would need for supper and breakfast. Wood was plentiful amid the brush and willows along Medicine Creek. It took him only a few minutes to gather enough to last all night. Darkness shrouded the countryside before his chores were finished, and Scott did not feel comfortable until he had built a fire large enough to throw a circle of light around his camp.

Afterward, he walked through the fifty yards of brush that separated his camp from the creek and took a bath. He washed the dust and sweat from the clothes he had worn and hung them on tree branches near the camp to dry. The cold bath and fresh clothing drove away some of his weariness, but he went to bed as soon as he finished supper.

The early-rising moon had wasted most of its color on a daylight sky and was already hovering over the western horizon. Scott cast a final searching glance over his surroundings, then lay on his back and stared at the limitless space beyond the stars twinkling in the indigo sky. At intervals during the day, the vision of his father lying dead in front of the Pioneer Bank had flashed through his mind, and the stillness of the dark basin reminded him again of the silence and grief that were the companions of death.

Scott shifted to his side and tried to force his mind to go blank so he could fade into the sleep he needed so badly, but his mind would not obey. His thoughts turned to Lily Vernoy, and he envisioned two pictures—one of her striking beauty as she stood nude under the wagon cover, and the other of the haunting fear in her gray-green eyes when he left her.

From early childhood, Scott had seen scores of wanderers in the West. Many moved across the broad expanses of the unsettled land with eager anticipation, confident of making a rich strike in the goldfields, dreaming of building great cattle herds on free land beyond the boundaries of Texas, or establishing mills and shops that would bring them wealth. There were others, however, whose belligerent attitudes and vague goals was a certain indication that misfortune or tragedy had forced them away from familiar surroundings and sent them searching for new hopes, with anger and desperation goading them on.

Lily Vernoy had been too quick to scream when he had innocently disturbed her privacy, and Jake and Lew Bender had been too eager to fight without waiting for an explanation. They were among the desperate people experience had taught Scott to recognize. He guessed that Jake and Lily had been left behind by parents who had passed away, and they now had to shift for themselves. Lew Bender was accompanying the Vernoys as Jake's friend, presenting himself as a man tough and worldly enough to see them safely to their destination.

As he looked back on the incident at the buckboard and the byplay between Lily and Lew Bender, he knew the reason for the tremor in her voice and the fear in her eyes. Lew Bender's real interest was Lily Vernoy, and the girl knew it. She was afraid Bender was going to rape her before they ever saw New Mexico Territory, and she had little confidence that her brother was strong enough to stop him.

Scott wondered if there was anything he should have done to help her. Perhaps she would have trusted him enough to go with him to Bluestem, where she could find a job to support herself or find relatives who would give her a home. He shrugged the thoughts away. These were alternatives Lily Vernoy was capable of considering for herself. Women were often the victims of this uncivilized land, but the strong survived, and Lily had shown a fierce, unyielding will when she had held Lew Bender at bay with her rifle. The wise thing for him to do, he decided, was to forget about Lily Vernoy and never again venture unannounced into a stranger's camp. It was unlikely that he would ever see the girl again, but he settled into his blankets with a silent wish that no harm would come to her.

The last thing he did before he went to sleep was to reach behind the saddle he was using for a pillow and run his hands inside his saddlebags. Before going to the creek, he had removed two slips of paper from his shirt pocket—the tally sheet with a smear of his father's blood on it and the I.O.U. Whit Kirby had signed for Billy Clyde Marcum. He was not sure he had put them where he intended, but they were there.

From a sound sleep, Scott woke up abruptly, his nerves tingling with a sense of danger. Someone had come close to his camp, and he was sure he had been watched for some time before he realized he was not alone. He did not know what had awakened him, but now he heard brush rustling and the ripping sound of a horse's hoofs dragging through the weeds somewhere out of his sight.

The campfire had burned out hours ago, and Scott was surprised that the night was gone. The grayness of dawn outlined the sagebrush and stunted pines like hazy ghosts, but the land was still too murky for him to see more than a few yards beyond his camp.

Except for his shirt and boots, Scott had slept fully

clothed. He peeled the blankets away from his saddle and grasped the loaded six-gun that lay beneath it. With the gun in his hand, Scott stayed hunkered close to the ground and ran for the cover of a matted briar patch twenty feet away, listening to a faint disturbance in the underbrush. In the space of minutes, the sky grew lighter. Sunrise was an hour away, but there was enough light for him to pick out clear spots in the chaparral. For a while the sound of movement faded, then grew louder again.

His sore mouth was a reminder of his fight with Jake Vernoy the day before. Lew Bender had wanted to take up the fight, but Lily had stopped him. Despite his sympathy for the girl, Scott knew nothing about the trio he had seen at the buckboard. Had Jake and Lew tracked him down to get even or perhaps to rob him of any valuables he might have? The stealthy approach of the person in the brush unnerved him and teased his mind with a flood of possible threats.

"Hello—o—o, the camp!" a man's voice called, startling Scott with its nearness.

He frowned, hesitating before responding to the traditional rangeland call. The voice was close enough to tell him the rider could see his camp while hidden from view. He did not recognize the voice, but he knew it did not belong to either Jake Vernoy or Lew Bender.

Staying where he was, Scott shouted, "Ride on by, mister! I'm about to break camp, and I don't have time for company."

"You'll want to talk to me, Rawley. I know who killed your pa!"

If the hidden man intended to lure Scott into a trap, he had spoken the right words. He was ready to accept any risk to learn the identity of his father's killer. His first impulse was to rush into the open and welcome the unknown visitor, but an instinct for caution overcame his eagerness.

Scott's eyes swept the trees and bushes in front of him, but he could not locate the man who had spoken.

"Come out where I can see you," he shouted.

A calm voice replied, "Sure thing."

Fifty feet away, the man stepped into a clearing. He had the fingers of one hand hooked into the bridle of a black mustang, which carried saddlebags and a bedroll. His other hand was raised shoulder high. Scott moved slowly forward to meet him at the campsite. After a few steps, he recognized the man and put his gun away.

"You're the whiskey drummer from the stagecoach! Your voice sounded different."

The man's lips twitched, and that was as close as he came to smiling. "I'm glad. When you saw me I was trying to talk like some dudes I've met, but it don't come natural. I'm eastern-born but western-raised. Name's Joe Pike."

The voice was a slow, mellow drawl, far different from the clipped tones Scott had heard while they traveled together. Scott eyed him suspiciously. "You told me your name was George Pratt."

"That's my whiskey drummer name. Sometimes I'm George Pratt, sometimes somebody else. My mother named me Joseph and my Pa's name was Lancelot Pike, so that makes me the honest-to-God, one-and-only Joe Pike."

The explanation sounded truthful, but Scott wanted to test the man and watch his reaction. He said, "If you gave me a phony name once, you could do it again. Maybe neither is right."

Joe Pike's expression did not change. "Anybody half smart would have to wonder. Thing is, my real name's known places where my face ain't, so I have to change my handle now and then. I've been following you most of the time since you left town, figuring you might lead me to something. I lost your trail yesterday after I spotted you and two other gents burying somebody. I thought I had time to circle around a bit, but when I came back you was gone. Last night I saw your fire, but I figured it'd be safer if I didn't bother you until daylight. I want to make you a proposition that'll be good for both of us."

Scott gave the man a calculative look. Aside from his laconic manner and the fluid ease of his movements, there was nothing about Pike to distinguish him from an ordinary cowboy. His face was burned brown, his expression unreadable, and his features were handsome in a rough-hewn way. Streaks of gray showed in the brown hair at his temples, but it was hard to guess his age—between forty and fifty, Scott estimated.

The salt-and-pepper suit of the whiskey drummer had been replaced by Levi's that had seen many washings. The brown buckskin vest he wore over an olive-green flannel shirt was without decoration and was shiny around the pockets. His tan Stetson was old but still held its shape, and the holstered gun on his thigh was a plain, iron-handled Colt .45.

Scott's wariness did not go unnoticed by Joe Pike. He said, "You don't take to strangers real quick, do you?"

"That depends," Scott replied. "You're the second man who's offered me a proposition. I'm waiting for you to tell me who killed my father."

"We'll get to that if you'll listen to my deal."

"If you'll make it short, I'll listen to it."

Joe Pike dropped the mustang's reins to the ground and hooked his thumbs in the lower pockets of his buckskin vest. He glanced at Scott's blankets and the ashes of the dead fire, then swung his gaze around as though he wanted to make sure there was no one else around. "You've made pretty good time since you left Blackwood," he said. "You must have a pretty good hunch about where you need to go."

The man was fishing for information, but Scott let the remark pass. He said, "That old prospector on the stagecoach and I had the same notion about you. Neither of us believed you were what you said you were. My guess is that you're a U. S. Marshal or a Ranger. If you are, I don't have time to waste with you."

"Not quite," said Joe Pike. "I work for the Pinkerton National Detective Agency."

"I've heard of it . . . sort of a fancy name for a bounty-hunting outfit," Scott mused. "If you're going to offer me a badge, save yourself the trouble. I turned down the same offer from Sheriff Bandy."

Pike withdrew a palm-sized leather case from his back pocket, removed a card from it, and handed it to Scott. "I don't have anything as fancy as a badge with me. Just cardboard with a name on it, but it carries considerable weight here and there.

"I'm the supervisor for the Austin region," he continued. "I've got four men scattered around these parts, and I've been checking with them to see if they're getting any closer to running down these two hombres we've been after for the past six . . . eight months. Pinkerton doesn't have a man in Blackwood. I came up on the stage looking to hire somebody who can hold his own in a fight and keep his mouth shut. You look to be that kind of man. I'd like for you to work with us."

Scott studied the card. Floating in space in the center of it was a lifelike drawing of a human eye. Beneath it was the slogan "We Never Sleep." Aligned with the curvature of the eye, the words "PINKERTON NATIONAL" were printed above the drawing, followed by "DETECTIVE AGENCY" below it. The left corner of the card listed Allan Pinkerton as principal, and gave the addresses of offices in New York, Philadelphia, and Chicago. Along the bottom edge, where the words "Issued To" appeared, Joe Pike's name was written in black ink.

Scott gave the card back to Pike. "If you've already got people around here, why do you want me?"

Shrugging, Joe Pike said, "It's a man's nature to be lazy, and my people are experts at it. They work first on the easy stuff, then get around to the tough cases. You're different. You've got a personal grudge to settle, and you won't give up until you get the man you're after."

"That's right," Scott agreed. "I don't need to be a Pinkerton man to do that and Pinkerton doesn't need me, since I'm going to get the job done for them, anyway."

"There's more to it," Pike drawled. "It's a matter of business. When them hombres are nailed, Pinkerton wants to claim the credit. That boosts our reputation and brings in more clients. It's business to Pinkerton, but it's more than that to me. I purely hate killers and thieves. I was on the hotel porch when the bank was robbed, but I saw what happened to your father."

Pike's head moved in a faint nod, as though he had made a silent decision. "I'm not going to hold out on you whether you turn me down or not. The robbers were the Sadler brothers. We've been chasing that pair for a long time. Mitch is the shooter, but Ned ain't any better. Either one of them will kill you if they have to, but Mitch'll kill you for the fun of it."

CHAPTER NINE

SCOTT LISTENED TO PIKE with the muscles in his throat constricting and turning his mouth dry. He did not doubt the Pinkerton man's description of the bank robber's cruelty. He had witnessed it for himself. Excitement quickened his pulse, and he felt encouraged. Pike had given him names and that was a step forward. From now on he could ask more specific questions. No man was a stranger to everyone, and if he inquired about the Sadler brothers often enough, he would find someone who had seen them.

"Are you sure it was the Sadlers?" Scott asked insistently.

"Maybe not a hundred percent," Pike conceded, "but

I'm sure enough to bet my saddle on it. It fits their pattern. They've been working their way back toward home grounds, robbing and killing, then laying low for a few weeks and popping up again. Mitch was let out of Huntsville prison about eight months ago. His brother Ned was in jail in Sagemore at the time, being held for trial on a rustling charge. He broke out a week after Mitch finished his time at Huntsville . . . faked a sick spell at supper time and got the jailer to come into his cell. He knocked him out with the fool's own gun, stole a horse off the street, and got away. Ned and Mitch have been working together ever since."

A troubled frown furrowed Scott's forehead. "There was three of them. Is there another brother?"

"Lord, I hope not!" Pike shook his head. "No, the third man seems to be different each time. Chances are he don't share in their loot. They probably hire anybody they can find to keep their horses ready for a getaway. Mitch and Ned don't always have help. There was only the two of them when they broke into the Wells Fargo office at Sagemore."

Pike's voice was even slower and deeper as he related the Sagemore incident. "It was after closing time, and they must've figured nobody was around that late. Trouble was, the agent was working late on his books. They shot him twice and must've figured he was dead. They pulled down their masks while they tried to get the safe open.

"Somebody scared them off and they didn't get a dime. Mitch left another corpse behind, but the agent lived 'til about daylight—long enough to describe the men he saw. I got a good description of Mitch from the warden at Huntsville and one of Ned from the town marshal at Sagemore. It was them that killed the Wells Fargo man, all right, and the quick look I got of them in Blackwood fits their size and shape."

Images of the robbery flashed through Scott's mind—a gunshot, people running along the street, and Frank Rawley writhing in the dust. He said, "Mitch must be the old one. He's the one who killed Pa."

Joe Pike walked over to Scott's blankets and sat down on one corner of the bedding, crossing his legs and tucking his feet between them Indian-style. Scott dropped down beside him and watched while Pike took papers and tobacco from his shirt pocket and worked on a cigarette.

"It was Mitch who did the killing all right, but he ain't old." Pike's words were muffled as he struck a match and puffed his cigarette alive. "He's twenty-six, and Ned's a couple years older. You must've been fooled by his hair. It ain't gray, it's blond—pale as sand. I don't know about their mother's habits, but Ned looks like he had a different father. He's dark, swarthy like a Mexican or Indian, only better looking. He ain't the ladies' man, though. Mitch is the one who's woman-crazy—and kill-crazy. He got sent to Huntsville for killing his wife. She wasn't much more than a young'un, but I hear he cut her up something awful."

Pike grew silent and thoughtful, and Scott wondered if the Pinkerton man was having doubts about talking so freely. He remembered Whit Kirby's I.O.U. in his pocket and Billy Clyde Marcum's lifeless body. He was eager to reach Bluestem, but Joe Pike possessed information that Scott needed, and he meant to stay with him as long as the Pinkerton man was willing to share it with him.

During the next hour, listening and asking questions, Scott learned as much as anyone knew about the Sadler brothers. From his own investigation and reports from other Pinkerton detectives, Joe Pike had compiled a history of their lives and crimes.

The Sadler brothers had grown to manhood near the cow town of Hub, but they lived in a number of places during their youth. Their father operated a sawmill, moving it every few years in search of new timber.

By the time Mitch was eighteen, the brothers stopped helping their father and struck out on their own, only occasionally visiting the strip-and-plank house that their parents had built near the mill. They were strong, quick to learn, and had no problem finding work on cattle ranches. They drifted from one job to another, sometimes together, sometimes going separate ways. When their parents moved on, Mitch and Ned stayed behind.

"Mitch's last riding job was with Charlie DeBord, who sent him along on a trail drive to Kansas City," Pike said. "He'd gone up with other herds, to Sedalia and Ellsworth, and each time he'd bring a woman back with him. Mitch can't seem to get by without a woman. Word we have is that some of them were nice girls who wanted to get out from under their parents' thumb, others just whores he took out of a brothel and promised a better life. They'd all leave after a while, slipping away when Mitch wasn't around to stop them."

There was disdain in the twist of Scott's lips. "He must

be as lustful as he is bloodthirsty. Do you think he might hide out with a woman somewhere?"

"Maybe, maybe not. He didn't have too much luck with the last one. On that drive to K. C.," Pike continued, "Mitch got acquainted with a storekeeper whose pretty young niece was visiting with him. Mitch fell in love with the girl, married her, and brought her to Hub. He kept his job with DeBord and rented a house on the stage road about a mile outside of town for them to live in. I've been told her name was Katherine, or Kitty, as most called her. Folks say they got along well, but Mitch was so jealous he'd start a fight every time another man looked at her the wrong way. She was probably the only person he ever loved."

"Then how come he killed her?" Scott asked.

"Bad mistake." Joe Pike made a clucking sound with his tongue. "Mitch came in early from DeBord's Square D spread one day and found a strapping young man standing stark naked in their bedroom. He didn't ask no questions. He pulled his gun and shot the man in the gut right away. His wife was in the kitchen slicing bacon for supper. Mitch didn't ask her no questions either when he stormed in where she was. He went plumb wild. He grabbed the butcher's knife from her hand and started cutting on her. They say she looked awful—an ear sliced off, fingers gone, her belly opened, and her bowels spilling out on the floor. Later—"

"Damn!" Scott uttered the word at the end of a shuddering breath. "How'd they catch up with him?"

Joe Pike took a deep drag on his cigarette and let the smoke out slowly. The sun wrinkles at the corners of his black eyes deepened as he spoke of the carnage inflicted by Mitch Sadler.

"Mitch was so sure no Texas jury would blame him for protecting the honor of his marriage that he went into the town of Hub and reported the killings to a deputy. He was a mite too quick in trying to set up his defense. Somebody else talked to the deputy later, and Mitch ended up in jail. The naked man that Mitch shot didn't die right away. He dragged himself out to the stage road and a horseman found him. He lived long enough to tell the rider who he was and what happened. The rider passed it on to the deputy. Turns out the young man was Kitty's brother, all the way down from Kansas to pay her a surprise visit. He'd taken a bath and was fixing to put on clean clothes when Mitch walked in on him."

The Pinkerton man unfolded his knees and stretched his legs. "The jury took into account that he thought his wife had been in bed with a strange man. They gave Mitch five-to-ten in the Hunstville pen, and five was all he served. It didn't teach him anything. He tied up with his brother Ned, and they've been on a rampage ever since."

"They should have hanged him!" Scott said.

"Probably," Joe Pike agreed. "It would've saved lives. Counting your pa, they've killed five people that I know of. There'll be more if somebody don't stop them."

He recounted the murderous trail of the Sadler brothers as he knew it. They had started by holding up a stage twenty miles outside of Huntsville, thinking it carried the prison payroll. They killed the driver, but there was no payroll aboard and their only loot came from a few dollars in gold they took from the passengers' pockets. Two more Wells Fargo stages had been hit, neither yielding much of value. Mitch and Ned apparently became desperate for money. They entered a saloon late one night in Caprock, where a high stakes poker game was in progress, and wounded two of the players before they scooped up a pot of four hundred dollars and rode away.

"The Sadlers have spilled a lot of blood without much to show for it," Pike concluded.

The whinnying of a horse cut through the air and reminded Scott that time was passing swiftly. He had picketed his bay in a clear spot fifty feet from the camp so its stamping and slobbering through the night would not disturb his sleep. The thick brush hid it from sight, but Scott knew the bay had grazed the grass thin and was ready to move on. He rose from the blankets, squinting against the first light of the day as the sun edged its way into a cloudless sky. Joe Pike stood up beside him.

"The Sadlers made a good haul in Blackwood," Scott said. "Most of it was from my pa."

Pike nodded. "I talked with the sheriff. He didn't say how much they got, but he hinted it was a goodly sum."

The Pinkerton man walked with him as Scott went to get his horse, and they continued their conversation. He was glad the Pinkerton man had found him. He liked Joe Pike, influenced by the fact that the man had not tried to hold back his knowledge of the Sadlers as a wedge to persuade Scott to join his organization. He decided to be equally frank, telling Pike the amount stolen from Frank Rawley and about the note that had to be paid to prevent

John Tripp from claiming the Crowfoot Ranch at an auction.

"Time's against you," Pike observed. "You might
make the bank's deadline, though. The longer the
Sadlers stay free, the braver they'll get. They'll start
taking chances sooner or later."

With Scott leading the bay by its bridle, they headed
back the way they had come. Pike had told all he knew
about the Sadler brothers and had little more to say. He
glanced sideways at Scott occasionally, and he appeared
to be somewhat sullen.

Scott guessed the reason for Pike's covert glances.
"You're wondering if I've been as open with you as
you've been with me."

Pike slowed his steps. "I noticed you've got a bruised
mouth."

Scott touched his lower lip. It was puffy and sore.
"Yesterday I had a fight with a man I'd never seen, and
when I heard you in the brush, I thought it might not be
over yet."

Scott described the brawl with Jake Vernoy, explaining
that his accidental glimpse of Lily in the nude had initi-
ated the fight. "I doubt that Jake has the stomach to
tangle with me again, but I'm not sure about his friend
Lew Bender. He was itching to get mixed up in it. I think
he wanted to prove to Jake and Lily how tough he is, and
I wouldn't be surprised to see him again. It's a personal
thing, and you don't have to get involved if he shows up
before I leave here."

"I'll keep that in mind," Pike drawled. "We ain't part-
ners yet."

"We probably won't be," Scott said, "but I'll show you this for what it's worth."

He took Billy Clyde Marcum's I.O.U. out of his pocket and handed it to Pike.

Frowning, his eyes flickering with interest, Pike studied the paper, then gave it back to Scott. "Maybe the man who signed that paper knows something we don't. This Billy Clyde feller might've been the third man at the holdup . . . maybe the one holding the horses. If he was, something went wrong on the getaway. Maybe the Sadlers didn't trust him, or maybe he pushed too hard for a share of the loot. That could get a man killed. Mitch is the kind who'd get his enjoys out of shooting a man in the back."

Scott walked on a few paces in silence. From the time Joe Pike had started talking about the Sadlers, Scott had worried about what appeared to be a contradiction. He could think of no reason that Pike would attempt to deceive him, but he had to be sure.

Watching Pike's face for any indication of evasiveness, Scott said, "You've given me something to go on that I didn't have, but you know so much about Mitch and Ned Sadler that it bothers me. How is it that you know they killed the Wells Fargo clerk, and are suspects in other hold-ups and killings, and Sheriff Bandy don't know spit? He has a box full of flyers on wanted men, but there's none on the Sadlers?"

"Bothers me, too." Pike admitted. "I spent an hour with Bandy, and I don't think he's hiding anything. Either he's careless with his mail, or he throws stuff away that he don't want to bother with. I talked with the sheriff over in the next county and two town marshals. They're not busting their britches to look for the Sadlers, but they know about them. I left Wade Bandy about as ignorant as I found him. I didn't tell him what I've told you, because he'd get in my way. He strikes me as a feller who wouldn't take kindly to a private outfit like the Pinkertons meddling in his jurisdiction."

Scott believed Joe Pike, and he felt more at ease with him. He said, "Wade Bandy wants to be a good sheriff, but he's got strange notions about how to go about it."

He glanced at the sun, annoyed because he had used up more time than he wanted to spare. It was a short walk to the bay's grazing grounds, but they stopped to talk so often it took them twenty minutes to get back to the campsite. Scott saddled the bay immediately and began putting together his bedroll.

Joe Pike stood quietly by his horse while Scott worked. He rolled another cigarette and seemed in no hurry to leave. Lashing the last rope in place around his tarp, Scott straightened and looked at the Pinkerton man. "I'm real anxious to meet this feller Whit Kirby and I've got to get going. I'm glad we got acquainted."

Pike reached out to shake hands, then stepped back and looked solemnly at Scott Rawley. "You haven't mentioned my proposition, so I reckon you're turning me down. That's not too smart for a man who's got a big job to do and not much time left to get it done. You're out here by yourself, already in trouble for meddling in the business between some hard-nosed drifter and a woman, and too damned stubborn to see that you need help."

"I don't see how carrying a Pinkerton card in my

pocket is going to make the job easier."

"That's because you didn't listen good," Pike said. "This is big country, and you can't be everywhere at once. I've got a detective crew roaming about. They'll be digging up what they can about the Sadlers, and I'll pass it on to you. Maybe we'll need them, maybe we won't, but if we do, it'll be like having your own posse. We can help you a lot if you'll help us."

Scott glanced at the sun, estimating the hour. The time Otis Potter had given him to pay the Crowfoot note grew shorter every minute, and he was eager to meet the liveryman who had written the I.O.U. for Billy Clyde Marcum.

"I don't want to be slowed down by big-shot orders," he told Pike, "and I don't want anybody bossing what I do."

"I won't lay down any rules for you. I can authorize pay of forty a month for you as a part-timer. If you nail the Sadlers, there might be more. Wells Fargo has offered Pinkerton a sizeable fee to catch the Sadlers. The state's got a reward out for them, too—five hundred on Mitch and two hundred on Ned. If you nail the Sadlers while you're with us, Pinkerton will claim the rewards, but you'll get a share."

Pinkerton's pay policy was of little interest to Scott, but he liked the sound of an independent posse who might be able to check on the outlaws' movements. He also liked the idea of having the help of a man such as Joe Pike. He shook Pike's hand again and agreed to become an agent with the Pinkerton National Detective Agency.

Pike did not give him a chance to back down. He quickly found writing materials and a packet of identification cards in his saddlebags. After the words "Issued To," he wrote Scott's name on one of the cards and handed it to him.

"That makes it official," Pike drawled, looking pleased. "Show it only when you think it'll help."

Scott pocketed the card and started toward his horse. He took one step, then stopped abruptly as a gunshot crackled through the air. He flinched as a bullet threw up dirt and plowed into the ground six inches from his left foot.

CHAPTER TEN

INSTINCTIVELY, they scurried for cover, diving on the ground behind the cedar scrub where Pike had tied his mustang when they returned with Scott's bay. The horses sensed danger, tossing their manes and whinnying. The mustang sidestepped around the tree, almost crushing Scott before settling down. The bay trotted away a few yards, dragging the reins, and stopped with ears up and nostrils flaring.

"Rifle shot," Joe Pike said. "Think it was Lew Bender or that girl's brother?"

"Could be," Scott said, "but Lily had the only rifle and I figure she'd never part with it as long as Lew Bender keeps leering at her the way he was when I saw him."

They did not say anything more for a minute or two while they waited to see if the bushwhacker would fire again.

"Want to see if we can find him, or let it go?" Pike asked.

"I want to find him," Scott said grimly. "I don't want to keep worrying about somebody shooting me in the back."

The single shot had come from the other side of the creek. Neither Scott nor Pike believed it was fired by the Sadler brothers. If the outlaws were in the basin, it was unlikely that they would want to draw attention to themselves. They surmised that a lone gunman had fired at Scott and was afraid to linger after his shot missed.

"You got any real bad enemies in Blackwood?" Joe Pike asked.

"None mad enough to kill me," Scott said.

He kept his horse still while they discussed a plan of pursuit. Afterward, Pike rode directly toward the spot where the shot had appeared to originate, on the far side of the creek. Scott headed across the basin on a route that would take him nearly a mile downstream. After crossing the creek, they would ride toward each other and try to pin the bushwhacker between them.

Scott forded Medicine Creek near the mouth of the basin. A rocky bench ran along the stream on that side, beginning as a foot-high ledge and rising to a height of fifteen feet a hundred yards farther on, where the creek took a sharp bend and went out of sight. There was a sandy shoreline between the trees, which bordered the creek and the bench.

He started upstream, peering intently at the ground ahead of him. The moist soil of the shore was unmarked except for a few scratchy lines that appeared to be bird tracks. There were no hoofprints. The bushwhacker had not yet passed this way, and Scott wondered if Pike had intercepted him.

Except for the swishing of the water, the land about him was still. He stopped his horse, considering the wisdom of riding past the bluff at the bend of the creek. It was a blind turn, and he did not want to be startled into a sudden gunfight that might result in his own death or the death of the man he sought. If he found the bush-whacker, he wanted him alive so he might learn if the sniper was involved with the outlaws or the bank rob-bery.

He thought he heard a sound, the faint noise a horse might make by throwing up dirt from its iron shoes. Scott's breath quickened. Reining the bay around as qui-etly as possible, he went back to the low end of the bench and urged his horse up the slope. He could now see that the high point of the bluff was actually the sandstone face of an eroded knoll, which rolled away from the creek and blended into the hills. The soil was thin and rocky, but it supported a scattering of sagebrush and small pines.

He moved far enough away to be hidden from the trail below, and rode along the knoll until he reached its crest. He tied his horse to a tree and walked part of the way back to the bluff, then dropped flat and wriggled forward on his belly until he reached its edge.

Lifting his head cautiously, Scott looked below. On either side of him, Medicine Creek flowed between green fringes like an empty street twisting through a des-olate town, visible for a while, disappearing around bends, then popping into view again.

Nothing moved along the sections that Scott could see. After scanning the shoreline, he scooted away and sat up, straining his ears for any hint of movement. Somewhere around one of the hidden bends of the stream a rider was coming toward him, and Scott was sure it was the bushwhacker. It was only a matter of time, he told himself, until he would find out who it was.

He thought about the question Joe Pike had asked him before they left the campsite. Perhaps he had been less than honest when he told Pike he knew of no one who would want to kill him. Deputy Pat Logan had tried to pull a gun on him after Scott kicked over his chair at the sheriff's office. It was the second time Scott had embarrassed the hot-tempered little lawman.

He had challenged Pat Logan for the first time six months ago at the Texas Star Saloon. It had happened on a Saturday night when Scott had come to town to have dinner with Della Grange. After bidding her good night, he'd gone to the Texas Star for a drink before riding back to the Crowfoot.

Business was dull at the Texas Star. One man stood at the bar, and four or five others were seated at tables. As soon as he entered, Scott heard an argument developing between two men near the side wall. The signs of an impending fight were obvious.

While Scott was sipping his drink, the voices at the table grew louder. Chairs scraped the floor, and the two men came to their feet, weaving on unsteady legs and mouthing curses. One of them was tall and slender, with a sharp nose and reddish hair. The other man was a head shorter. His face was round, covered with a stubble of black beard, and the tail of his flannel shirt had slipped from the belt around his bulging stomach.

With fists clenched, they stood a yard apart and screamed violent threats at each other. Finally, the red-haired man threw a looping punch at the fat man's chin. He missed his mark, staggered forward, and fell face-down on the floor. Blinking bleary eyes, the fat man stared vacantly, puzzled that his companion was no longer standing where he should be. He spotted him on the floor and moved clumsily toward him.

It was not the kind of fight anyone would want to stop. The Texas Star patrons gathered around, laughing at the feeble efforts of the combatants and waiting for the altercation to wear itself out.

Deputy Pat Logan heard the disturbance as he passed in front of the saloon. He burst through the batwing doors, swinging his head around in search of the trouble. He strode swiftly toward the cowboys. Without asking any questions, he drew his Colt and smashed the butt against the side of the fat man's head. The big cowboy fell to one knee and pitched sideways to the floor, with blood oozing from a cut on his temple. With the gun upraised, the deputy lunged toward the redhead, who had remained where he fell.

Scott Rawley had seen enough. Two quick strides brought him to Pat Logan's back. He grabbed the wrist of the hand that held the gun, yanking the deputy's arm back and forcing it up between his shoulder blades. Logan cursed and let the gun drop.

"They didn't pin a badge on you so you could beat up

on helpless drunks," Scott said sharply.

Logan picked up his gun and shoved it in the holster. He glared at Scott, his yellowish-brown eyes bright with anger. "You're asking for trouble, Rawley! You're interfering with the law."

"Arrest me," Scott said flatly.

Logan pretended not to hear Scott's words. He yanked the red-haired man to his feet and marched him toward the door, supporting him with an arm around his waist.

"Couple of you fellows grab that fat hombre and tote him over to the jail for me," he said to the onlookers.

No one moved. As he went out the door, Logan said over his shoulder, "Maybe it'll be better if I come back for him myself."

Later, Scott regretted his interference, but he did not regard the brief incident as serious enough to generate a long-lasting feud. He was more uncertain about the Crowfoot's relationship with John Tripp. Was the Bar 40 owner a deadly rival, or merely a tightfisted man who wanted to increase his wealth the easy way? Tripp would not risk his reputation by killing a man to accomplish his aims, but he might get it done another way.

Cal Baylor probably had more than a foreman's interest in the success of the Bar 40 Ranch. If history repeated itself, the foreman was the heir-apparent to the Bar 40 fortune. If Tripp ordered it, Cal Baylor might kill Scott to prevent him from recovering the stolen money in time to stop a forced sale of the Crowfoot.

Scott's speculation about enemies ended. He heard a horse slobber, and this time there was no mistaking the sound. It was distinct and nearby. Scott's five-minute wait atop the bluff was about to pay off. Sliding on his stomach, he inched to the edge of the bluff again. He removed his hat, left it on the ground, and peeked at the trail below.

He acted just in time. The horseman was fifty feet to Scott's right. Although he had been thinking of the bush-whacker as a stranger, he was not surprised to see a face that he knew quite well.

The man riding along the edge of the creek, sitting stiffly erect in the saddle with both hands gripping the reins, was Deputy Pat Logan. The lawman had chosen caution rather than haste in his getaway. He kept his horse at a slow pace, casting furtive glances over his shoulder, then searching the land ahead of him and cocking his head to listen for any telltale sounds.

Scott waited until Logan was directly below him. He swore under his breath and dived at him, his arms spread to encircle the deputy's neck. His timing was off. He struck the horse's back with his elbows and chest, a hand's width behind the saddle. The impact from the short leap hardly jarred him. He slid off the horse's rear and landed on his feet.

The unexpected jolt scared the horse and it reared up on its hind legs, whinnying in alarm. Pat Logan was a skilled rider. He dropped the reins, swung one leg high, and stepped lightly to the ground.

He whirled about to face Scott Rawley, his eyes widening with recognition. "What do you think you're doing, flying out of the sky on top of me like that?"

"I'm catching me a bushwhacker, that's what I'm doing!"

The color faded from Pat Logan's face. "I don't know what you're talking about. I'm out here trying to pick up some sign of them outlaws you wanted us to catch. I don't know nothing about no bushwhacker."

Scott took a step toward the man. His crow-black hair hung in ringlets across his forehead and the frosty blue eyes shone fiercely. He ground out his words through clenched teeth. "You're lying, Logan. You tried to kill me a few minutes ago. You'd better start spilling your guts, or I'm going to pound you with my fists until you do."

Logan held up a restraining hand. "I'm not taking anything off you today, Rawley. You're a foot taller than me and forty pounds heavier. You're too big for me to fight, but I'm better with a gun than you think. You caught me off guard at the sheriff's office, but I know what's coming this time. If you lay a hand on me, I'll kill you!"

The deputy's hand hovered inches above the butt of his gun. He backed away and stared at Scott, his eyes blinking rapidly while he tried to steady his nerves.

A split second was long enough for Scott's mind to filter scores of fleeting thoughts. The deputy's defiance was unexpected. Scott wanted to avoid a gunfight, which would thwart his purpose. A frightened man was more dangerous than any gunman, desperation driving him to accomplish feats beyond his abilities. Scott wondered if he would have to draw and fire by instinct, or whether he would have enough time to aim a shot where he wanted it.

Pat Logan had old scores to settle and they were on his mind. His voice cracking, he yelled, "You're always trying to make me look like a fool, and it's going to cost me my job. I'm not going to take a beating from you. I'll kill you first. I can explain that easy. You pulled a gun on me, and I had to defend myself. There ain't no witnesses!"

The deputy's hand darted downward. Scott's hand was faster. His move seemed almost effortless as his gun came up and fired. The roar of his Colt echoed along the rippling water and reverberated from the hills.

A yelp of pain came from Logan's gaping mouth. His gun was only half out of its holster. It fell at his feet and the deputy sank to the ground, clutching his right thigh.

Scott walked to Logan's side. There was a tear in the deputy's Levi's below his holster. Logan ripped the slit wider and inspected the wound. Scott's bullet had gone where he'd aimed it, cutting a furrow through the flesh of Logan's leg. It had sliced deep enough to injure part of the muscle, and the ragged gash was covered with blood.

"You'll pay for this!" Logan cried.

"Shut up!" Scott snapped. "You tried to kill me and I want to know why."

Logan shook his head. "I'm out here doing my duty as a deputy sheriff and that's all I've got to say."

Scott's gun was still in his hand and the acrid odor of powder wafted from its barrel. He cocked the Colt and pointed it at Pat Logan. "I'm going to put a bullet in your other leg, then I'm going to put one in each arm and keep putting holes in you until you tell me what you're up to. You'll—"

The thudding of hoofbeats caused Scott to break off

the sentence and look upstream. Joe Pike had heard the gunshot and was pounding toward them. He slowed his mustang when he saw that Scott was safe, approaching at a trot. The Pinkerton man dismounted and left his horse in front of the limestone bluff.

"What happened?" Pike asked.

Scott nodded toward the deputy, who sat rocking back and forth and holding his bleeding leg. "I found our bushwhacker. He had his mind set on killing me, and he got sort of a lead burn for his trouble."

"What're you going to do with him?"

Scott's lips drew close against his teeth. "I want to know whether he's trying to satisfy a grudge or whether he's got other reasons for shooting at me. I'm going to keep putting bullet holes in different parts of his carcass until he tells me what I want to know."

"That's what I'd do," Joe Pike said.

Bubbles of sweat popped out on Pat Logan's forehead. He cowered down, shielding his face with his forearm as Scott cocked the six-gun and aimed it at the deputy's right arm.

"Wait!" Logan's eyes were wide, pleading. "It—it was all Sheriff Bandy's notion. That's right! He wanted me to try to slow you down so we'd have a chance to catch them bank robbers before you did. I wasn't trying to kill you. I was trying to shoot you in the leg . . . maybe lay you up a few days or scare you off."

Tilting his head skeptically, Scott said, "Wade Bandy wouldn't give an order like that. He sticks too close to the law books. You're lying, Logan."

The deputy grimaced. He grabbed his thigh again and

pressed his thumbs down on each side of the wound. "My leg hurts bad! All right. It was my idea to slow you down, but it's what the sheriff would do if he had any guts. I—I need the money, and I didn't want you to beat me to the rewards. I'm going to give up this badge and try to get ahead. Dave Rankin has agreed to sell me the Texas Star Saloon if I can raise a thousand dollars for a down payment. That's all I'm trying to do . . . trying to amount to something. You ain't hurt, so why don't you leave me alone?"

Scott's threat was a bluff He could not shoot a wounded, unarmed man, and Pat Logan had said all he was going to say. For a few seconds Scott towered over the man, wishing he could make him suffer more for his cowardly act. Logan watched Scott's face fearfully, until he saw him ease the Colt's hammer back in place.

Picking up the deputy's fallen gun, Scott opened the cylinder and shook the cartridges out on the ground. He handed the weapon to Logan. "Tie your neckerchief around that scratch on your leg and get out of here. If you ever cross me again, I'll kill you."

"You going to let him go?" Joe Pike asked quietly.

"I don't know what else to do with him. I can't haul him around with me, and I don't have time to march him back to Blackwood to face Sheriff Bandy right now."

"See what you mean," Pike said. "Fooling with a lawman is touchy business." He stared into Pat Logan's eyes, then looked toward the deputy's horse. He gave Scott a knowing look and said, "Keep him where he is a minute. Sometimes a man's traps will tell you things his mouth won't. I'm going to look in his saddlebags."

126

Pat Logan forgot about his wound. He rose on his good knee and cried, "Stay out of my stuff! You're messing with official business, and I'm still wearing a badge!"

Scott put his hand on his gun and snapped, "Sit down!"

Cringing, Logan slumped back to the ground.

Years of dealing with lawless men had honed Joe Pike's intuition. He ran his hand around inside Logan's saddlebags and withdrew a sheaf of papers. Throwing aside the string that bound them, he shuffled through the papers, pausing to read a few lines from each one.

"He's been holding out on his boss," Pike said, handing the papers to Scott. "He's got all the posters and letters other lawmen have told me about—a rundown on the stage holdups, the Wells Fargo killing, and Ned Sadler's jailbreak. There's a letter from the U. S. Marshal listing the rewards. There are descriptions of the Sadlers in that bundle, too."

Scott inspected the documents, and renewed anger traced hard lines around his mouth. He looked down at Pat Logan and growled, "You bastard! You've been protecting those killers!"

Shoving the papers into his pocket, Scott lifted his Colt from its holster and slapped the barrel against his palm. He ran his glance over the deputy's body as though he were trying to decide where to place a bullet. It was all the encouragement Pat Logan needed to start talking again.

Sheriff Bandy had assigned his deputy the task of picking up the official mail and telegraph messages. Logan had the first look, and he kept everything that mentioned cash rewards.

In a shaky voice, he again said that his shot at Scott had been a bluff, and his only other wrong had been to deceive his boss.

Running his tongue over his lips, the squatty little deputy made a final effort to regain his dignity. "You ain't heard the last of this. You shot a deputy sheriff, and I aim to tell everybody about it. Us lawmen stick together, and there'll be others looking to pin something on you."

"You're a fool," Scott said dryly. "You'll have a hard time explaining that wound to Wade Bandy. He's not going to believe I shot you for no reason. I'm keeping these papers, and I hope you'll be there when I show them to the sheriff."

CHAPTER ELEVEN

SCOTT TURNED HIS BACK on the man and walked away, heading downstream to look for a way to the top of the bluff, where he had left his hat and his horse. Joe Pike stepped into his saddle and slow-walked his horse alongside. Neither of them looked back. They had no fear that the frightened deputy would try to stop them. When they reached the low end of the bench, Pike waited while Scott retrieved his horse, then they rode back together.

When they arrived at his campsite, Scott loaded his bedroll behind the bay's saddle and prepared to leave. Joe Pike lingered beside his horse, holding the reins loosely between his fingers, and Scott knew he had more to say.

Scott paused with one hand on his saddlehorn and looked at the Pinkerton man, waiting for him to speak. Pike pushed his hat brim back with his thumb and said, "I've been thinking about that girl and those two hombres you ran into up the creek a ways. Mitch Sadler has got a way with women, and maybe she's one of them. Jake Vernoy could have started that fight to sidetrack you before you looked around too close. They'd make a good smoke screen for the Sadlers to lay low with for a while."

"I don't think so," Scott said, shaking his head. "I don't think Lily would go along with hiding outlaws. They're probably what they say they are—pilgrims looking for something solid to tie onto."

He looked in the direction that he had met the Vernoys and Lew Bender. "Ever since you told me the kind of woman-chaser Mitch Sadler is, I've been thinking, too, but not about those people at the buckboard being friends with the Sadlers," Scott continued. "I've been thinking about something my pa said. He told me the way to get the best of a man is to find his weakness and work on it. Mitch Sadler's weakness is women. It's not much to go on, but it's more than I've had up to now. I'm going to start checking out all the whorehouses around these parts. If he's as wild about women as you say, he's likely to show up at one of them sooner or later."

Joe Pike nodded approvingly. "You're going to make one hell of a Pinkerton man! That's a prime notion, and there's a bordello of some sort in every town I've seen."

Rubbing his hands together, Pike paced back and forth, nodding his head in approval. "It's too bad we can't start our own bordello. That way, anytime Mitch showed up we would be there waiting for him."

"That's impossible," Scott said. "I need more than Mitch's hide nailed to the wall. I need my money, too. I'm sure the Sadlers have stashed that away somewhere. First I need to find them, then figure a way to make them lead me to the money."

Pike shrugged. "I didn't say it was possible. I just said it might be a sure deal. Time's your problem, and we'd better start doing something about it. The only telegraph close by is in Hub, and I need to send some wires to headquarters to let them know where I am and what I'm up to. There's got to be a bordello there, and it's the Sadlers' old stomping grounds. I'm going to head cross-country from here and nose around Hub for a while."

He strode to the mustang, which was tethered to a nearby tree. "I'll catch up with you in Bluestem. You know this country well enough to find the town?"

"I know the general lay of the land, but it has been years since I've been to Bluestem. It might take me a while to pick up the trail."

Pike waited long enough to give directions. "I've worked around here a few times. Follow the creek across the prairie and you'll spot the stage road on the opposite bank about three miles out. Hold to it and it'll take you toward town. You'll come to the crossroads after an hour or so, and there ought to be signposts. From there it's five miles to Bluestem and five miles to Hub. The right fork goes to Bluestem. You might want to get a room at the Elkhorn Hotel."

"See you in town," Scott said.

Pike sent his mustang cantering toward Medicine Creek, heading north toward the town of Hub. A few minutes later Scott rode toward Bluestem, where a man named Whit Kirby had signed an I.O.U. for Billy Clyde Marcum. If Billy Clyde had become acquainted with the Sadlers while he was working at the livery, Whit Kirby was bound to know something about them.

Under the blazing mid-afternoon sun, the streets of Bluestem were almost deserted. Only those who had a pressing need to be outside ventured forth on such a day, but Scott doubted that the heat accounted for the town's inactivity.

The condition of the dozen buildings that strung along each side of the main street spoke of Bluestem's lack of prosperity. Several shops were vacant, and others displayed wooden awnings that sagged on rotting supports. Storefronts were patched with scrap lumber, and several windows were boarded over where glass had been broken and never replaced.

After reaching the stage road, Scott had lost sight of Medicine Creek for most of the way, but now he could see the line of trees that marked its course south of Bluestem. The town's residential area had grown up along the stream. A score of houses, some of painted clapboards and some of chinked logs, were visible from the street.

As a boy, Scott had visited the town with his father, but it did not look familiar. His only clear memory was of the two-story Elkhorn Hotel, where he and Frank Rawley had spent a night long ago. He looked for it as he rode slowly down the street.

Bluestem was not completely devoid of life. A buck-board was drawn alongside the boardwalk in front of Monroe's Mercantile and a few saddled horses waited at other hitching rails. There was a scattering of pedestrians along the boardwalks, most of them near the Dry Run Saloon. A few people stopped to gaze at the tall rider, making no effort to conceal their curiosity about the arrival of a stranger in town.

"Sorry-looking place," Scott murmured aloud as he passed the buckboard.

The false fronts of the Dry Run Saloon and Monroe's Mercantile blocked Scott's view for a while, but after he passed them, he saw the upper floor of the Elkhorn Hotel rising above the other buildings. He was glad the ride was over, and he grunted wearily as he dismounted in front of the Elkhorn and secured his horse at one of the hitching rails.

The hotel was set back from the street far enough to allow an expanse of green lawn between the hitching rail and the gallery porch. A walkway of flat stones led to the steps, flanked on each side by beds of red, yellow, and purple flowers. Two pin-oak trees shaded the front of the building, their leaves and patches of blue sky reflecting from the spotless glass windows of the dining room.

"The place must be run by a woman," Scott said to himself as he put his bedroll across his shoulder and went inside.

His assumption proved correct. The woman behind the desk was about Scott's age, tall and shapely with a broad-cheeked face, a gently rounded chin, and shiny black hair that brushed the shoulders of her crisp white blouse. Her eyes were a peculiar brown, like the color of old gold, and they sparkled when she greeted him in a brisk soprano voice.

"Welcome to the Elkhorn!" she said as Scott dropped his bedroll on the floor and approached the desk. She surveyed him with a frank, appraising stare that began at his scuffed boots and rose until she looked straight into the ice-blue eyes.

"My name's Millie Adcock—owner, manager, cook, and cleaning woman." She smiled at Scott. "It's plain to a Texas girl that you're not rolling in money, so you ought to know how I operate the Elkhorn. We don't get many visitors in Bluestem and I make sure I get all I can from them when they stop here. The rate isn't as cheap as most places, and I expect to be paid each day until I know you better. Are you sure you can afford to stay here?"

Scott returned her smile. He did not like the sound of the Elkhorn's prices, but he was not about to let Millie Adcock know the truth about his limited resources.

He returned her smile and said, "Yes, ma'am. As a matter of fact, I was thinking about buying the place. What's it going to cost me?"

"For the hotel?"

"Just the room right now," Scott replied. "Maybe we can make a big deal later."

Millie Adcock tossed her hair and laughed. "There are days when I feel like getting rid of the place, but I know you're teasing me." She explained the rates—two dollars a night, with breakfast and supper included. Obviously proud of the hotel's reputation, Millie Adcock spent a few minutes talking about the Elkhorn's facilities, then handed him a key.

"You'll be in Number 10, upstairs near the front end of the hallway. It's next to the room I use, but don't jump to any conclusions because I'm putting you there. We get the church crowd in here for supper on Sundays and Wednesdays, and they're always looking for sin." She put her hands to her cheeks and giggled. "I'll try to drop a hint that there's a handsome man sleeping in the room next to me. I like to keep them guessing about whether I'm good or bad."

Scott chuckled, enjoying her sense of humor. He handed her the twenty-dollar bill that his father had given him when they sold the Crowfoot cattle. Unfolding the bank note, Millie Adcock inspected it carefully before she gave Scott his change. She dipped a quill pen in an inkwell and handed it to him. "You need to sign the book, but I ain't particular about names."

"I'll use the one my mother gave me."

As he turned to leave the lobby, Millie Adcock said, "We've got a shed in back with four stalls if you want your horse out of the sun, but if you want feed, you'll have to go to the livery."

Scott nodded. "That works out all right. I need to see a man named Whit Kirby."

"Well, if you go to the Bluestem Livery, you'll see him, hear him, and smell him."

Her tone indicated she did not like Whit Kirby, but her opinion of the livery man was of no interest to Scott. He looked around to familiarize himself with the layout of the hotel. The Elkhorn lobby was square in shape, well lighted from the three windows that faced the street. A hallway leading to the ground-floor rooms was to the right of the registration desk, and the stairway was on the left. A doorway near the stairway provided an entrance to the dining room. A half-dozen cane-bottom chairs were placed at intervals around the walls, and a horse-hide sofa in front of the rock-faced fireplace.

The Elkhorn had only a few guests. A heavy-jowled man with muttonchop whiskers sat at one end of the sofa. He paid no attention to Scott and did not look up from the newspaper he was reading as Scott walked by him. Two other men were engaged in conversation with the slick-haired bartender in the dining room, but Scott suspected they were townspeople whiling away time in the Elkhorn's quiet surroundings.

He climbed the stairs to his room, but stayed only long enough to toss his pack on the bed and check his shirt pocket to be sure he had Billy Clyde Marcum's I.O.U. He saw his reflection as he passed the dresser mirror and stopped short, surprised at his appearance.

Scott had not shaved before leaving his night camp, and the stubble on his face darkened his skin beyond its normal tan. The contrast of the sky-blue eyes above the beard was like fiery stars shining in a black sky. The swelling was gone from his lips, but the inside of his mouth was still raw.

He looked at the water pitcher and bowl on the wash-stand, considered rinsing his face before leaving, but decided it was more important to meet with Whit Kirby. He did not want to appear before the liveryman with the look of a vengeance-crazed killer, but he could not wash away the anger and grief that had aged his face and put the wild look in his eyes.

It was a short ride to Whit Kirby's livery barn. Scott had obtained directions from Millie Adcock before leaving, and he was pleased to learn that the livery was located on a narrow road two hundred yards from the rear entrance of the Elkhorn Hotel.

Scott was about to dismount to open the gate in the rail fence that enclosed the livery's main lot, when a man stepped from a side door of the barn and came toward him. He stayed in the saddle while the man lifted the bars, swung the gate aside, and waved him in.

"I sure like to see business come from strangers," the man said, bobbing his head. "Ain't enough money in Bluestem to keep a man in business, and it's a damn sorry business I'm in, anyway. Name's Whit Kirby."

Scott slid to the ground and handed the bay's reins to the liveryman. Whit Kirby was a small man, his head rising barely above Scott's shoulders. His cotton shirt and hickory pants, held in place by a wide belt with brass studs, smelled of hay, sweat, and caked dust. He surveyed Scott's long frame over rimless spectacles, which rested midway along the ridge of his sharp nose. "I reckon you won't be giving your name. Damn few with your looks ever do."

The liveryman was a talker. The surly expression portrayed by his shrunken, bony-cheeked face and slanted, blue eyes was evident in his tone. Whit Kirby's voice was curt and twangy, peppered with profanity. He licked his lips each time he started to speak, reminding Scott of a snake at bay.

"I've never been ashamed of who I am," Scott said, introducing himself.

"Damn stranger to me. I never heard of no Rawleys and I know everybody around. 'Course, there ain't been a new person settle in Bluestem since Noah floated the ark. This place is going to hell in a handbasket and we're all going with it. We got no town board, no mayor, no town marshal . . . no nothing. Fools who settled here thought the Missouri Pacific Railroad was coming, but it went on to Red Butte Junction instead. Fools then, fools now."

Kirby pushed at his shapeless black hat with one hand while he held onto the bay's reins with the other. "The board for the bronc is fifty cents a day. You pay me now. Just drop the money in my shirt pocket and I'll take care of the horse. Don't take no offense because I don't trust you. I don't trust nobody. Don't like nobody much, and damn few like me. After you pay me for the first day, I'll trust you for the second if you want it. That don't make us friends, though."

"I'll keep that in mind," Scott said. He put a dollar in Kirby's pocket and caught the odor of stale whiskey on the liveryman's breath. "I want to talk to you about something."

Whit Kirby's tongue darted across his lips, and the corners of his slanted eyes appeared to droop lower. "You do, eh? Somebody told you I was a damn nosy old busybody, did they? Well, they told you right. I mind everybody's business just so's we'll be even when they start minding mine. Wait on the bench on the shady side of the barn."

After stabling the horses, the liveryman returned and sat down beside Scott with a grunt. He appeared to be in his seventies, his legs stiffened by rheumatism and his disposition soured by hard times. He peered at Scott over the top of his spectacles. "You got a badge in your pocket?"

Kirby's voice was less strident, somewhat cautious. He either feared the law or respected it, and Scott tried to make a good impression. He said, "I'm nobody's official, but I've signed on with the Pinkerton National Detective Agency."

He showed Kirby the Pinkerton card Joe Pike had given him. It was the wrong move.

The liveryman gave the card a cursory glance. He uttered a string of curses and spat into the dirt. "By God, a Pinkerton man!" he snorted. "I despise them bastards! Spies and carpet-baggers, that's what they are. Old Allan Pinkerton was hired by Abe Lincoln in person, some say, to work for the Yankees and spy on the Confederacy during the late war. Them Yankee skunks done dirt to a lot of Texans, and I ain't having no truck with any damn Pinkerton man!"

"I'm not here to fight the war again," Scott said. "I want to ask you about Billy Clyde Marcum."

Whit Kirby looked away and cursed. "Never heard of the sonofabitch."

CHAPTER TWELVE

ITH AN IMPATIENT JAB at his shirt pocket, Scott took out Billy Clyde Marcum's I.O.U., spread it open, and laid it on the bench beside Whit Kirby. "Billy Clyde's dead, but I took this off his body. You signed it."

News of Billy Clyde's death came as a shock to the liveryman. Scott saw the droopy eyes widen slightly, but it was only a fleeting change in the man's dour countenance.

"So I lied to a Pinkerton man," Kirby snorted. "That won't cost me no sleep, by God. If you're here to collect Billy Clyde's debt, I'll give you two dollars and send you on your way, but I ain't telling you nothing. What do you say to that, Mister Pinkerton man?"

Scott's eyes were like frosted glass. He stood up, put his hand on his gun, and towered over the wizened liveryman. "Billy Clyde used to be a friend of mine. He was riding with a couple of outlaws who killed my pa and robbed him. They had to come here to find Billy Clyde, and you must have been around at the time. You're going to tell me all about it. If you keep on being stubborn, I'm going to pound this Colt on your bony head until you change your mind!"

There was no sign of fear in Whit Kirby's face. He lifted his hat and rubbed one hand through his wispy gray hair, then clamped the hat back in place. "In seventy-two years," he said dryly, "I been shot, stabbed, and gun-whipped, and I ain't partial to none of them. If you're going to be that damn ornery, sit and we'll talk."

Scott sat down, leaving more space between them this time so he could watch Kirby's face. "No more lies," he said firmly.

Kirby dipped his head and looked at Scott over the top of his glasses. "Hate to hear about Billy Clyde. I was close to liking that damn wild-eyed maverick. How'd he die?"

"Shot in the back." Scott told the liveryman where he had found Billy Clyde Marcum's body and of the subsequent burial on Matt Latham's Anchor Ranch. He also recounted the story young Jeff Latham had told him about seeing three riders headed toward Blackwood and described the bank robbery that had resulted in Frank Rawley's death.

"That's all you need to hear from me," Scott concluded. "I want to hear about Billy Clyde."

"One of them rolling stones that didn't gather no moss," Whit Kirby began. "That's sure as hell what he was. Down on his luck and happy as a man with good sense, by God."

Billy Clyde had come into Bluestem afoot a month ago, with a saddle on his shoulders and blisters on his feet. He walked in from the Hub crossroads, which was as far as the stage driver would let him ride on the money he had.

His first stop had been at the livery barn. He told Kirby he had been working for two years on a ranch near the Rio Grande, saving his wages to pay a debt to an old friend. When he had accumulated the money he needed, he headed north. While he had been asleep one night in a cow town hotel, someone knocked him over the head and took his money.

Hoping to recoup his loss, Billy Clyde sold his horse to raise a stake and tried his luck in a poker game. Within an hour, he was down to his last twenty dollars, so he gave up and used the remaining money to buy a stage-coach ticket.

After listening to Billy Clyde, Whit Kirby had been convinced the bearded cowboy knew more about horses than any man alive. The liveryman hired Billy Clyde as a helper, furnished his meals, and fixed him a place to sleep in the harness shack.

"Any man who talks as much as Billy Clyde most often is full of lies," Whit Kirby said. "I reckon you could believe about half of what he said. He didn't lie about horses, though. Hell of a bronc-buster, he was. A feller wandered in here last week with a wild mustang he'd spent a month trying to tame, and it was still ornery. Offered to pay me ten dollars to tame him or sell him to me for twenty. Billy Clyde was listening, so he called me aside and said—"

"I don't care about that." Scott cut in impatiently.

"I'm trying to tell you about the I.O.U., damnit. I want to clear that up."

Scott shrugged and Kirby continued.

"Billy Clyde told me to buy the horse and he'd tame him for me. I figured it's a sixty-dollar horse if he's saddle-broke, and that's a good profit off of twenty dollars. Next day, I bet Billy Clyde two dollars he couldn't stay on the mustang, and he won. I was going to add it to his regular pay so he wouldn't blow it right away, but he wanted it in writing, so I wrote that I.O.U. you found on him."

"So much for that," Scott said. "I want to know how he got tied up with the men Jeff Latham saw him riding with on the way to Blackwood."

Whit Kirby sighed. "You're a hard-nosed hombre, ain't you?"

"Usually I'm not." Scott said. "I'm looking for a killer and I don't have the rest of my life to find him."

"I can tell you what they looked like." Kirby said. "One was your size, tall, cold-eyed with sorta faded straw hair. The other one's maybe a head shorter, dark as an Injun with a grin that looks like he knows something nobody else don't. They was right friendly all around. Billy Clyde takes to that sort. They rode in about noon, told me to give their horses a good feed of grain, then walked up the road to Big Betty's Place."

"Big Betty's Place?"

"Damn high-class bordello up the road a piece from here. They stayed up there two hours or so, then came back for their horses. I saw them jawing with Billy Clyde for a spell, and after a while Billy Clyde asked me for a couple days off. He said he could make an easy ten bucks by helping move some horses from one place to another. Damn my hide, maybe I should've . . ."

The liveryman's voice trailed off into unintelligible mumbles. He turned away, pretending to notice something unusual about the horses prancing around one of the corrals.

"You were about to say more," Scott prodded.

Rising stiffly, Whit Kirby turned his back on Scott and

walked away. "I've told you what you asked."

Scott moved to the liveryman's side and grabbed his arm. "You knew those men!"

Kirby pushed at his glasses and looked up at Scott. "You're mean enough to gun-whip a man if he riles you, ain't you?"

"You can bet on it," Scott snapped.

"The Sadler brothers," the liveryman blurted out. "That's who was here. I knowed them when they was damn young colts, knowed them when Mitch killed that little woman of his. It took me a while to recollect the faces, but I knowed them. I should have warned Billy Clyde to stay away from them."

Kirby took a step forward to avoid looking at Scott. He said, "My mouth runs off like a horse with the scours, by God, but folks hereabouts know I spread lies and gossip. A man can get killed telling the truth about some things, and I ain't saying no more."

"Good enough," Scott replied. "I'm obliged to you. Don't tell anybody I showed you that card."

Whit Kirby glared at him. "Tell about it? Hell, I wouldn't want any self-respecting Texan to know I ever said spit to a Pinkerton man."

"I'm a Texan," Scott countered. "I expect I'll always be one."

Scott left Whit Kirby and walked back toward the Elkhorn Hotel, wondering if his visit at the livery had accomplished anything. At least, the conversation had restored some of his respect for Billy Clyde Marcum. He suspected Billy Clyde had saved his wages to repay the money he had stolen from Scott long ago, and he was almost certain his former partner was unaware of the real nature of the job the Sadlers had hired him to do.

His final words to Whit Kirby echoed in his mind. When the liveryman had indicated that a loyal Texan would not become associated with the Pinkerton agency, Scott had felt defensive. He had declared himself a Texan, and a man who expected to remain one. His doubts about returning to the Missouri River had grown from the moment he saw Billy Clyde Marcum's body. Billy Clyde died before he was thirty, leaving behind nothing but a two-dollar I.O.U.

Scott thought of the vast difference between his father and the bearded, carefree cowboy he had hoped to emulate. As a Ranger, Frank Rawley had helped tame a wild and lawless frontier, and as a cattleman, he had stood proud upon the land his sweat had paid for, undaunted in his belief that it would provide him the success and contentment which were the keystones of a working man's life.

Frank Rawley had lived life to the fullest, determined to prevail over the land that defied him to conquer it. Billy Clyde Marcum had not lived life; he had hidden from it, and Scott knew now that Billy Clyde's way was a coward's way.

A decision about his future had been forming slowly in his mind for days, Scott realized, and he had almost put it into words when he'd taken Whit Kirby's remark about self-respect as an insult.

He would not go back to the Missouri and the *Nebraska Queen*. By the time he was forty that kind of life would end, and traffic on the river would be forced to a trickle by the more efficient movement of goods over the ribbons of steel the railroads were threading through the West.

Someday Scott hoped to have children of his own, and he wanted to offer them more than his memories of the lonesome wails of steamboat whistles, the feel of the river spray in his face, and the revelry of drinking sprees in the port villages. They would expect more from him than bawdy tales of a carefree life, which he now admitted had been his excuse to avoid the hard choices his father would have put before him someday. His children deserved something they could see and touch— something like the good Texas rangeland of the Crowfoot. Suddenly, his battle to save his father's ranch became the only challenge he had ever faced that was worth winning. He would make peace with Hobe Calder, and together they would build the Crowfoot into the prosperous spread Frank Rawley had set as his goal.

The Crowfoot would not be his to build, however, Scott thought as he trudged back to the Elkhorn, unless he could track down two vicious outlaws and find a way to keep the ranch out of John Tripp's hands.

Everyone he had ever known seemed to walk through Scott's sleep during the night. His dreams took him back to the Big Muddy, and he heard the hiss of steam boilers and the groan of paddle wheels pushing the riverboats upstream. He was a boy again, kneeling in the grass while Frank Rawley taught him how to hog-tie a steer for branding. Billy Clyde Marcum sat with him beside the well and fired Scott's imagination with tales of far-away places.

In the illogical world of his subconscious, he moved swiftly through time and space. His mother came alive, singing in the kitchen and calling for him to help her with a chore. Images of Lily Vernoy standing nude in the filtered light under a wagon cover warmed him with desire, but Della Grange appeared and wagged her finger at him, pulling him away. Gunshots roared in his head and he saw blood on Frank Rawley's face. Hobe Calder cursed him and cuffed him in the face, and Scott came awake at the sound of his own voice shouting, "I'm not dumping the Crowfoot! I'm not dumping the Crowfoot. . . ."

He sat up in bed, shaking his head and rubbing the stubble on his face. It took him a moment to realize he was at the Elkhorn Hotel and not at the Crowfoot Ranch. He slumped back on the pillow, too unnerved to sleep for a while.

The single window in the room faced west, and the thumbnail moon was a sliver of yellow on the horizon. Scott estimated that it was close to midnight and that he had awakened after sleeping only three hours.

After he returned from Whit Kirby's livery barn, he had eaten a leisurely supper in the Elkhorn dining room with an unexpected companion. There was not enough business to keep Millie Adcock busy in the early evening. When Scott came down from his room after scrubbing his hands and face at the washstand, he found Millie leaning against the registration desk and staring idly into space. She came quickly toward him, and he was keenly aware of the way the curves of her body filled her clothes and the easy stride of her walk.

"You shouldn't have to eat alone on your first night in a strange town," Millie said brightly. "I haven't eaten yet, so why don't we get better acquainted?"

Millie Adcock was pleasant company and Scott was glad she invited herself to join him. She had learned early that a man enjoyed a woman's company when he was the center of attention, and she appeared to be sincerely interested in knowing more about Scott Rawley. She asked him about his home, if he was a cowhand or a rancher, if he had traveled much, and if he was in Bluestem on business or just passing through.

Scott did not resent her curiosity. Millie was not prying, she was just trying to entertain him and make him feel comfortable with her. He told her about the Crowfoot, mentioned that it was near the town of Blackwood, and smiled with fond recollections when he talked about the time he had spent on the riverboats of the Missouri River. He stated that he had come to Bluestem on business, but he did not tell her at the moment what it was, and Millie did not press him.

After a while she said, "There's a look of sadness in your eyes. You hide it well, but I think you're in trouble or someone has caused you trouble."

"Maybe both," Scott admitted. "My father was killed and robbed by a couple of cutthroats who hit the bank in Blackwood a couple of days ago. It was a bad thing to see."

"I'm so sorry," Millie gasped quickly. "Were the robbers arrested?"

Scott shook his head. "No. It happened so fast

nobody got close to them. I think I know the men who did it, though."

"Now I know why you're in Bluestem." Millie frowned and reached across the table to touch his hand. "You're going to run them down yourself."

"Hope to," Scott said. She had managed to learn enough about him that Scott saw no reason not to be more frank with her. He was sure the Sadler brothers wouldn't be reckless enough to check into a hotel, but he described them and asked if Millie had seen them.

She had not, and she had never heard of them. She lowered her eyes, slid her plate back and forth on the table for no reason, then said, "There must be some pretty girl in Blackwood who's worried sick about you."

"Probably," Scott said. Now Millie Adcock was prying, and Scott was aware of it. He grinned, finding an impish joy in satisfying her curiosity. "Her name's Della Grange."

Still fiddling with her plate, Millie changed the subject and shared information about her own life. Her father had founded the Elkhorn, but Millie never knew him. He died when she was a year old. Her mother took over the business and operated the hotel for more than twenty years, but she had passed away six months ago.

"I know how you feel," Millie said sadly. "I'm beginning to think straight at last, but you never get over losing your folks. I grew up in the Elkhorn and I know the business. I'm glad I have something to keep me busy, and you're lucky that you have a ranch to run."

"If I can keep it," Scott replied, deciding he might as well tell the girl about the bank note and why his search for the Sadler brothers needed to end quickly.

A pretty girl brought more coffee, and he and Millie had little more to say while they finished their meal. Scott was beginning to feel restless, thinking back on his meeting with Whit Kirby. The Sadler brothers had passed through Bluestem only a few days ago, and while Scott's heart told him he should not waste any time in trying to pick up their trail, his body demanded rest.

Since morning he had been involved in a gunfight, covered fifteen miles on horseback, and forced a grizzled old liveryman to reveal Billy Clyde Marcum's role in the Sadler brothers' raid on the Pioneer Bank. He was physically and emotionally drained, and he was too tired to do any more.

After leaving the dining room, he sat in the lobby and waited for Joe Pike. Scott was eager to find out if Pike's trip to Hub had turned up any new information about Mitch and Ned Sadler, but the Pinkerton man failed to appear. At nine o'clock he gave up and went to bed, wondering if tomorrow would be any more profitable to his cause than this day had been.

CHAPTER THIRTEEN

SCOTT WAS UP AT DAYBREAK, feeling almost as tired as he had been when he went to bed. He had pushed the dreams out of his mind, but the pressure and fear that he would not find the Sadler brothers in time to pay off the bank had kept him awake most of the night.

At the far end of the second-floor hallway, he found

the bathing room Millie Adcock had boasted about as one of the many conveniences provided by the Elkhorn. It was clean and spacious, furnished with an oblong brass tub, barrels of water, and a polished metal mirror. He bathed and shaved, then put on clean clothes and went downstairs to see if he could find Joe Pike.

Millie Adcock saw him looking around the lobby and called to him. "We had a new guest sign himself in late last night and help himself to a room key. He's an old acquaintance, though, so I didn't kick him out this morning. He wants you to meet him in the dining room."

"I waited up for you last night," Scott said as he slid into a chair across the table from Joe Pike. "You must have had a busy day."

Pike rubbed his fingertips across his eyes. He appeared tired and sleepy. "Busy, but not much to show for it. I sent my telegraphs, nosed around town a while, then heard about a place called the Line Shack. It's a bordello on the back side of Hub. I spent a long evening there. I left about nine, but it's more'n a two-hour ride back here, and you folks had turned in. They've got a couple of pretty women at the Line Shack, the kind Mitch would like, but I didn't see no sign of the Sadlers."

"They've been in Bluestem," Scott said. "They rode away from here four days ago with Billy Clyde Marcum, must've camped somewhere overnight, then robbed the bank the next day. Whit Kirby told me they went to a whorehouse here. If Mitch liked the place, he's likely to come back to it. I need to keep my eye on the place, but I was too petered out to check on it last night."

Pike nodded. "Figures. When you start a manhunt,

then get mixed up in fistfights, gunfights, and long-winded palaver with a Pinkerton man, it takes the sand out of a man."

"I'm finding that out," Scott said, pausing to give his order as a waitress came to stand beside him. He waited until she was gone before he continued. "Whit Kirby has a reputation as a gossip, but I think he told me the truth about Billy Clyde and the Sadlers. If he didn't, I'll go back and talk serious to him."

"Do you think he knows more than he's telling?"

"He's a cranky old cuss, and it's hard to say what he knows. He knows about the Pinkerton Agency. He thinks Pinkerton caused the South to lose the war. If I was you, I'd stay away from him."

Scott managed a small smile as he watched Pike's face. The Pinkerton man drained his coffee cup and put it down without a change in his expression. He shrugged and said, "Being disliked by some hard-nosed liveryman ain't big on my list of worries. Thing is, though, he's got a point. It's a fact that old Allan Pinkerton was asked to set up a secret service for the Union Army. Spies is what they was, but that was war, and it's over for everybody 'cept a few die-hard rebels.

"Pinkerton got acquainted with Abe Lincoln early on when his agency started furnishing guards for the Illinois Central, and Lincoln was lawyering for the same railroad. In '61, so the story goes, them spies found out somebody was going to assassinate Lincoln on a train between Baltimore and Washington City. Allan saved the President's life by putting him on an earlier train. That got the Pinkerton Agency in solid with the head man, I imagine. Too bad Pinkerton wasn't around when Wilkes Booth showed up at Ford's Theater to kill Lincoln."

The hint of a grin twitched at Pike lips. "If all you learned from Kirby is that Texans don't always take to a Pinkerton man, it wasn't worth your time."

The other diners were beginning to finish their meal and leave. Scott lowered his voice as people passed close to their table, many of them casting glances at the grim-faced men they knew to be strangers in town.

"My time with Whit Kirby was worth it to me," he told Joe Pike. "I feel better about Billy Clyde, and Kirby gave me a better description of the Sadlers than we had before. I'll know Mitch and Ned if I see them."

They stopped talking while Scott finished his meal. Joe Pike drank his coffee and, as though it were an after-thought, apologized because he had not waited for Scott before going to breakfast. Presently, he said, "We'll know in a day or two if Sheriff Bandy is making any progress from his end."

"How're we going to know that? I can't waste time running back and forth."

Pike shrugged. "Carson Rowe will let us know."

"Who's Carson Rowe?"

"A Pinkerton man . . . one of my detectives. Maybe you saw him hanging around. Dignified-looking feller with muttonchop whiskers. He's been in Bluestem a week or so, trying to pick up the Sadlers' trail. I guess Whit Kirby wouldn't talk to him."

"Damn!" Scott's eyebrows lifted and he shook his head. "I saw that man, but I pegged him for a drummer or a preacher. He can give us a hand while we're watching Big Betty's Place. We could stay at it around the clock with the three of us taking turns."

"Rowe's gone," Pike said. "Now that I'm here, I don't need him in Bluestem. I sent him on to Blackwood to check on Wade Bandy. I told him to send me a telegraph to the Hub office if he learns anything that might make us go in another direction."

Reaching for tobacco and papers, Pike rolled another cigarette before they left the table. He stopped in the lobby to strike a match to it and said, "I'm going to ride over to Hub. I want to check at the telegraph office and spend some time scouting around the Sadlers' old home place. Maybe they're hiding out there. I reckon you're itching to look at that whorehouse Kirby told you about."

Scott took a deep breath. "Yeah. I'm tired of talking about the Sadlers. I want to find them and get rid of this knot in my belly."

"We'll find them," Pike said, and headed down the hallway to his room, apparently to get the gun that Scott noticed he had not worn to the dining room.

Scott left the hotel, walked up the stony road to the Bluestem Livery, and let himself in through the gate. Whit Kirby stepped from the doorway of his living quarters with a half-eaten biscuit in his hands. He stared at Scott while he chewed on the food in his mouth.

"You here to hassle me again?" he growled.

Scott grinned. The liveryman's cantankerous nature was beginning to amuse him more than it annoyed him. "Did you ever try saying 'good morning' to a paying customer?"

"What the hell's good about it?" Whit Kirby looked at the sky and shook his head. A thin layer of gray clouds had moved in overnight, and the sun was a diffused circle of white behind them. "The Lord's promising us rain, but he ain't going to give us one damn drop. He's got no use for this place, and I ain't either."

Scott told him he had come for his bay, and Kirby headed for the rear of the barn. Before the liveryman had gone far, Scott called, "I wanted to ask you something."

Kirby's shoulders sagged as he turned to face Scott. "Now we're at it, by God. You've milked my brains dry, cowboy, so it won't do no good to pester me with questions."

"It's nothing that'll hurt your head. I just want to know how to get to Big Betty's Place."

The sound that came from Kirby's throat was like a hacking cough, but it was actually a laugh. "Damn, I'd like to be young!"

It took the liveryman several minutes to give the information Scott wanted. First, spitting and cursing between words, he recited what he knew of Big Betty's history and habits, then gave directions to her house. Scott could take a path from the rear gate of the livery lot, walk down a brushy slope, and reach Big Betty's on foot in a few minutes. If he wanted a comfortable ride on horseback, he would have to avoid the narrow path and follow the trail that continued past the livery, take a wide sweep to avoid the trees, and descend the slope at a lesser grade.

"The trail joins up with the stage road out past Big Betty's," Kirby explained. "It's a good mile out of your way if you go on horseback."

Scott chose to ride.

"Been' thinking," the liveryman said as he handed over the horse's reins. "You ain't horny this early in the day. You're checking on the Sadlers again."

"That's why I'm in Bluestem," Scott said.

Whit Kirby took a step back and gave Scott a speculative stare. "You any good with that gun you're packing?"

"Fair."

"Maybe you'll be able to handle Mitch and Ned if you find the bastards," Kirby snorted. "I've learned that most men who brag about being good with a gun ain't, and them that says they're fair are usually faster'n lightning."

"I wouldn't know about that," Scott replied, and turned his bay down the wagon trail that led away from the livery stable.

Big Betty's house was located in a grove of trees a hundred feet north of the dirt road. It was large and imposing, a two-story structure of clapboards with four white columns that stretched from the second-story roof to the ground-level porch. A well-beaten path, marked by hoofprints and carriage wheels, led from the road to the porch. There was a small barn and several outbuildings visible beyond the house, and a hitching rail near the front door.

As Scott tethered his horse and walked toward the porch, his surroundings were so quiet he could hear insects buzzing in the grass. Birds chirped in the post-oak at one corner of the porch, and somewhere in the distance a dog yelped plaintively but there was no sound or sign of life from inside the house.

His knock drew immediate response, however. The front door swung half open, and a petite woman in her mid-thirties looked up at him while she held the door close to her side. Her brown skirt was belted tightly around a narrow waist and the white blouse above it revealed the slope of a generous bosom. Her blue eyes were red-streaked and Scott could tell she had been crying.

"We're not open today," she said quietly. "Most folks know we don't open until noon unless it's for a special customer, and we're not going to do that today. Actually, I don't think we'll ever be open again. You must be a stranger in town."

"Are you Big Betty?"

"I'm Betty Kelton," she replied. "You can call me 'big' if you want to. My girls are still asleep and won't be up for hours. They won't like it when they find out I'm thinking of closing this place, and I'm in no hurry to tell them."

Scott grinned as he surveyed Betty Kelton's trim body, recalling that in St. Louis he had once met a seven-foot giant of a man called Tiny. He introduced himself and said, "I—I'm not here for . . . I'm not a customer, but I wanted to ask you some questions about two men who are."

She brushed a hand through her hair, which lay in auburn ringlets around her face. "I can't be of any help to you, but if we're going to talk, let's get off the porch."

She stepped back, and Scott followed her into the parlor. The odor of steaming coffee in the adjoining kitchen wafted through the room. Betty Kelton's parlor was not the kind of room Scott had expected to see in a brothel. It was much like many he had seen in ordinary homes. A mohair sofa faced a stone fireplace, and beside it were two leather-covered arm chairs with lace doilies draped across the backrests. The pine floor had been scrubbed so thoroughly it was almost white, and the pictures on the walls portrayed small children at play and vases of colorful flowers.

A double-width doorway at the end of the parlor revealed a larger room beyond, with a half-dozen small tables and a gleaming oak bar along the far wall.

"Would you like some coffee?" Betty Kelton asked as she took a seat on the sofa and invited Scott to sit beside her.

Despite the tempting aroma, Scott declined. He wanted the coffee, but the woman was not pleased by his presence and it was an effort for her to be hospitable.

"I'll get to the point and try not to wake your girls. I was told that Mitch and Ned Sadler visited your place a few days ago. Maybe you overheard something that will help me find them."

"I've heard of them, but I don't know them. A lot of men come here."

Scott had expected her to be evasive and secretive. Men who visited the brothels of the West knew those who served them observed their own ethical code. What the girls heard in moments of relaxation or passion was not repeated outside the brothel walls. It was the only way they could lure their customers back again. It was also the only way they could stay alive. To appear manly in the eyes of the women, bankers and businessmen boasted of financial coups; cowboys talked about their riding and roping skills; and gunslingers and rustlers tried to make an impression by reciting their prowess in killing, robbing, and evading the law.

Hoping to appeal to her sense of justice, Scott told her about the Blackwood bank robbery and the murder of Frank Rawley. He described the Sadler brothers and said flatly, "You can play 'possum if that's your way, ma'am, but I'm not leaving until you help me or convince me you can't."

While Scott talked, Betty Kelton sat stiffly beside him, staring idly at her hands. She did not respond to his stern declaration, and he realized she had not been listening.

Her face was pale and her hands were shaking. Scott touched her shoulder and asked, "Are you all right, ma'am?"

"What?" She shook her head as if to clear it, and she tried to smile. "You'll have to forgive me. I didn't hear what you said. I—I'm really not myself today. A man rode over from Hub and woke me at daybreak to give me some bad news. He told me the deputy sheriff at Hub was shot dead last night."

"The deputy must've been a good friend."

"Yes, he was," she said. "I lived in Hub for a long time before my husband ran off with another woman and left me without a dollar in my purse or a speck of food in the house. My life seemed so hopeless until I found my wonderful deputy sheriff. I—I—"

Tears glistened in the corners of her eyes. She brushed them away and gave Scott her attention. "Do you want to go over what you were talking about?"

Scott shook his head. Although the deputy and the young madam were strangers to him, Scott was touched by sadness. He knew the hurt and grief that came in the wake of a violent death, and he waited in silence until the woman regained her composure.

After a few seconds, he asked, "Was the deputy who got killed the same lawman who arrested Mitch Sadler some years ago for killing his wife?"

She nodded, her eyes growing brighter. "Yes. Doyle Joyner. Did you know him?"

"No, but I have a hunch I know who killed him."

Apparently, it had not occurred to Betty Kelton that Deputy Doyle Joyner's death might be tied to events of the past. She gave Scott a puzzled look, then exclaimed, "Oh, my goodness! You think one of the Sadlers killed Doyle!"

A nervous tremor shook Scott's stomach. He had expected the Sadler brothers to lie low for a while after the Blackwood robbery, but he was sure Mitch had been unable to harness his craving for revenge against the man who sent him to prison.

"That's what I think, ma'am. Mitch Sadler's going to keep on killing until somebody stops him."

"Oh, my goodness!" Betty Kelton whispered again. She reached her arms toward Scott and leaned against him, her shoulders shaking as she sobbed.

Uncomfortable and at a loss for words, Scott put his arms around her and held her lightly while she cried until she had no more tears. Her weeping subsided and she drew away, wiping moisture from her cheeks.

"I—I'm sorry I showed myself this way in front of a stranger," she said softly. "I wasn't completely honest with you before. The men you described were here three or four nights ago. I never tell anyone who our customers are, but if they were the Sadler brothers . . . well, that's different. It was their second visit. They were here about a month ago. One of them—the blond good-looking man—seemed to be crazy about Polly Wexler, and I thought he'd probably come back to see her."

"That was Mitch," Scott said. "He's got a reputation for liking pretty women. I came here to see if the Sadlers might have dropped a hint about where they're staying, or if they're moving on, or anything that will help me find them. Maybe Mitch let something slip while he was with Polly Wexler."

"It's possible, but she wouldn't tell you. My girls don't mention customers' names even if they know them, and they never talk about what they hear in their bedrooms."

She glanced over her shoulder toward the stairway, which led from one corner of the large bar room to the second floor. "Polly might be different. She might give you some information if you'd pay her for it. I think she'd do anything for money. She's trying to save enough to go back home to Mississippi, and our business has been so bad she's getting desperate."

"Maybe I'll come back tomorrow when you're open for business and have a talk with her," Scott said.

Betty Kelton shook her head. "I'm serious about closing the place. We had a terrible drought on the Bluestem range last year, and the cattle business has been bad. The ranchers cut their crews, and money is scarce among the cowboys. I'm barely able to break even these days. I've been thinking of quitting for a long time, and now I don't have the heart for this business. You might be able to see Polly sometime tonight, but I won't be here. I'm not sure my girls will, either. When I tell them I'm quitting, they may pack up and leave today."

From the moment he'd suggested that Mitch Sadler might be responsible for Doyle Joyner's death, Betty Kelton's resentment had evaporated. Their conversation seemed to take her mind off her grief, and she grew more relaxed and friendly.

The sadness returned to her eyes, however, when Scott said, "I hope Polly won't leave until I can talk with her. I hope you'll find something better, too, ma'am."

Scott's sympathy was sincere. She saw it in his eyes and wanted to reassure him. "I'll be all right. Doyle and I were going to be married next year. We've been making payments on a small ranch east of the Hub cross-roads, and I've saved enough to pay it off. Doyle had already built a four-room cabin out there, and we have fifty head of cattle. That's where I'll be living now. The ranch was Doyle's dream and I'm going to make it come true."

Her voice faltered and she took a deep breath. "I hope you find Mitch Sadler and kill him!"

A knot of muscle swelled along Scott's jaw. "Someday I'll do that, but I need my money now. I was hoping you'd be able to tell me something that would help me flush him out in a hurry."

"I would if I could. Until you described them, I didn't

know those men were the Sadlers. I'd never heard of them until Doyle told me how Mitch had butchered his wife. I was so hemmed in at home, Mitch Sadler had been in jail for a year before I ran into Doyle and heard the story. How did you track them to my place?"

"They knew they were going on to Blackwood and wanted their horses well fed. They left them at the livery, and Whit Kirby told me they came here."

Betty Kelton's face colored and she made a wry face. "Oh, that old goat. I rent this house from him. He comes out here once a month and offers to forget the rent if I'll go to bed with him. I can't convince him that I run a business and don't sleep with anybody—much less him. At least, I'll be rid of that problem."

She glanced at a clock above the stone fireplace, and Scott realized he had stayed too long. He said, "I'll try to see Polly tonight if I get back from Hub in time. If Mitch was Doyle Joyner's killer, maybe somebody spotted him and knows which way he headed. I'm going to Hub and see if I can learn anything. Would you like to come with me?"

She touched his hand and smiled wanly. "Thank you for asking, but I'm going over later with the friend who brought me the news. Doyle didn't have any family, so I suppose I'll have to—to handle things."

Scott picked up his hat, which he had placed on a chair, fiddled with the brim a moment, then turned toward the door. "I'm sorry I came at a bad time, ma'am."

She patted his arm and said, "It's all right. I'm sorry about your father."

Nodding a farewell, Scott put on his hat and walked

outside. Before he reached his horse, he stopped and stared thoughtfully at the ground, recalling Joe Pike's remark about the advantage they would have if they owned a brothel that might attract Mitch Sadler. He went back to the porch and knocked on the door.

Betty Kelton appeared surprised and puzzled by his return. "Yes? Did you forget something?"

"You'll have to forgive me for talking business, but I was wondering if you'd be willing to let me take over this place for two or three weeks. It would give the girls time to make plans, and I'd pay you a fair price plus any profit we have."

"Oh, my goodness!" Betty Kelton murmured. "I don't know. I'd have to think about it. Whatever do you want with it when it's not worth your time?"

Scott's face settled into grim lines, and his voice was cold and hard. "I hope it'll be a trap for Mitch Sadler. I know something of Mitch's habits. It appears he falls in love right regular and likes to have a woman with him all the time. If he's taken by Polly Wexler, I've got a gut feeling he won't leave her alone. I want to be around if he comes back."

Frowning, moving her hands impatiently, Betty Kelton said, "I can't get my girls mixed up in something like that without talking to them first. I'd like to help them, but they may not like the idea of working where there's likely to be shooting. You might have to talk to Whit Kirby about the house, too. I can't make a decision right now. I—I've got to go to Hub. I suppose we'll bury Doyle late this afternoon, and I'd planned to stay at our—the ranch cabin for a few days. It's just—"

"I don't have much time, ma'am. I'm going to lose everything if I don't get the money the Sadlers took from my pa. Mitch may never come back here, but I've got to gamble that he will."

She pressed her fingertips to her temples and appeared to be fighting back tears as the time drew near for the sad journey ahead of her. "I hate to turn you down, but I've got so much to think about. I—I'll decide something overnight. I'll come back for an hour or two tomorrow and let you know. Meet me here about four o'clock and we'll talk again."

"I've got a partner who'll be putting up whatever money you ask," Scott said. "If you don't mind, I'll bring Joe Pike with me tomorrow."

"That will be fine. I'll talk to you tomorrow."

Brushing at her eyes, she stepped back and closed the door. It opened again almost immediately, and Betty Kelton said, "If you're not here, I'll be worried. I'll know you learned something in Hub that put you on the Sadlers' trail."

"I hope I'm that lucky," Scott said. She gave him a long look, shook her head sadly, and eased the door closed.

CHAPTER FOURTEEN

THE TOWN OF HUB was twice as large as Bluestem and more active, but it was like dozens of cow towns Scott had seen over the years. There were four or five saloons, a large general store called the California Emporium, half-a-dozen smaller shops, and a sprawling stockyard that had attracted an unusual amount of attention.

There was a cluster of buggies, buckboards, and idle horses in the field south of the business district, apparently left there by spectators at a cattle auction or horse sale. Farther down Main Street, Scott saw a flat-roofed brick structure with a "County Jail" sign jutting out over the doorway, and he chose that as his destination.

A knot of range-dressed men and a few in business suits were gathered at the jail. Even at a distance their animated gestures told Scott they were involved in something more serious than casual conversation. He expected to find the shooting of Deputy Doyle Joyner the talk of the town, and he was sure it was the subject on the minds of the group at the jail. He was eager to join them and learn the details of the deputy's death.

His route along the street took him closer to the stockyard, which was adjacent to a large livery barn. He slowed his bay and looked toward the livery. A cloud of dust rose in a swirling plume above the heads of the people standing shoulder to shoulder around the pole fence. Shouts, yells, and whistles blended in a clamorous din, but Scott was able to control his curiosity until one voice rose above the others, yelling, "Ride 'im, cowboy! Ride 'im to the ground!"

It was a cry Scott could not resist. It revived memories of his experiences north of the Trinity with Billy Clyde Marcum. The crowd at the stockyard was no longer a mystery. Wild horses were being sold, and some rider was trying to tame them enough to bring a good price.

Scott admired the skills of bronc-busters, and he

decided he could spare enough time to watch at least one ride. He turned the bay into a vacant lot and took a shortcut to the stockyard. He dismounted fifty feet before he reached the crowd, dropping the bay's reins to keep it in place until he returned.

He was tall enough see over the heads of most of the crowd, but he had to move around to get a clear view. A man of Scott's size saw him and said, "Here's a spot, partner."

The man crowded against his neighbor to make space, but Scott could barely squeeze in. The excitement was about over. A lean, red-faced cowboy was in the process of bringing a lathered, snorting roan to a halt in the center of the lot. A wrangler dashed out to grasp the animal's bridle, bracing his heels in the dirt as the horse tried to pull away. The rider lifted his hand in a triumphant salute, stepped out of the stirrups, and waved to the cheers of the crowd. He walked toward a gate, trying to appear nonchalant, but Scott noticed a slight buckling of the man's knees. A bronc-buster had to look confident after a good ride, but Scott knew the pain the man felt in his bones.

"Damn good ride," the man beside Scott declared. "I ain't seen nobody who could ride that good since Pat Logan left these parts."

Scott whirled, eager to question the man, but he drew a deep breath and waited a minute before he spoke. He was in a strange town among strange men, and he had to be careful not to arouse any suspicion about his motives.

"Seems I've heard of Logan," he said casually. "Have you seen him around lately?"

The man shook his head. "Not for quite a spell. I hear he's a deputy sheriff over in Blackwood now, but he was just a plain cowpoke like me when he was around Hub. Rode a spell for old man DeBord's Square D spread, then drifted on."

"It's a small world," Scott murmured.

His companion looked at him and frowned. "What say?"

"Never mind," Scott replied, backing away from his spot at the fence. "I was thinking about something else."

Since the day his father died, Scott had been troubled by the unbelievable coincidence that had timed a bank robbery to occur on the very day he and Frank Rawley returned with money from their cattle drive. Was it a coincidence, or had someone told the outlaws when the Rawleys were scheduled to return to Blackwood? Was the Pioneer Bank the primary target, or was the holdup staged as a smoke screen to cover up the deliberate murder and robbery of Frank Rawley?

The questions kept passing through his mind, and he doubted that fate had arranged such convenience for the outlaws. He had been suspicious of the circumstances from the start, and now he was convinced that his father's death had not been the result of bad luck or unfortunate timing. Someone had wanted Frank to die— either to settle an old score or to prevent him from taking the open range away from John Tripp's Bar 40 Ranch.

The casual remark from a cowboy watching a bronc-buster ride wild horses raised a storm of speculation in Scott's mind. The spectator who had stood next to him was an admirer of Pat Logan's horsemanship, having mentioned that the deputy once worked at Charlie DeBord's Square D Ranch. According to Joe Pike, Mitch Sadler had been riding for the same spread at the time he cut his wife to pieces. Was Pat Logan trailing the Sadlers for the rewards on their heads when he had shot at Scott on Medicine Creek, or was he on his way to warn the two that Scott Rawley had vowed to kill them? Scott had no way of knowing Pat Logan's intent, but it was another question that would stay in his mind.

The group in front of the jail had doubled in size while Scott was at the stockyard, now numbering eight or nine people. Most of them were men, but Scott saw two women in bonnets among the crowd. Their voices were muted, but as he tied his horse at the hitching rail, he was able to hear a few words. ". . . Got to have some kind of law here at a time like this . . ." ". . . Ain't up to us to say who he chooses . . ." ". . . Looks plausible enough to me . . ."

A few minutes later, Scott was able to make sense of the snatches of conversation. The thick door of the jail swung open, and Sheriff Wade Bandy stepped onto the boardwalk. He was surrounded immediately by curious, worried men who bombarded him with questions.

Wade Bandy was a man whose deliberate, hard-eyed manner and deep Texas drawl managed to convey a sense of authority and competence. He tugged at his hat brim, set his hands on his hips, and talked quietly while he moved his eyes from face to face. Scott could not hear what the lawman was saying, but he saw an air of calm settle over the group, and the voices grew quieter. Presently, Bandy waved his arms in dismissal, and the people began to drift away in twos and threes.

Scott stood beside his horse at the edge of the board-walk and waited for the crowd to disperse. Busy with their own concerns, none of the men had noticed him when he dismounted in front of the jail, but now a few of them looked him over suspiciously as they left. Sheriff Wade Bandy remained in front of the doorway, the lines of his leathery face deepened by worry. With his view of the street no longer obstructed, the lawman looked directly at Scott.

He ran his fingers along the edge of his vest and heaved a sigh. "What're you doin' here?"

"Looking for a killer—three or four, maybe. I heard about your deputy getting killed, and I should've expected to see you but I didn't."

The sheriff's lips were so tight they were barely visible beneath his mustache. "It's my job. I'm the county sheriff. Some low-life bushwhacker put a bullet in Doyle Joyner's back. Cowardly bastard shot him right between the shoulder blades in the dark. He was a good man, barely thirty-five, and he worked for me. Why wouldn't I be here?"

"Just something I didn't think of when I decided to ride over here. Did you bring that other fine deputy with you?"

"You talkin' about Pat Logan?"

Scott nodded. "Yeah, little feisty-britches. I need to talk to you about him."

"Well, he ain't here." There was a note of exasperation in the sheriff's voice. "I had to fire Pat . . . took his badge yesterday before all this mess come up. He's a lyin',

169

mail-stealin', money-grubbin' fool. Everything's goin' wrong all of a sudden, and I had to bring a temporary deputy with me to see if he can settle folks down while we try to find Doyle Joyner's killer."

"Seems you'd want to handle that yourself."

"Hell's bells, man! I can't be everywhere at once. That damned circuit-ridin' judge is openin' court in Black-wood Monday, and I got to be there. I've got a passel of paperwork to do in two days, and Judge Kirkwood don't put up with no excuses. A deputy marshal showed up to present some cases, too, and he talked to me first thing yesterday morning. He wanted to know if I'd followed up on the telegraph messages he sent me on some sus-pects. I don't have no messages, but I figured out what happened to 'em."

The lawman paused and looked around, aware that his voice had grown loud and irritable. "Damn Pat Logan's hide! He was hidin' my mail. About midday he shows up, and I was layin' for him. I badgered him 'til he admitted what he'd done, holdin' on to my telegraphs and flyers so he'd get the first shot at any rewards."

"I think there's more to it than reward money," Scott said.

"Maybe there is. Hell, I don't know. While I was cussin' him out, I noticed he was favorin' one leg. Said he banged it up when his horse throwed him onto a splin-tered pine stump. I run him out of the office while I thought about what to do about him, then I seen him headin' for Doc Eversole's place, so I followed him over there. That's when I took his badge. Turns out his bad leg was from a bullet wound, and he wouldn't tell me how he got it, so—"

"That was my bullet," Scott cut in. "I shot him, and I've got your mail and telegraph messages."

"What!" Wade Bandy's mouth dropped open. He waved a thumb toward the door of the jail. "Come inside. I want to hear more about this, and maybe my new deputy needs to hear it, too."

Even a stranger could learn something about Deputy Doyle Joyner's personality by looking at his office. Following Wade Bandy, Scott stood just inside the doorway while his vision adjusted to the gloom of the building's interior, then he moved forward and surveyed the room.

Three barred cells, all unoccupied, formed most of the office's rear wall. There was a clean brass cuspidor in front of each cell door. A potbellied stove with a cold coffeepot atop it sat next to a doorway, which opened to a hallway leading to the deputy's living quarters. A few feet from the outside entrance, near the barred window that faced the street, was a rolltop desk. Envelopes and folded papers were tucked into its pigeonholes, but the working surface of the desk was uncluttered except for a Bible.

On the wall to the left of the cells was a large bulletin board with posters and messages tacked to it in neat vertical rows. A range-dressed man in worn boots, with a dirty brown Stetson pushed far back on his head, stood with his back toward the room while he studied the bulletin board.

"I think you're acquainted with the man I brought with me," Wade Bandy said.

"Barely," the man murmured. He was in the gloom on

the far side of the room. The single window provided only dim light from the cloudy sky, and Scott was not sure of the man's identity until he spoke. The man turned around, and Scott saw that the new deputy was John Tripp's Bar 40 foreman, Cal Baylor.

Scott glared at Wade Bandy. "Why in hell did you pick him?"

"He was there when the telegrapher brought me word of Joyner's death," the sheriff said defensively. "Him and John Tripp was in town for a meetin' at the bank, and they come by lookin' for Pat Logan. Pat's been breakin' some horses for the Bar 40 in his spare time, and him and Cal got to be friends. I was wonderin' where I could find a deputy on short notice, and Baylor said he'd help me out if it was all right with Tripp. Tripp said I could borrow Cal for a spell, so I took him up on it."

Bandy appeared uncomfortable under Scott's disapproving stare. He continued talking with his eyes focused on the floor. "Hell's bells, I don't have time to do no long search for an experienced lawman right now. Cal's a bright youngster. He's had good schoolin' and Tripp says he can handle a gun. I figure he'll do until I find somebody. I didn't ask you in here to tell me how to run my office. I want to know what's goin' on between you and Pat Logan, and where my papers are."

"Seems to me your first order of business ought to be Doyle Joyner's killer. Have you asked around to see if anybody spotted the Sadler brothers in town?"

The sheriff squinted his eyes. "You're tryin' to tell me again how to do my job. People keep talkin' about the

Sadler brothers. All I know is what the marshal who's visitin' in Blackwood told me. He says they're suspects in a Wells Fargo robbery and some killin', but that's all—just suspects. There's nobody to testify against them. I don't know nothin' about all that, 'cause Pat stole my papers and now you have 'em."

"They're with my stuff over at Bluestem," Scott said. "I'll get them to you. Did you know that Doyle Joyner's the man who sent Mitch Sadler to prison?"

"Sure I know that. I'm not a fool! I was laid up with lumbago when all that was goin' on. I didn't hear the trial, and I wouldn't know Mitch Sadler from a Comanche squaw."

Cal Baylor stood aside quietly while Scott and Bandy talked. When it appeared they had finished, he said to Scott, "You don't know me very well, but I want you to know I'll do all I can to—"

Scott's voice was sharp as he cut off Cal Baylor's words. "I'll listen to you in a minute." Still glaring at Wade Bandy, he said, "I found another man shot in the back on my way to Bluestem, and I'm sure he was killed by Mitch Sadler. It must've crossed your mind by now that Mitch Sadler had a good reason to kill Doyle Joyner. You've either thought of it or you don't want to think of it, and you've picked a deputy who won't help any. He'll take orders from John Tripp instead of you."

The sheriff's chest rose and fell, and he kept his voice low. "Hell, Cal Baylor ain't goin' to be here forever—and what's it to you, anyway?"

"Nothing that I can't handle," Scott said angrily. "I

wonder how he'll go about arresting himself or John Tripp!"

The sheriff's head jerked upward. His brush mustache bristled like miniature porcupine quills. "What's that supposed to mean?"

"John Tripp had good reason to want my pa dead, and his foreman ain't my idea of a deputy you can trust. If things tie together the way they're beginning to shape up, I'll probably kill him."

Milder words than those spoken by Scott Rawley had triggered countless brawls and gunfights on the western frontier, and Scott was not surprised by Cal Baylor's reaction. The Bar 40 foreman swore quietly and lunged at him, aiming a fist at Scott's chin. Scott whirled aside to let the man go by, and the blow missed. He kept turning, flinging his right arm behind him to backhand Baylor across the mouth. The momentum of his body powered the blow, and he felt Baylor's lips and teeth grind against his knuckles.

Baylor stopped as if he had been caught by a rope. He was stunned, but only for an instant. His lower lip was split and blood trickled down his chin, but he was not ready to give up. He settled into a crouch, his fists raised, and took a cautious step forward. He circled around and leaned close, inviting Scott to swing at his chin. Scott tried to hit the target, but it was a mistake. While his arm was outstretched, Baylor countered with a paralyzing punch that landed over Scott's heart.

A choking pain shot through Scott's chest and cut off his breath. He forced a smile, determined not to show that he was hurt. Cal Baylor knew his punch had sapped some of Scott's strength, and he tried to pursue his advantage. He lowered his head and charged forward, pointing a shoulder at Scott's midsection that would knock him off his feet.

Already, Scott regretted the words that had angered Cal Baylor. He had spoken impulsively, showing his hand prematurely, but he was not going to waste time in a lengthy fight. He did not try to avoid the man's charge. He waited until Baylor's face was a foot away from him, then jerked his leg upward and jammed his knee beneath the man's chin. Baylor's head snapped back and he went to his knees. He fell over on his side, gagging and spitting. He was tough. He pushed himself up and started toward Scott again.

The fight ended abruptly. With surprising agility, Wade Bandy stepped between them. He shoved the Bar 40 foreman aside and whirled on Scott Rawley.

"Your smart mouth is beginnin' to wear on my nerves," Bandy growled. "If you want to tell me somethin' that'll help, then say it. If you ain't goin' to do that, get out of my sight."

Cal Baylor dabbed at his bruised mouth with the tip of his neckerchief. He looked at Wade Bandy, and his tone sounded strangely apologetic. "He's got it in for me because Mr. Tripp wants to keep the grazing land the Crowfoot Ranch is buying out from under him. I'm sorry Frank Rawley got killed, but Mr. Tripp don't hire killers. I won't stand by and let people talk about him. It beats me why he's accusing us of working with outlaws."

Scott swallowed hard, forcing himself to say things he

did not mean. "Foolishness, Cal," he said. "Just plain foolishness. I shouldn't have been shooting off my mouth that way. I'm sorry."

"That's better," Wade Bandy said, glaring at Scott. "I warned you when you left Blackwood not to try doin' things your own way, and my guts tell me you're keepin' things from me. What about this friend you found back-shot?"

Scott took a moment to catch his breath. "His name was Billy Clyde Marcum. We wasn't the best of friends, but he used to ride for us. He was working at a livery in Bluestem when two men made some kind of deal with him, and he went off with them. I know it was Mitch and Ned because the liveryman saw them, and he's known them since they were boys."

Wade Bandy listened with an air of boredom while Scott gave him a brief account of what he had learned from Whit Kirby and Matt Latham's son Jeff. Scott did not mention Joe Pike or the Pinkerton Agency's interest in the Sadlers.

"What you've got is more suspicion and no proof," the sheriff said. "Seems like the whole world is fallin' in on me. The bank's been robbed, people are gettin' killed all around, and I've got an election coming up. Maybe you've got reason to believe the Sadlers killed your friend, but that don't explain why you started mouthin' off about John Tripp and Cal Baylor bein' suspects, too."

"I said I was sorry about that. Pat Logan tried to bush-whack me for some reason. I found out today he and the Sadlers used to work on the same cattle spread. You told me Logan and Cal Baylor are also friends, and maybe I tried to make too much out of it."

"You sure as hell did," Cal Baylor murmured. "I'm not a thief or a killer. Give me a chance and I'll do my best to help you."

Scott ignored Baylor and asked the sheriff what he had learned about Doyle Joyner's death.

"We don't know nothin' about what happened, except that he's dead," Bandy said. "Doyle was a hard worker, checked around town every night until it was quiet, then turned in. His best friend, Corey Millsap, owns the Running Iron Saloon across the street. Him and Doyle spent some time together most every night, just talkin' or havin' a nightcap. It was Corey that found Doyle."

"Did he hear the shot or see Joyner talking to anybody?"

"Nobody heard nothin'. Corey brought a bottle over to share with Doyle. There was a lamp burnin' in the office and one in Corey's room down the hall, but Doyle was nowhere in sight. There's a one-stall shed in back where Doyle kept his horse. On his last turn every night, he'd ride down to the stockyards and back. Corey checked to see if Doyle's horse was gone so he'd know if he was on his rounds. He found Doyle dead with a bullet in his back. That don't leave me nothin' to go on."

The sheriff folded his hands across his belt and picked at a rough fingernail. "As soon as the funeral is over, I'm headin' back to Blackwood. You hold on to my papers."

"Lot of good that'll do now," said Scott. He stood up and hitched at his gunbelt. "I need a drink."

He started toward the door, his eyes on the Running Iron Saloon across the street. He stopped when Cal

Baylor jumped to his feet and fell in step beside him. "I've got no hard feelings if you don't," Baylor said, extending his hand.

Scott hesitated, then shook hands, but the frosty glint of his eyes left a look of doubt on Cal Baylor's face.

CHAPTER FIFTEEN

I T WAS NOT OFTEN that Scott drank so early in the afternoon, but his nerves had been shaken by the events at the jail, and he wanted to talk with Doyle Joyner's bartender friend. He was irritated at himself, at Wade Bandy, and at Cal Baylor—at himself because he had forewarned Cal Baylor of his suspicions; at Cal Baylor for pretending an interest in justice that he did not have; and at Wade Bandy because the sheriff seemed more interested in his campaign for reelection than in finding the Sadler brothers.

The death of the deputy sheriff and the mustang sale at the stockyard had drawn an unusual number of people to Hub. A dozen or so men sat around the tables at the Running Iron Saloon, talking in muted tones and nursing their drinks.

The bartender was alone at the bar, standing with his arms folded and his back against a mirrored wall. He was a big man in his thirties, with a broad, freckled face and coarse red hair, which was parted in the middle and combed back from his forehead in deep waves.

He greeted Scott at once, behaving as if he had been expecting him. He gave Scott a firm handshake and said, "Welcome to Hub. I'm Corey Millsap."

"I figured you were," Scott said, and introduced himself. "The sheriff told me you found Doyle Joyner's body."

Millsap's eyes clouded. "I wish I'd gone over sooner last night. Maybe I could have done something. He'd been expecting trouble for days. A peddler from Sagemore came through town last week and mentioned to Corey that the Sadlers were robbing and killing again. He wondered why the sheriff hadn't sent him word about what was going on. Doyle was worried, but he wasn't afraid. I guess he didn't think anyone would lay for him at his own jail."

Corey Millsap rubbed a hand across his forehead and shuddered. Scott ordered a drink, and the bartender set out a glass and poured it half full of whiskey. Across the room, a man called for a bottle, and Millsap took one from the shelf behind him and carried it to him.

Scott sipped his drink, scowling as the whiskey burned his stomach. He noticed his image in the mirror behind the bar, and the man with the saddle-brown skin, frosty eyes, and crow-black hair who stared back at him was like a stranger. He looked wild, bitter, and tired.

The bartender returned and took up his customary stance. Pushing his drink aside, Scott asked, "Do you think one of the Sadlers killed your friend?"

"No doubt about it. It had to be Mitch Sadler. He ain't the kind to let bygones be bygones, and Doyle had a hunch he'd try to get even with him some day for sending him to prison."

"Has anybody spotted the Sadlers around here?"

"Who knows?" The bartender moved closer and

leaned his elbows on the bar. "You've got two kinds of people here: them that'd protect the Sadlers because they think it would help them to be friends, and them that's too scared to admit they saw them."

Scott gave the man a searching look. "What about you? Would you tell me if you knew where the Sadlers might be hanging out?"

Color flooded Corey Millsap's face. "Damn right I would. They're around here somewhere, that's for sure. Their old man used to have a place eight . . . nine miles out in the hills along what he called Sawmill Springs. He cut timber for a while out that way, and the old house is still standing. Doyle and me rode out there last week and looked around, but we didn't cut any sign. That doesn't mean they're not around there somewhere."

"Maybe I'll take a look around Sawmill Springs," Scott said thoughtfully.

"You want me to go along and show you the way?" Corey Millsap sounded eager to help. "I can get somebody to look after this place for a while any time you say."

"I guess not. Just tell me how to get there."

The bartender looked disappointed, but he gave Scott detailed directions to the old Sadler house. Scott thanked him and took out money to pay for the whiskey.

Corey Millsap pushed his hand away. "The drink's on the house and will be from now on. This town's on edge, and I'm sure glad you're here. Look around and you'll see what I mean. All these people are killing as much time as they can because they feel safer in numbers. When they leave, they'll bye alone and wondering if the

Sadlers have anything against them . . . wondering if they might get robbed or killed. They'll rest easier knowing you're here."

Scott had wondered about Corey Millsap's gracious manner, and he grew more puzzled. "I don't know why they'd expect anything from me. I'm just trying to find out what's going on. I won't be staying here."

The bartender stepped back and rubbed his forehead again. "Ain't you the new deputy the sheriff brought in?"

"No. The new deputy is a man by the name of Cal Baylor. He'll probably be in to see you."

The bartender's freckled face froze. "Hell, I could've been running off my mouth to Mitch Sadler's best friend. I've got to be more careful."

"Not with me," Scott said. "Mitch Sadler gunned down my pa when he and his brother robbed the bank in Blackwood. I'm not his friend. I'm the man who's going to kill him."

Relief brightened Millsap's eyes. "In that case, the drink's still on the house."

"Thanks." Scott touched his hat brim and turned to look outside. Through the front windows he could see that the sky was still murky, and he heard a rumble of distant thunder above the drone of voices. As he started to leave the bar, the batwing doors swung inward and Joe Pike came inside. The Pinkerton man spotted Scott and strode toward him, his thumbs hooked in the lower pockets of his buckskin vest.

"Thought I recognized your bay outside," he said as he came up beside Scott. "I didn't know you was coming this way."

"Something came up that I wanted to look into."

Corey Millsap saw that the two men were acquainted, and he watched them with interest. Joe Pike fixed his dark eyes on the bartender, stared at him until he took a step backward, and picked up the bottle that Millsap had left sitting at Scott's elbow. "I'll pay for this," he drawled, waited for Corey Millsap to hand him two glasses, then headed for a table next to the far wall, motioning for Scott to follow.

"Are you Joe Pike or George Pratt today?" Scott asked.

Pike shrugged, poured whiskey in both glasses, and took tobacco and papers from his shirt pocket. "It's been a while since I worked around here, so I'm going to be myself. I'll lend you the George Pratt name if you have need of it."

"Thanks a heap. Did you know somebody killed one of Wade Bandy's deputies here last night?"

"Heard it first thing. Folks think Mitch Sadler got him. They're too scared to say it out loud, but they're whispering it amongst themselves. They're afraid Hub won't have any law for a while, and they're as jumpy as a mule in a cactus patch. I'm a mite jumpy myself. I got here about noon and asked around about where the Sadlers used to live. I backtracked halfway to the crossroads and rode out to Sawmill Springs. I didn't see anybody, but I had a feeling somebody was looking down a gun barrel at me all the time. I came back to pick up my telegraph messages and felt like I needed a drink. There's a lot of worried faces in here. Thing is, most folks don't give a hoot about the law until they get scared."

"They've got a lawman," Scott said. "The sheriff's in town and he brought a new deputy with him—Cal Baylor. I told you about him and John Tripp. Cal volunteered for the job, and that strikes me odd. I think Tripp wants to be sure there's a deputy around who won't try to find the Sadler brothers."

"You're making up your mind awful fast about him. You must've learned something we didn't know."

Scott pushed his hat back to let the air cool his head. "I stumbled onto some interesting connections today and got in trouble by talking too much."

He told Pike about his visit to the stockyard, his conversation with Wade Bandy, and the fight with Cal Baylor.

Pike sifted tobacco into a thin paper, rolled it in his fingers, and sealed it with a lick of his tongue. He lighted the cigarette and inhaled slowly. "Death has a way of disrupting things. A man like Doyle Joyner gets killed, and it causes moves that wouldn't be made otherwise. It brought you to Hub, brought Cal Baylor here, and you learned things that might not have come out if death hadn't stirred the pot. Thing is, it might not amount to anything. Because Cal Baylor's a friend of Pat Logan, and Logan's a friend of the Sadlers, and Baylor is John Tripp's foreman don't mean Tripp's behind the robbery."

"They're in it together," Scott insisted. "I've had a hard time swallowing the fact that the Sadlers just happened to decide to rob the Pioneer Bank at the very minute we got back to town with a satchel full of money. I kept wondering if the Bar 40 had anything to do with it. I was about to believe it was a coincidence. We didn't know the Sadlers, and I couldn't figure how they'd know when we'd be back from the cattle sale, but I think I know now."

"You think Pat Logan tipped off the Sadlers that your pa would be carrying a lot of money."

"That's what I think," Scott said firmly. "John Tripp runs a big herd of horses as well as cattle, and sometimes he's pushed for help when he has to fill his contract for Cavalry remounts. Wade Bandy wants to stay in good with Tripp. He's been letting Pat Logan do some bronc-busting for the Bar 40. Logan and Cal Baylor got to be good friends, and that's where the robbery was planned."

Pike took a deep drag on his cigarette and left it drooping from the corner of his mouth. "There's one bad apple in that barrel—Pat Logan. He's wearing a badge to see what he can get out of it. I didn't buy his story that he wanted to slow you down so's he could beat you to the reward money. I think Logan meant to kill you. He just got off a bad shot. He's a lowlife, but I don't know about the others."

"I know about them," Scott said. "John Tripp didn't want the Crowfoot to buy up the free range he'd been using, but he didn't know how to stop it as long as Pa could pay for it. I think somebody mentioned that to Pat Logan and offered to pay him if he could help squeeze us out. Maybe Tripp wouldn't do that himself, but he could get Cal Baylor to talk to his good deputy friend about it. Pat Logan wants a lot of money. He can't get it from rewards, and he thinks he can get rich as a saloon owner. He wants to buy the Texas Star but can't raise the cash for the down payment. I think he looked up his old saddlepards, Mitch and Ned Sadler, and tipped them off to a good deal. They killed Pa, solved Tripp's problem, and Pat Logan got paid for setting it up.

"A lot of people knew our plans—people like Della Grange and Milam Huff. Folks talk about what their friends are doing. Pat Logan would know when we were coming home, and from there on it was up to Mitch and Ned Sadler. Robbing Pa wasn't enough, because he'd find a way to hold on to the land as long as he was alive, so they had to kill him."

Scott stopped talking and watched Pike's face for his reaction. The Pinkerton man blew smoke through his nostrils and crushed the cigarette out on the floor. He finished his drink and stared past Scott's shoulder as if he had not been listening.

"What do you think?" Scott asked impatiently.

"Who do you plan to kill first?"

There were times when Pike's drawling monotone annoyed Scott with its veiled meanings. He leaned close to the man, his face turning a shade darker. "You're making light of me, and I'm not in the mood for it."

"Didn't mean it that way, but I'm not in the mood to go chasing my tail around a tree, either. You can't prove nothing or solve nothing until we find Mitch and Ned Sadler. Thing is, you've laid out a whole stack of maybes. Maybes can turn into possibles, and possibles can run into sure bets, but I ain't got time to play out that hand. My job is to run down outlaws who are a threat to the good name of Wells Fargo. If you want to clean out a wolf pack, you get rid of the lead dog first. In our case, that's Mitch Sadler. There's another problem to think about. You don't want the Sadlers dead until you find out if they've still got your money, and how to find it if they do."

Scott propped an elbow on the table and rested his chin in his hand while he stared at Joe Pike. "I've been working on that. Maybe I feel so pushed for time I'm getting things out of order, but I'm not sure there is any order. I'm already down to seventeen days before my ranch gets sold. I thought I didn't care about the Crowfoot, but I was wrong. I want to keep Pa's ranch."

"That's sensible, but how are you going to do it?" Pike asked. "You said you had an idea that might get your money back."

"I thought of something that might work if Mitch Sadler has found a girl he wants to hold on to for a while, and I think he has. She's at Big Betty's Place. I need to know something from you."

"What's that?"

Scott told Pike of his conversation with Betty Kelton and his proposal to rent her bordello. His main interest, he explained, was in Polly Wexler, the girl who had become Mitch Sadler's favorite. During his ride to Hub, Scott had thought about the girl and her need for money, and he was sure she could be useful to them.

"What I need to know from you is about money," Scott said. "I'm counting on Pinkerton to pay Betty Kelton if she'll rent the place to us, and I'm hoping we can get Polly Wexler to work with us if we pay her enough. Would Pinkerton be willing to give her part of the reward . . . say, the five hundred posted on Mitch?"

"Depends. Pinkerton will want to know if she was a

principal in the capture, as they say, or just passed on information."

"She'll be a principal all right," Scott assured him. "If she needs money bad enough to string Mitch Sadler along until we can nail him, she'll be right in the middle of it."

Pike looked at Scott from beneath lowered eyebrows. "We're dealing with a man who don't think no more of killing than I do of spitting. You willing to risk her life for this?"

Scott's reply was a grim whisper. "I'm willing to risk my life, yours, hers—whatever it takes to get Mitch Sadler."

A cagey and careful man, Joe Pike wanted to know more about Scott's plans before he agreed to part with any of Pinkerton's money. He poured himself another drink, swirled the whiskey around in his glass, and scowled. He sat that way for a minute, then took a swallow and pushed his hat higher on his forehead.

"Nothing can break up friends or family faster than greed or jealousy," Pike said. "I'm guessing you want to find a way to get Mitch and Ned to distrust each other, make one of them believe the other's going to cheat him out of the money they took from Frank Rawley."

Scott was somewhat amazed that Pike had anticipated his thoughts. Because of the Sadlers' attraction to it, he was sure Big Betty's Place could be helpful to him. During his ride to Bluestem, he had turned over the possibilities in his mind, mentally searching for a way to lure the Sadlers into a trap and uncover his money at the same time. He was not sure how this could be done, but his instincts told him Big Betty's Place was the key to forcing a showdown with the outlaws.

"Betty Kelton told me Mitch is really stuck on Polly Wexler," Scott said. "I don't know much about Polly except that she wants to give up whoring and go home, but she's broke. Big Betty thinks she'll do about anything for money. You told me Mitch likes to have his own woman, and maybe he's decided Polly Wexler fits that bill. She might be able to get Mitch to do things nobody else can. I want to pay her to help us get him in a trap."

"How?" Pike asked skeptically.

"I haven't got that far yet. Maybe Polly Wexler will have some ideas. First we need to meet her and size her up, and see if she wants to go home bad enough to take some chances."

"Some good and some bad in that plan," Pike drawled. He pulled his hat brim back to its usual position close to his eyebrows. "Mitch has got a history of falling in love real easy—or at least pretending he is if he wants a woman to stay with him. If this Polly girl has got a good grip on him, he won't leave her alone. That's good. We'll know where to watch for him. Thing is, it ain't likely that a professional girl is going to give away any secrets she's learned from the men she entertains. If she's as smart as most women, she's been able to spot the mean streak in Mitch Sadler, and she'll be looking to protect her hide."

Scott's eyes narrowed thoughtfully. "Polly's from Mississippi, and there's something about Southern folks that draws them back to their roots. We'll have to see how money hungry she is. Maybe she can talk Mitch into paying her fare home or going back to Mississippi with her. He wouldn't leave without his loot, and when he goes for it we could follow him, get Polly away from him, and find my money."

"You're leaving out something. Ned figures half the money they stole belongs to him. He won't sit by and watch his brother ride off with all of it. We'll have to deal with Ned, too."

"I've been thinking about that," Scott said. "If we can get Ned and Mitch fighting over who gets to the money first, they'll get careless and we ought to be able to trail one of them to it."

"Lot of loose ends to tie up before we'll know how to make any of this happen." Pike studied the hope in Scott's eyes, but his expression gave no hint of approval or disapproval. "We're banking on a woman we don't know and two men we know well enough to scare the britches off of anybody with good sense. Mitch is a nervy bastard, and he's likely to keep coming back to Big Betty's as long as he feels nobody has tied him in with the bank robbery and the other killings."

"Nobody around here has mentioned the robbery," Scott said. "In this country a man figures anything which happens thirty miles from his front door ain't any of his concern."

Pike continued to stare at him, and Scott saw doubt in the tightening of his lips. "Thing is," he said after a brief pause, "I ain't sure about trusting outsiders when I'm trailing a killer, and I don't like to put all my eggs in one basket. If we wait around Big Betty's and the Sadlers don't come back, we'll end up empty-handed and you'll run out of time on your bank payment."

Scott frowned. He shared Pike's worry that his plan for Big Betty's Place might result in failure, and he was not counting on it as his only pursuit. He said, "Maybe we won't have to depend on Polly Wexler to trap the Sadlers. If my guts have ever told me anything, they tell me Cal Baylor is mixed up in this some way. Pa's death makes things work out too good for John Tripp and the Bar 40. If we get Big Betty's Place, I'll be around there at night when the Sadlers are most likely to show up, but I'm going to spend all the time I can in Hub and keep my eye on Cal Baylor. I've got a hunch he's got a payoff coming from the Sadlers. He might even know where they're keeping the money. I'm going to watch for visitors he might have who don't have anything to do with his deputy's job."

A sound that might have been a mumbled curse escaped Joe Pike's lips. He fiddled with his drink and appeared to be staring at something beyond Scott's shoulder. He was silent so long the clinking of glasses and the hum of voices from the other tables in the bar seemed magnified and distracting. From the corner of his eye Scott could see that some of the other patrons were casting curious glances toward them, and he became aware of the mingled odors of cigarette smoke, sweaty men, and open whiskey bottles.

Finally, the Pinkerton man's cold, probing stare settled on Scott's face. "However it comes about, there's going to be a gunfight sooner or later. I hope you're not setting up some excuse to be out of sight so I'll have to face the Sadlers alone."

"Excuse? What do you mean by that?"

Pike's glance did not waver. "I tied in with you because I figured you had enough hate pushing you to help me get things done. You've done that. I wouldn't have known Billy Clyde Marcum from Billy the Kid. That I.O.U. you found on him wouldn't have meant anything to me, but it's put us on a warm trail. I figured you were smart, but I didn't know about your guts. I still don't."

CHAPTER SIXTEEN

A FLASH OF ANGER darkened Scott's face and a ripple ran along his throat as he swallowed hard. "I didn't ask you for help. You did the asking. If you don't like what I do, then do things your own way."

For several seconds they stared at each other, neither blinking. They had worked together for only two days, and it was a time for testing and measuring—a time to cement their friendship or a time to part. Scott knew this and Pike knew it.

"I could do that," Pike said flatly. "It might take me a week or it might take me a year, but I'll get Mitch and Ned Sadler. I'd arrest them or kill them the first time I saw them, but I was willing to stall for time until we find your money. They sure ain't carrying it with them. I don't have no ranch to worry about, no deadlines to meet. My job is to do what I can to protect the good name of Wells Fargo and satisfy my own feelings about cold-blooded killers."

"Do as you please," Scott countered.

Pike's shoulders stiffened and white lines appeared at the corners of his mouth. He pushed his chair back and stood up. He picked up the bottle and started toward the bar, intending to show Corey Millsap what was left and pay the bill.

He took one step, then changed his mind and sat back down. He poured another drink, gulped it down, and tapped the bottom of the glass on the table. "It don't make sense for us to argue between ourselves. That's what we want Mitch and Ned to do. We'd best stick together. It couldn't cost too much to rent a house in a dry hole like Bluestem, and I'm willing to give Polly Wexler a share of the reward money if she helps us. That settle things?"

"Not quite," Scott said. "If you hint again that I'm a coward, I'll bust you in the mouth."

"That's what I'd do." The grim expression softened and Pike's square face looked younger despite the graying temples.

Scott grinned. "I guess we understand each other. We won't know until tomorrow whether or not Betty Kelton will rent us the bordello, but I'd like to have a talk with Polly Wexler today. We might not need the bordello without her."

"Then let's get at it." Pike glanced at the clock above the bar. "It's better than a two-hour ride to Bluestem, and I hope we can make it before Big Betty's girls pack up and leave for new jobs."

Pike pushed his chair back and stood up, and Scott could see that he was still troubled by their conversation. "I promised I wouldn't tell you what to do or how to do it, and I won't. It appears to me, though, that you've made up your mind Cal Baylor is guilty, and you don't aim to rest until you prove it. This is the Sadlers' home country, and you ain't likely to learn much by hanging around this town. No matter how mean a man is, he's always got friends in his own pasture—people who don't believe he's as bad as the law claims and people who want to do him a favor so they'll be in his good graces. You'd best be careful about what you say and do in Hub."

"I'll keep that in mind," Scott said.

They were turning away from the bar after paying for the whiskey when the batwing doors of the Running Iron swung inward and Cal Baylor strode inside. He paused midway across the floor, running his eyes first over Scott and then Joe Pike. He pulled at the brim of his shapeless Stetson and came on toward them, stopping again when he was in front of the two.

Nodding to Scott, he extended his hand to Joe Pike and said, "I'm Cal Baylor."

Pike shook the deputy's hand, introduced himself, and added as he turned away, "Always glad to make the acquaintance of the law."

When they were outside, Pike said, "He was fishing, wondering who I am and what I'm doing with you. Baylor has a strange look about him—like he's hurting about something or hiding something."

"That's what I saw in his eyes," Scott murmured. "He's not nearly as curious about you as I am about him. Something more than his interest in justice made him take this job, and I want to find out what it is."

Pike had left his mustang at the hitching rail next to Scott's bay, and they were swinging into their saddles when Scott remembered what Millie Adcock had said about the way the Pinkerton man checked into the Elkhorn Hotel. There had been a lilt in her voice and a secretive look in her eyes when she spoke about the new guest who had arrived in the middle of the night. Scott had been too busy to think about minor incidents, but the woman's manner had aroused his curiosity at the time.

"Millie Adcock must know you pretty well to trust you to help yourself to a room." Scott looked at Pike with a teasing smile. "She made me pay before I could look at a key. I take it that you're an old hand at the Elkhorn."

Pike's hard stare was the look of a man who treasured his privacy. "I've stayed there off and on, but not for two or three years. Millie's probably been talking more than she had any cause to. She recognized my name, and that's all there is to that."

"I wouldn't bet on it," Scott said. "She seemed right pleased that you showed up."

Shrugging, Pike slapped the reins of his mustang and Scott knew the subject of Millie Adcock was closed for the moment.

As they rode out of Hub, Scott felt a strange pang of loneliness and a sense of guilt about having spent too little time with his parents. He said, "My mother would turn over in her grave if she knew I was thinking about taking over a whorehouse."

Pike looked across at him and lowered his chin close to his chest. "Mine, too. My folks were missionaries, came west from Ohio when I was eleven. They stayed six years, then gave up and went back. Thing is, they figured they'd never make the Indians believe in the white man's God as long as the white man was killing their game, raping their women, and stealing their land."

It was the first time Pike had revealed anything of his personal life. Scott would not have guessed the Pinkerton man came from a religious background. He started to offer a sarcastic comment, but the sadness in Pike's face changed his mind.

"Maybe I should have gone with them," Pike continued, "but by that time I'd learned a lot about Indians, so I lied about my age and got a job as a Cavalry scout. One thing led to another, and I ended up with Pinkerton. Folks passed away a couple of years ago, but I didn't hear about it until three months after they was buried. I hadn't seen them in nineteen years."

Scott studied Joe Pike's lean jaw, the blunt chin, the hard lines around his mouth, and the steady black eyes. "The way that adds up, you're thirty-six years old. Hell, I thought you were at least forty, maybe fifty."

"Wear and tear," Pike said.

"I guess you're not too old for Millie Adcock after all." Scott watched the man's face, expecting the remark to draw one of Pike's cutting glances or a snort of denial.

Pike's lips twitched and he almost smiled. "Maybe not."

For a long time they rode in silence, but before they reached Bluestem, Pike grew more talkative than usual. He reminisced about his exploits with the army and recalled a few of the cases he had worked on for the Pinkerton National Detective Agency. At first Scott thought the whiskey Pike had consumed at the Running Iron was responsible for his behavior, but the man's voice was clear, and his seat in the saddle was firm and steady. They became more at ease with each other, and Scott talked about his own life—about his father, the Crowfoot Ranch, John Tripp's resentment toward them, and his years on the riverboats.

Two miles past the crossroads that marked the halfway point between Hub and Bluestem, they turned off the stage road and proceeded along the wagon trail Scott had followed that morning from Whit Kirby's livery stable to Big Betty's Place. A few minutes later they came within sight of the bordello. Scott had expected the yard of the big white-columned house to be as deserted as it had been on his first visit, but two horsemen came around a corner of the gallery porch as he and Pike approached.

The riders saw them coming and waited. They were cautious men. The sudden squaring of their shoulders, a quick lift of their heads, and hands sliding toward holstered guns on their thighs told Scott they were wary and dangerous. One of the riders was tall and lean, dressed in stiff new Levi's, a black flannel shirt, and a pearl-gray Stetson. Even in the dreary light of dusk, the thatch of pale hair on the back of his neck glistened like polished silver. The other man was shorter but powerfully built, a black-hatted, swarthy man who kept his lips slightly parted so the edges of his teeth were visible, giving his face an expression that could be either a grin or a sneer.

"Damn!" The word came from Joe Pike at the end of a long breath, spoken softly and warily. "You know who we're looking at?"

"Yeah, I know," Scott said hoarsely.

"Don't do nothing foolish. It ain't the right time."

Joe Pike's whispered warning was a faint sound, drowned by the roar of blood racing through Scott's head. His face felt hot and sweaty. His throat muscles were cramped too close to allow a reply, and the hand gripping the bay's reins was squeezed so tightly his fingernails were digging into his palm. A flash of memory showed him the blood gushing from his father's mouth as Frank Rawley fell dead in front of Blackwood's Pioneer Bank, and fury blurred Scott's vision as he slow-walked his horse toward the two mounted men.

He crossed the last thirty feet of the yard, stopped with his hands folded on the pommel, and had his first face-to-face meeting with Mitch and Ned Sadler.

The chance of encountering the two outlaws in the yard of Big Betty's bordello so soon had never crossed Scott's mind, and it was difficult for him to face them and keep his senses. He forced an image of calm indifference, but his insides were churning and the faces in front of him seemed to float in a dreamlike haze.

He sat loosely in the bay's saddle, his eyes roaming over the faces of the men who were responsible for his father's death. As the seconds dragged by, Mitch Sadler's horse fidgeted and the blond-haired outlaw patted its flank, tightened his hold on the reins, and relaxed. The uncertainty that had causcd the Sadlers to halt their horses abruptly when they saw Scott and Joe Pike was gone. Swift, searching glances had sized up the visitors. Mitch and Ned were looking for a badge or any sign of interference with their passage, and when they saw none they were at ease.

Mitch Sadler broke the silence, unaware of the hate and shock in Scott's eyes. Lounging in his saddle, he spoke as pleasantly as a neighbor passing on helpful information to a friend. "I'm afraid you're out of luck, gents. The place is closed."

"Oh?" A single, questioning word was all Scott could manage from a throat writhing with bitterness.

Mitch bobbed his head regretfully. "Big Betty's gone into mourning for a deputy who got himself killed over in Hub last night. I didn't know she had that much to do with badge-toters, but it turns out she was real sweet on Doyle Joyner. That's what Earl McKay was telling us a few minutes ago. Earl's standing guard in the house to see that things go the way Big Betty wants them."

The outlaw had directed his remarks to Scott Rawley, but he kept glancing sideways at Joe Pike, who had brought his mustang to a halt on the other side of Ned Sadler's mount. Tilting his head, Mitch looked directly at Pike. "I don't favor getting too close to lawmen myself. How about you, mister?"

There was a purpose behind the question. At first glance, the Sadlers had accepted Scott as an ordinary pleasure-seeking cowboy, but Mitch was suspicious of the taciturn man on the black mustang.

"I can take them or leave them," Pike said dryly. "Mostly, I favor leaving them."

The quick grin on Mitch Sadler's face indicated he was satisfied with Pike's reply, but his brother was not. Ned's parted lips hardly moved as he growled, "He talks like a man who's on the dodge, but that's what you'd expect. If I was to pick a man who's got a badge hiding under his vest, I'd pick him."

As he spoke, Ned's fingers inched toward his Colt, and Scott saw Joe Pike's right hand drop to his side. Mitch Sadler saw both moves, and he spoke quickly.

"Don't pay any attention to my brother." Mitch cast a warning glance toward Ned. "He's ornery because he won't be having himself a woman tonight. It's nothing to us who carries a badge, but you gents might as well ride on. There's nothing going on here."

With a nudge of his spurred heel, Mitch eased his horse forward. Ned skirted Joe Pike and took the lead, appearing to be eager to leave. The horses moved ahead a few yards, and then Mitch halted his mount and looked back at Scott and Pike as though he expected them to go on their way at the same time.

"You can push Earl McKay out of the way and go on in," he said, "but it won't do you any good. That's what we did, but the girls won't come downstairs. They've got too much respect for Big Betty to work at their trade tonight."

The few minutes of conversation had given Scott time to swallow down the lump in his throat and find his voice. He wanted to scream out the loathing he felt for the Sadler brothers, whip out his gun, and blast them into eternity, but he had to wait. He might be able to avenge his father's death before the outlaws had a chance to ride away, but it would cost him everything except the satisfaction of seeing the Sadler brothers dead.

He could benefit from the meeting, however, if he could taunt the man enough to determine the depth of

Mitch Sadler's feeling for Polly Wexler. Shrugging, Scott said, "I'm here on a personal matter. I spoke to Betty Kelton about Polly Wexler this morning, and I think Polly is expecting me."

"Personal matter with Polly?" Mitch looked surprised. He toyed with his horse's reins a few seconds, then ran his glance over Scott as though he were seeing him for the first time. "If I were you, I wouldn't get too personal with Polly. When I'm around here at business hours, I'm going to see that Polly's' time is reserved for me. I wouldn't like it if I found out she's setting aside private time for somebody else."

Mitch's voice was hard-edged and threatening. It was what Scott wanted to hear and it encouraged him to keep talking. He said, "She's a working girl, and I figure it's first come, first served in a place like this. If I was here for pleasure, I figure she'd take my money as easy as yours, but I'm not here for that. I've got other business to talk over with her."

Mitch straightened in the saddle, gripping his horse's reins so tight his knuckles turned white. "You got a name, mister?"

It was a question few men in the West asked of another stranger, but Mitch Sadler meant it as a challenge. He was asking because he wanted Scott to know it was something he would mark in his mind and not forget. Scott meant to be equally bold, letting Mitch know he had no fear of the challenge. He started to speak, then felt his skin crawl as he realized how close he had come to making a serious mistake.

He hesitated only long enough to take a deep breath,

then said, "Yeah, I've got a name. It's Pratt—George Pratt. How about you?"

There was no hesitation in the blond-haired outlaw. "Mitch," he said. "If we meet again, you can call me Mitch."

"We'll meet again," Scott said, and immediately regretted that he had spit out the words as if they were venom.

Apparently, Mitch Sadler read nothing unusual in Scott's reply. He was silent for a moment, then he chuckled. "You're right about Polly, George. She's a fool about money, and I can't control what she does when I'm not around. If you come back to Big Betty's and find me here, don't try to make any deals with Polly."

Before Scott could respond, Ned Sadler said impatiently, "You going to spend the night visiting with strangers?"

"I'm ready to go," Mitch said. He gave Scott a final, searching glance. "You're not from Mississippi, are you?"

"Texas," Scott said.

"Thought so," Mitch grunted. He jiggled his horse's reins, signaled to his brother, and the two of them rode quickly toward the trail that led to the stage road.

CHAPTER SEVENTEEN

EXCEPT FOR THE BRIEF EXCHANGE with Ned Sadler, Joe Pike had remained silent while Scott and Mitch talked. He had sat aside like a disinterested spectator, but Scott knew the Pinkerton man was watching every move, ready to act if anything went wrong.

As they dismounted and tied their horses at the hitching rail, Pike said, "That was a little hairy, but you did good."

"I wanted to kill them," Scott said.

"You scared the hell out of me when I thought you was about to tell Mitch your name. By now there's been newspaper reports about the bank robbery, and the Sadlers would know Scott Rawley is the son of the man Mitch killed . . . know you're after them. That would've started a gunfight for sure. I'm glad I loaned you a good name."

Scott drew a deep breath. "I almost slipped up, but Mitch Sadler doesn't seem to care who knows his name."

"Lot of men named Mitch in this country. Either he figures it won't mean anything to us, or he's giving us notice that he's not afraid of us and we'd better not get any notions about collecting the reward on his head. He's mean and cocky, and he knows there's no law in Bluestem. That makes him right nervy."

Still nervous and frustrated, Scott seemed unable to draw enough air into his lungs. He backed up between the two horses and rested against the hitching rail. Pike moved up beside him, watching as Scott looked across the trampled ground that separated Betty Kelton's house from the trail that ran from the back side of town to the stage road.

While they paused to let the tension drain from their nerves, Scott wondered aloud about the advisability of trying to follow the Sadler brothers. There was no dust on their clothes, no lather on their horses, and he was sure the outlaws had established a hide-out camp somewhere close to Bluestem. It was possible, he reasoned, that his quest could come to an end this very night if the Sadlers were carrying Frank Rawley's cattle money with them or had it stowed with their belongings at their camp.

The scowl on Pike's face betrayed his thoughts before he spoke. "If you don't learn some patience, you're going to mess things up," he said. "We don't want to tip our hand and let the Sadlers know what we're up to. If they spot us sneaking along behind them, there'll be a showdown and we'll have to kill them—or get killed. Your money won't be at their camp. They might be carrying the few hundred they got from the bank, but the big haul they got from your pa is hidden somewhere else."

Scott shifted his feet irritably. "You keep saying that like it's gospel. What makes you so sure?"

"Experience. I've run down a lot of thieves, and I know how they think. The Sadlers know there's a chance they'll get arrested anytime on one charge or another. If they have to go to jail, they want to be sure the money is waiting for them when they get out. They don't want it on them if they run afoul of the law."

Scott looked away, shaking his head, and Pike changed the subject. He said, "You was smart enough to learn how Mitch feels about Polly Wexler, so let's find out what she thinks of him."

A hand-lettered placard that said "TEMPORARILY

CLOSED" was tacked to the front door of Betty Kelton's house. Scott's first three knocks were ignored, but he kept pounding on the wood panels until a sandy-haired man in range clothes finally opened the door and looked out at the two men on the porch.

He pointed to the sign. "That means what it says. Why can't you waddies believe what you read?"

"You must be Earl McKay," Scott said. "I talked with Betty Kelton this morning, but she didn't mention that she had a bodyguard for this place. We won't keep you long."

"You ain't going to keep me a-tall," Earl McKay snapped. He was in his mid-thirties, a well-built man with a clean-scrubbed look about his face and his clothes. The six-gun that was holstered low on his right thigh looked as if it had just been oiled and polished. He rested his hand on the gun butt while he spoke. "I don't know you and I don't know how you learned my name, but I'm not exactly a guard. I help out with a lot of things around here, and today I was told to make sure the girls didn't entertain any guests while Big Betty's at a funeral. That's what I aim to do. Get away from here and leave us alone."

Earl McKay started to slam the door, but Joe Pike's left hand shot out and pushed it back. His right hand came into sight at the same instant, and Scott was as surprised as Earl McKay when he saw the blued-steel Colt clutched in Pike's fist, with its barrel inches from the tip of McKay's nose. He had never seen Pike draw a gun and he had not seen him do it now. The move was so quick and effortless that the Colt seemed to materialize out of the air.

"Some people can't seem to listen good unless they've got a gun in their face," Pike drawled, and looked aside at Scott. "Go ahead and tell him what we came for."

The sun wrinkles at the corners of Earl McKay's gray eyes deepened. Color drained from his face, and the freckles on his forehead and across the bridge of his straight nose stood out like tiny spots of blood. His fear was only momentary, and then he squared his jaw defiantly. "I thought I just got rid of the two who're the most likely to make trouble, but I reckon the more they come the worse they get. If you're going to force—"

"We're plumb friendly folks," Scott cut in. "Betty knew I was coming back to see Polly, and she probably told her. I'm not interested in Polly's favors—just her opinion of the two men who left here a few minutes ago."

McKay's glance flicked from Scott to Joe Pike. "She might not come downstairs. Do you want me to give her your name?"

At the moment Scott was not sure Betty Kelton would rent him the brothel, but he was taking no chance that the Sadlers would learn his identity. He told Earl McKay his name was George Pratt and introduced Joe Pike. The Pinkerton man put his gun away and gave Earl McKay a friendly pat on the shoulder. "It's been said that a man should never pull his gun unless he means to use it, but you can't always believe that. Sometimes it's only a bluff. I was bluffing you."

Earl McKay grinned, feeling more comfortable with the two visitors. "You couldn't prove it by me. When a man pulls a gun on me, I get helpful in a hurry."

Swinging the door wider, he invited them inside, and they followed him to the parlor where Scott had talked with Betty Kelton earlier in the day. They sat down on the wine-colored mohair sofa, holding their hats in their hands, and waited for McKay to inform Polly Wexler of their arrival.

The sandy-haired man started toward the opening to the barroom, then came back to stand in front of them. He did not like being characterized as a bodyguard, and he spent a few minutes explaining his association with the bordello. He was a gunsmith by trade and was employed at a small shop in town. Business was bad, his pay was low, and he needed extra income. After the gun shop closed each afternoon, he came to Big Betty's Place, where he served as a bartender and general handyman.

"It's not my line of work," he concluded, shaking his head, "but it helps pay my room and board. I can handle loudmouths and drunks, but I don't get paid enough to tangle with people like those two you met outside. They look like gunslicks to me."

"You know who they are?" Joe Pike asked quietly.

McKay shook his head. "Around here we hear only first names. One of the girls told me they call themselves Mitch and Ned."

"Mitch and Ned Sadler," Pike said. "Ever hear of them?"

"No," McKay replied. "Big Betty has told us we're not to meddle in the private affairs of her customers, and I don't."

Pike said nothing more, and McKay headed for the stairway that led from a corner of the barroom to the second floor. Scott looked at the Pinkerton man, wondering why he had not told McKay more about the Sadlers. Pike read his thoughts. "It's good that he don't know nothing about Mitch and Ned. We might need his help, and I don't want him to get spooked by the Sadlers' reputation."

"We're going to need somebody," Scott agreed. "I'd like to be sure we can trust somebody to find us if the Sadlers show up here when we're not around. If McKay won't do it, you'll have to call in that Pinkerton posse you was telling me about."

A frown replaced the bland expression on Pike's face. "I was hoping you wouldn't bring that up. We can't count on my posse. One of the messages I picked up in Hub was from Carson Rowe, the detective I sent on to Blackwood. He's had word from the Chicago headquarters, and they've ordered him to hold down the Austin office until I get back there. There's some kind of feud going on over in New Mexico Territory which is about to break out into a range war. The governor has asked Pinkerton to see if we can flush out the ring leaders and make peace before it explodes. Pinkerton has sent my men over to Lincoln County for a while."

"Damn!" Scott said with disgust. "You sold me a pig in a poke and I bought it. I was counting on that so-called posse to help us corner the Sadlers if it comes to that."

"Don't fret about it. There's two of them and two of us. That's better odds than I'm used to. Thing is, I want to be sure you'll be with me when the showdown comes."

The stare that Scott fastened on Pike's face came from ice-blue eyes with a sparkle of hate in them. "I'll be there. Someday, somewhere, I'm going to kill Mitch Sadler."

Footsteps thumped on the stairway, and Scott's attention was drawn to the barroom. Earl McKay came into sight, and with him was a young woman in a bright red skirt and lime-green blouse. They paused briefly on the square landing three steps from the floor, then came quickly into the parlor.

McKay said, "This is Polly." He introduced the visitors as George Pratt and Joe Pike, then turned and walked through the kitchen toward the back of the house.

Polly Wexler looked first at Scott. She held out her hand, palm down, as though she expected him to kiss it, smiling when he grasped it lightly instead. She went through the same motions with Joe Pike, then sat down on the sofa and gestured toward the two leather chairs as an invitation for them to be seated.

"Miss Betty told me to expect a gentleman caller today," she said, "and I've been dying of curiosity and feeling a little frightened as well. I said to myself 'I'll bet my Daddy has sent someone to track me down again,' and I'll simply die of shame if that's who you are. I won't go with you, though, and you mustn't tell him you found me in a place like this. As soon as my circumstances improve, I'm—"

"We don't know your daddy, ma'am," Scott interrupted. "We're not here to take you anywhere."

Polly Wexler took a deep breath and smiled, her even

white teeth glistening between full, sensuous lips. Her voice was a vibrant, cultivated soprano with the slow, melodic inflections common to southern speech. "Will you listen to me, just running on about things before I know the nature of your business. I declare, I live in fear of my daddy finding me before I can go back in style to Three Oaks Plantation in Pearl River Landing, Mississippi. The Wexlers of Pearl River Landing are known from Three Oaks to Jackson as a family of property and influence, and I know my daddy has been sending people to find me for the past three years."

She paused, and Scott sensed she was disappointed that they were not messengers from her father. She lowered long lashes to conceal the sadness that appeared for a fleeting moment in the midnight-blue eyes, which had been so lively when she'd first seen the two men.

"I reckon you're getting mighty homesick," Joe Pike said. "I take it your folks don't know the profession you've taken up."

Touches of color showed on the high cheeks of her oval face, streaking up into her thick chestnut hair. "Mercy, no, they don't know! Mama would just die and Daddy would move away in disgrace. I want to go home, but I won't do it until I have enough money for some pretty clothes and the fare for first-class accommodations all the way to Pearl River Landing. I must look successful! I've written them so many letters full of lies, I—I—"

She stopped abruptly, apparently aware that she was revealing too much of her personal life. "What is the business you wanted to discuss with me?"

In less than ten minutes, Scott had learned many things about Polly Wexler. She was beautiful, intelligent, well-educated, and possessed with a dignity rarely seen among women who earned their living at a bordello. In addition, she was disenchanted with her profession, longed to see her parents, and was in dire need of money to satisfy that desire.

Scott was encouraged. Without hesitation, he answered her question frankly. "I've got a score to settle with a man who's been coming here to see you. The word I hear is that he's pretty stuck on you, and maybe you like him too much to talk about him. His name is Mitch Sadler. How do you feel about him?"

"I purely hate him!" She breathed deeply again, her eyes flashing. "I don't know his last name, but I know Mitch. He's an animal, and I hate him."

A surge of excitement warmed Scott's veins. He leaned back in his chair and smiled at Polly Wexler. He had found the kind of ally he needed and, perhaps, the ideal bait for a trap that would bring him to terms with Mitch Sadler.

Until he was sure Betty Kelton would rent him the bordello, however, Scott was not ready to confide any further in Polly Wexler. This was the only place Mitch Sadler and the girl were likely to meet, and without it and the ability to control its activities, Scott's tentative plans were useless. He could not take a chance that Polly would change her mind about Mitch Sadler over a period of time and alert the outlaw of Scott's intentions. Before he told her more, he had to be assured of her loyalty to him—loyalty he could buy for a price or gain willingly because of Polly's desire to get even with Mitch Sadler for mistreating her.

Scott had been pleased by the girl's fiery reaction to his question about her feelings for the outlaw, but Joe Pike was not satisfied. It was not Pike's nature to accept outward appearances as a reflection of the truth. He stared steadily at Polly Wexler, watching her eyes, the turn of her lips, and the fluttering of her hands while she spoke.

"Most sporting girls I know don't let personal feelings interfere when they find a man who singles them out as his personal stock," Pike commented wryly. "They'll hang on to him until they milk him for every dollar he's got. What's wrong with Mitch's money?"

Life in frontier bordellos had hardened Polly Wexler and conquered any inclination toward shyness. Her quick mind read Pike's suspicions, and she dispelled them quickly. "If you think I'm trying to mislead you so you won't tie me in with anything Mitch has done, you're wrong. I may be a sporting girl in Texas, but I was raised as a lady at Three Oaks Plantation. In my own way, I'm still a lady. Mitch tried to make me do things I won't do. When I refused him, he slapped me and pushed my arm behind my back so hard he made me cry. I'll declare, I thought he was going to cry, too, right after that. He fell on his knees, held my hands, and begged me to forgive him. He gave me twenty dollars and promised he'd be an absolute gentleman if I'd scc him again.

"A few days ago he came back, but I turned my nose up at him. I guess he had to have someone, and he finally went to bed with Rose. He had to pay her five dollars, but I'll swear he came right back and offered me any amount I wanted if I'd let him make love to me. I need money so desperately right now and Mitch seems to have plenty of it, but I'll stay in Texas forever before I'll let him in my bed again! I'm afraid of him."

"You need to change professions," Pike said dryly.

Polly Wexler nodded wistfully, looking young and fragile, and she voiced a dream many young girls of her time carried in their heart. She said, "I know. I want to go home and fall in love with a fine southern gentleman who owns good cotton land. When I save enough money, I'm going home as fast as I can. Travel is so expensive and I'm so far away. I'll have to go by stage-coach, then by train, and then Daddy will meet me at the station in Jackson in our own carriage. I wish I could go today."

Shrugging, Pike leaned back in his chair. He was convinced the girl's disdain for Mitch Sadler was real, and he grew silent.

Polly was not offended by Pike's manner, but she was curious. So far, Scott and Pike had spent their time prying into her affairs without explaining the purpose of their visit.

She looked from one man to the other. "What was the important business Miss Betty said you wanted to discuss with me?"

Scott had to think of an answer. His original interest in meeting her was to find out if Mitch Sadler had revealed any information about his campsite, or whether he had given any hint that he intended to remain in the immediate area or move on. Joe Pike felt that locating the Sadlers' camp would be of little value, but Scott was still not sure. At some point he might have to try to catch them off-guard and see if a threat to kill them would persuade the brothers to lead him to his money.

After a moment's hesitation Scott started asking questions, hoping they would at least serve as a reason for his visit. He and Pike talked with the girl for ten minutes, but Polly's comments were of little help. She knew nothing about the outlaws' habits, and she showed no interest in what Mitch and Ned did outside the walls of the bordello.

She surprised Scott as she bowed her head and rendered a girlish curtsy when they bade her farewell and started outside. By the time he left her, Scott wanted to do all he could to help Polly Wexler find a way to return to her home in Mississippi.

Each preoccupied with his own thoughts, Scott and Pike were silent until they were on the wagon trail that led to Whit Kirby's livery stable. It was an hour before time for the sun to set, but the overcast that had lowered the sky all day pushed an early dusk down upon them. As they rounded the brushy slope and came within sight of Bluestem's colorless buildings, Pike said, "That Polly girl is full of spunk and good breeding. When you hurt a woman's face you hurt her all the way through, and Mitch made a mistake when he slapped her. She's ready to make him suffer for that. If we have to count on somebody to help us, I'd bet on her."

"I don't want to get her killed to settle my own problems," Scott said uneasily.

"A few hours ago you didn't care about that."

Scott smiled, but his eyes were worried. "All I knew

about her then was her name. There's a difference in knowing a name and knowing a person. I keep thinking about what Mitch did to his wife, Kitty, and it makes my skin crawl."

"Let's don't lose any sleep over it. Thing is, we don't have a deal with either Big Betty or Polly yet. Tomorrow we might have a whole new set of things to worry about."

CHAPTER EIGHTEEN

THEIR DISCUSSION ENDED as they reached the livery. Whit Kirby saw them coming. He limped out from the doorway of his quarters and took the reins of their horses while they dismounted.

The liveryman wanted to talk with Scott, but he watched Joe Pike speculatively as the Pinkerton man walked away a few paces, stretching his arms and stamping his feet to relieve some of the fatigue from almost a full day of riding. Kirby waited until Pike was beyond the range of his voice before he said, "By God, you've got the gall of a good Texas man. I'll credit you for that. You're a damn fast worker. Big Betty come by here with some stringbean in a buggy on their way to a funeral in Hub. She said you was askin' to take over her business and wanted my feelin's about it. Hell, that's up to her. Her rent is paid until the first of the month, and that's three weeks away. What happens between now and then is between you and her."

"You surprise me, Whit. I figured you'd be a hell of a landlord to reach any kind of agreement with." Scott's eyes narrowed. "If Big Betty lets me have the place, I don't want you around there. You know my name, and if you run into the Sadlers, you're likely to let it slip and get me killed."

Kirby spat into the dirt and cursed. "I know what you're up to. I'm ignorant as hell, but I ain't stupid. I ain't takin' any chances that might tip off Mitch and Ned that I was the one who told you I seen them goin' to Big Betty's Place the same day they rode off with Billy Clyde Marcum. You won't be bothered with my company, by God. You can——"

The liveryman cut off his words as Joe Pike came up to them. Pike reached beneath his waistband, fumbled inside a money belt, and offered Whit Kirby a dollar. "This will take care of the horses we're keeping here."

Kirby shook his head. "Look's like you fellers are goin' to be around for a while. I'll trust you to pay me when you pull out."

"Suits me," Pike said, and put the money in his pocket. Assuming by the liveryman's manner that he wanted to talk privately with Scott, Pike walked back toward the gate.

Leaning closer to Scott but still peering at Pike over his rimless spectacles, Kirby asked, "Is he a Pinkerton man, too?"

"Why don't you ask him?"

Kirby continued to study Joe Pike's easy-moving figure for a moment. "I told you I wasn't stupid. I ain't askin' that hombre no questions that might offend him," he said, and led the horses toward the stalls.

Halfway along the stony path that ended at the rear of

the Elkhorn Hotel, Joe Pike took his money from his pocket, thumbed through it, and handed Scott a twenty-dollar bill. "Here's half of what I promised you as a part-time Pinkerton man. I don't usually pay in advance, but I figure you're about broke. You'd go hungry before you'd ask me for it."

Scott thanked him and accepted the money. "I ain't much for asking favors, but I might need this."

There were four or five people moving around the lobby when they entered the Elkhorn, and Scott noticed that the bar at the rear of the dining room was crowded. "Looks like business is picking up around here."

"Too many people crying hard times in Bluestem," Pike commented. "It makes me think they're talking things down to keep anybody from moving in and cutting into their business."

"It's been done," said Scott.

A bright smile spread over Millie Adcock's face when she saw them. She waved gaily and gestured for them to come to the counter.

"I'm relieved to see my two favorite men back here alive and well," she said, still smiling. "After what Joe told me this morning, I'll be worried sick every time you go out."

Scott fastened an accusing stare on the Pinkerton man. "Looks like somebody else has been talking more than they had cause to."

Tugging at his hat, Joe Pike gave Millie Adcock a long look and said, "She always sticks her nose in my business, but she keeps things to herself. Thing is, once a cat has got its head out of the bag, you might as well let its

216

tail out, too. She told me about having supper with you, and there wasn't much she didn't know before I saw her."

Slapping playfully at Pike's shoulder, Millie began asking questions, most of which they answered vaguely. Scott noticed that her copper-flecked eyes clung to Pike's face most of the time while she talked, and he suspected they were closer friends than the Pinkerton man had wanted to admit. Millie began discussing people she and Pike had both known in the past, and Scott soon excused himself and went upstairs.

He enjoyed Millie's company, but he was tired, worried about his lack of progress, and needed time to himself. He was eager for this night to pass. Betty Kelton had promised to meet him at four o'clock tomorrow and let Scott know whether or not she would rent him the bordello. He wanted to rest before supper and think about what his next step would be if Betty Kelton declined his request.

An hour later, feeling refreshed after a bath and a brief rest, Scott met Joe Pike and Millie Adcock in the dining room. A peaceful atmosphere, good food, and the sight of a pretty face could do much to lift a man's spirits, and Scott enjoyed his supper. They sat at table near the front windows, and for a while it was like a get-together of old friends. Pike assured Scott that Millie could be trusted, and they talked freely about their activities during the day, including what they hoped to accomplish at Big Betty's Place.

Millie looked at Pike through half-lidded eyes. "Is Polly Wexler a very pretty girl?"

"She's a real beauty, but a girl is what she is," Pike replied. "She couldn't be more than seventeen . . . eighteen years old. Somewhere along the way she made a wrong turn and she knows it. She's bound and determined to get back to her Mama and Papa some way. I hope she makes it."

As time passed, it became obvious that Joe Pike wanted to make the evening last as long as he could, but Scott was growing weary of it. Anxiety dwelled constantly in his mind, and he was too restless to while away the time with idle chatter. When Pike beckoned to a waitress and ordered more coffee, Scott waved his aside and stated that he was too sleepy to stay. As he left, he looked back and saw Joe Pike and Millie Adcock sitting with their heads close, and Pike was smiling.

Early the next morning Scott rode to Hub. He was up before first light and was the dining room's only customer when he ate breakfast. He was able to saddle his bay and get away from the livery stable without being delayed by one of Whit Kirby's harangues. In the coolness of dawn the ride passed quickly, and Scott arrived in Hub before the full heat of the sun began to beat down from a cloudless sky.

There was not much activity in the town for the first hour. As the shops along the main street opened one by one, people began to transact business, and a number of wagons stopped to load supplies at the side or front of various stores. As the day grew older, a few horsemen appeared to take up space at the hitching rails near the saloons.

For Scott, it was a time of looking and listening. With

spurs rattling on high-heeled boots, his Stetson pulled close to his eyes, and his bone-handled Colt brushing at the seam of his faded Levi's, he acted like a cowboy who had nothing more to do than kill time. He strode casually along the boardwalk, pausing to gaze at goods displayed in the windows. Each time he saw two or more men talking together, Scott found a reason to pause where he would be close enough to eavesdrop. He heard a lot of talk about stock prices, dry weather, nagging women, and lazy cowboys, but no one mentioned Mitch or Ned Sadler. He watched the side streets and rear alleys for any sign of skulking men or two riders who appeared unduly cautious, but he saw nothing suspicious.

Once, as he was coming out of the California Emporium after browsing through racks of wool suits and shelves of boots he could not afford, he saw Cal Baylor coming toward him. The flash of the deputy's star in the morning sunlight caught Scott's attention first. When he saw who was wearing it, he crossed the street to avoid meeting him.

It was a boring day, but Scott was convinced his patience would be rewarded. He moved his bay from one hitching rail to another so it would not have to stand too long, loosening the cinch and bridle each time to make the horse more comfortable. In the early afternoon, he went to the Running Iron Saloon. He bought a glass of beer and sat down at a table near the window, which gave him a view of the town jail across the street.

Scott sipped the beer and gazed idly at the traffic on the street. The brew was warm and bitter, and he had taken it only as a reason for his being at the saloon. Two cowboys stood at the bar, nursing their drinks and gossiping with Corey Millsap about a range war in Lincoln County, New Mexico. They showed no interest in Scott, and he was relieved that they had no curiosity about him.

Half an hour later, Deputy Cal Baylor finished his rounds of the town and came back to the jail. He stood a moment in front of his office door, set his hands on his hips, and swung his gaze up and down the street before he went inside. The angle of the sun allowed Scott to see the interior of the office clearly, and he watched Baylor fiddle with a stack of papers on his desk, hitch at his gunbelt, then disappear into the hallway that led to his living quarters.

Noticing the clock above the bar, Scott swore at himself for paying less attention to time. It was two o'clock, and he was going to be late getting back to Bluestem. He pushed his drink aside and stared again at Cal Baylor's office. The front table in the Running Iron gave him a perfect spot for surveillance of the jail, and he planned to return to it often.

Scott rose abruptly and Corey Millsap looked questioningly at him. He waved to the bartender and went outside, wondering if Millsap had guessed why he was spending time in Hub. He had more pressing concerns than a bartender's curiosity, Scott told himself as he rode out of town. If Betty Kelton was patient enough to wait for him in Bluestem, he would soon know whether or not he and Joe Pike would gain control of Mitch Sadler's favorite whorehouse. If they were successful, it would be time to talk frankly with Polly Wexler . . . time to find out if she hated Mitch

Sadler enough to double-cross him.

Reaching an agreement with Betty Kelton turned out to be quick and simple, and Scott's tardy arrival did not affect it. He knew it was past time for the four o'clock appointment when he turned off the stage road onto the wagon trail that traversed the back side of town. It was the route he had taken from Whit Kirby's livery stable and was a shortcut to the Elkhorn Hotel. Scott assumed Joe Pike would be waiting for him there, pacing and swearing because he had not arrived on time.

On his way to the hotel he had to pass Betty's Place, and he debated whether he should stop or go on. His quandary was settled when he came within sight of the bordello and saw a familiar horse tied at the hitching rail in front of the big clapboard house. It was Joe Pike's black mustang.

He guided his bay across the stretch of hoof-marked ground that lay between the house and the wagon trail and left it beside Pike's horse. Betty Kelton looked tired when she answered Scott's knock, but her voice was pleasant and friendly. "Hello again!" she said with a strained smile. "We've been expecting you."

"Sorry I'm late, ma'am."

"It's perfectly all right," Betty Kelton said. "I wanted time to talk to my girls before I gave you my decision, and I got back early enough to do that. When I saw Mr. Pike waiting beside his horse outside, I assumed he was the friend you mentioned. I invited him in, and we've got everything settled."

She led Scott into the parlor. Joe Pike sat in one of the leather chairs and Earl McKay was slouched in the other, brushing his unruly hair away from his freckled forehead and looking bored and ill at ease. They stood when Betty Kelton came into the room and waited until she and Scott were seated on the sofa before they sat down again.

Scott cut a quick glance at Joe Pike. The Pinkerton man's chin moved in an almost imperceptible nod, a signal that his bargaining had gone well.

"I assume you're renting us the place," Scott said.

"Yes." Betty Kelton was dressed in a black dress with a high-necked lace collar and a row of pearl buttons down the front. Her skin looked pale against the dark fabric, and there was a quaver in her voice. "I think you've met Earl. Since we're not signing any documents, I asked him to sit in so there would be a witness to our agreement. It's not that I don't trust you. It's something Doyle Joyner told me I should always do in business matters—even with friends. Mr. Pike has paid me, so there's not much left for me to do."

Scott nodded. "We're obliged to you, ma'am. We'll leave everything as good as we found it. You're mighty kind to let us take over your business for a while."

"I wouldn't call it kindness. I have my reasons. I don't want to put my girls out on such short notice, and we both want to see the same man dead. If renting this place helps, I'll be glad."

She drew a long breath. "I hope you won't think I'm impolite, but I need to pick up a few more of my things and get back to the ranch cabin before dark. Right now I only have three girls working for me. You've met Polly Wexler, and I want to introduce you to the others. Earl can show you around after I'm gone."

Within fifteen minutes, the formalities involved in the transfer of the bordello's operation were completed. Betty Kelton brought the girls from their rooms. Scott and Joe Pike met them at the foot of the stairs in the barroom. Unsure of the degree of secrecy desired by the two men, Betty Kelton stood discreetly aside while greetings were exchanged.

The women stepped forward, shaking hands with both Scott and Joe Pike as they introduced themselves. Scott studied them carefully, noting characteristics that would help him remember their names: Rose Spring, with straw-blonde hair, sultry brown eyes, and a soft purring voice; Iris Blue, short and slender, with flaming red hair and breasts that looked too large for her petite frame; and Polly Wexler, whose milk-white skin and round blue eyes gave her fine features the appearance of a porcelain figurine.

Smiling at Rose and Iris, Scott said, "Looks like Miss Betty is about to start a flower garden here."

The girls giggled and some of the uneasiness faded from their eyes. They were worried about their jobs, uncertain of their security under the supervision of the two range-dressed men who looked unsuited for the brothel business, but they had to accept the circumstances and make the most of them. Rose laughed and said, "You seem to doubt that we're giving you our real names."

"No, ma'am," Scott replied. "Sure as my name is George Pratt, I'm going to believe everything you tell me." Scott rubbed his hand across his chin, moving it to hide his mouth as he smiled to himself at the irony of the assurance he had given under a fictitious name.

After shaking hands with Scott and Pike and wishing them luck, Betty Kelton left them and went toward her bedroom at the rear of the house. She took Earl McKay with her to help load the buggy she had brought from the ranch cabin Doyle Joyner had built as the first stage of a family home.

"We need to know where we stand," Rose Spring said. She was in her thirties, the oldest of the women, and obviously trusted by the others to further their aims or defend their faults.

A flurry of questions followed, only one or two from Polly Wexler but several from Rose and Iris. Pike supplied the answers. His early arrival at the bordello had given him time for a lengthy discussion with Betty Kelton and Earl McKay, and had allowed him to anticipate the anxiety that the girls were now expressing. No, he and Scott would not remain indefinitely; they were merely filling in for Betty Kelton until she made a final decision about the future of the bordello. Yes, the fees would remain the same, and the girls would continue to receive sixty percent of the money and the house would keep forty. Earl McKay had agreed to take time off from his job and become a full-time bartender, cashier, and handyman. When Scott and Pike were not on the premises, the girls were to take their orders from McKay.

Finally, the questions ended and the girls started back to their rooms. Before she left, Rose asked, "Are we going to be working tonight?"

Pike looked at Scott, saw that he was waiting for him to reply, and said, "That's up to Earl McKay. If it's all right with him, it's all right with us. We won't be back today, but we'll be here tomorrow and from now on."

When they were outside, Pike said, "I figured we'd leave them alone tonight while they get used to the idea of the new setup. I didn't mean to hog the show out here, but I didn't know where you were and when you'd show up. I was going to hang around outside and wait, but Miss Betty saw me and called me in."

"I've got no objections. We're spending Pinkerton money, and you should handle the details. You worked things out in a hurry."

Pike nodded. "Miss Betty's a nice woman, easy to deal with. She figures Mitch Sadler killed that feller she was going to marry, and that made it easier. She wants us to get him. There's a pretty good stock of liquor in the bar, enough food for a month, and all the furnishings except what's in her bedroom go with the house. We settled the whole thing for ninety dollars."

On their way to the livery stable, Scott told Pike about his day in Hub, conceding that he had accomplished nothing. "I left this morning without telling you because I figured you'd try to talk me out of wasting my time."

"Not necessarily. We ain't bound to stand in each other's shadow. You do what you think best, and I'll do the same. Thing is, we know our best chance of getting the Sadlers to make a move will likely happen at Big Betty's Place if we can work out a deal with Polly Wexler. I thought you'd want to talk with her."

"I figured like you," Scott said. "She needs some time to wonder what we're up to. She knows our questions about how she gets along with Mitch Sadler meant something, and she's waiting to find out what. I'll know tomorrow how bad she wants to go home and how much nerve she's got."

"Have you hit on a way yet to get the Sadlers to go after the money?"

"I think so," Scott replied. "We'll talk about it at supper."

Pike dropped the subject, content to wait until a quieter time. He said nothing about how he had spent the day, and Scott did not inquire.

CHAPTER NINETEEN

THE LOBBY LAMPS in the Elkhorn Hotel were alight and a dozen big-hatted men, clustered in groups or lounging in chairs, filled the room with cigarette smoke and the rumble of separate discussions. Millie Adcock was at the desk, watching the activity with a look of satisfaction.

Millie was in an exuberant mood when Scott and Pike went to talk with her. She pointed at the lobby and chuckled. "The Stockman's Association meets here a couple of days each year, and I try to get rich off of them before they leave."

Scott laughed at her frankness, then apologized for leaving at an early hour without paying for his night's lodging. Millie patted Scott on the arm, then told him she was changing her policy just for him and that he could pay when he ended his stay.

As they walked away, Joe Pike offered a cheaper alternative. Betty Kelton would not be using her bedroom at the bordello, and there was a spare bedroom next to it. "We could both stay out there if we wanted to," Pike said. "She also told me she'd been keeping a couple of horses on the pasture that goes with the house. She's taking the pinto with her, but she's leaving a dun for a while. She said we're welcome to use it if we need a spare horse. We could save a few dollars if you'd like to stay at Big Betty's Place."

Scott shook his head. "I don't think so—I'd be mighty uncomfortable out there with all those women."

"Likewise," drawled Pike. "I've got enough bad habits without taking up more."

With Millie too busy with the crush of business to join them, Scott and Pike finished their evening meal quickly. They talked little while they ate, but before they went to their separate rooms, they had agreed on a scheme to deceive Mitch Sadler if Polly Wexler was willing to help them put it into effect.

Since the day his father was killed, Scott had dreaded the nights. They were a time of loneliness and doubt, a time when his thoughts turned to the Crowfoot Ranch and memories of his mother and father.

After leaving Pike, he lay wide-eyed in his bed and worried about what course he would follow if the bank sold his ranch. Otis Potter felt that John Tripp would bid only slightly more than the bank indebtedness, and the Crowfoot had other smaller bills to pay. After an auction, there would not be enough money for Scott to start another spread, and work on the riverboats no longer held any appeal for him. He would survive, but with a lifelong sadness that Frank Rawley's years of hard labor and undaunted ambition would count for nothing.

He thought about Hobe Calder, wondering if the Crowfoot foreman had forced a confrontation with John Tripp or any of the Bar 40 riders. Hobe was protective of the Crowfoot's rights, angry that John Tripp's cattle still grazed on land in which Frank Rawley had made a large investment, and had promised to meet any threat from the Bar 40 with gunfire. Scott hoped Hobe was safe and had not made matters worse than they were.

Scott bunched the pillows under his head, folded his arms across his chest, and clamped his jaws fiercely together. He was irritated that he had allowed himself to drift into a mood of self-pity and pessimism. As long as there was an hour left before time for the bank to foreclose on the Crowfoot, Scott had a chance to save it. Much of that chance rested on his hunch about Cal Baylor and the plans for the bordello, which he and Pike had discussed at supper.

Pike was confident that the showdown with the Sadlers would come at Big Betty's Place—and soon. Scott went to sleep with that hope in mind, but it still worried him that he was betting his future on the weakness of a cold-blooded killer and the strength of a disillusioned, homesick girl from Mississippi . . .

Polly Wexler was not surprised to learn that Mitch and Ned Sadler were outlaws. She listened with only mild interest while Joe Pike recounted the details of the Wells Fargo clerk's death in Sagemore, the bank robbery and killing in Blackwood, and the ambush slaying of Deputy Doyle Joyner in Hub.

"Everywhere I've been in the West," Polly said, "I've run into a lot of plain white trash. Sometimes I think men like that are our best customers. Mercy, you only see most of them one time, and I don't care what they do to earn their money as long as they'll give some of it to me. I knew Mitch was no good the first time I saw him, but that didn't bother me until he hurt me. I'm certainly not going to have anything more to do with him while I'm waiting to get away from here."

Joe Pike and Scott Rawley exchanged glances, communicating the common thought that Polly Wexler would not become their ally in the interest of justice. Despite her tender years, Polly had seen the violence, cruelty, and tragedies of the frontier and she skirted the edge of them, concerned only with self-preservation.

They sat with her on the slatted settee on the gallery porch at Big Betty's Place. Scott and Pike had arrived at the bordello shortly after dusk and found more business than they expected. There were five horses at the hitching rail, and when they entered the barroom, they were greeted by the noise of boisterous talk, clinking glasses, and the presence of cowboys who were taking turns squeezing and kissing Rose Spring and Iris Blue.

Earl McKay was behind the bar. He wore a white shirt, string tie, and red sleeve garters to keep his cuffs away from the water while he rinsed glasses in a pan of water beneath the bar. Now that he was a bartender, McKay had changed his style of dressing.

He told them Polly was busy with a partner upstairs. Scott and Pike took a seat at a corner table and waited until she returned, arm in arm with a grinning young man who kissed her lightly, then headed for the bar. Polly started toward a table where two men were eyeing her hungrily, but Scott intercepted her. He took her by the arm, told her he and Pike needed to talk with her, and invited her to go with them to the porch for privacy.

While they talked, Polly kept looking over her shoulder toward the sounds coming from the barroom, impatient because she was missing the opportunity to earn money. After again expressing her animosity for Mitch Sadler, she said, "I know y'all want something from me, and I wish you'd tell me what it is so I can go back to work."

"We want you to make Mitch Sadler fall in love with you," Pike stated bluntly. "Make him so wild for you he'll agree to take you home. Do you think you can do that?"

Polly Wexler wriggled her shoulders and smiled. "You should know the longer a woman holds a man at bay, the more determined he is to have her. I've got Mitch where he'll do anything I ask, but I wouldn't go to a dogfight with him. I can't imagine why you're talking about such strange doings, and I don't see why I should get involved."

"To help us put the Sadler brothers where they belong," Pike replied. "Either at the end of a hang-noose or in a grave. They're killers and thieves, and they're going to hurt a lot more people if something ain't done about them. We took over Big Betty's Place for that very reason. First, we need to find out where they're hiding what they stole in Blackwood. When that's done, we aim to take them in to the law, or shoot it out with them if that's what they choose. You're our best bet for getting them things done."

A narrowing of round blue eyes, a tightening of muscles in a delicate chin, and a pursing of full red lips told Scott and Pike that Polly Wexler suspected she was being deceived. She pointed out that they had passed up an opportunity for a showdown with the Sadlers when they met them at the hitching rail the day before. It was her opinion that Scott and Pike were outlaws themselves, thieves less successful than the Sadlers. They knew Mitch and Ned had accumulated money, she reasoned aloud, and were waiting for an opportunity to take it from them.

"You sure do see through a man real quick," Joe Pike said. "We're after money all right, but it don't belong to Mitch and Ned. It belongs to George Pratt here, and I'm trying to help him get it back. Otherwise, I'd just throw down on the Sadlers and try to stop them from robbing and killing. That's what Wells Fargo is hiring my people to do."

"Aha!" Polly Wexler exclaimed, and there was a note of triumph in her voice. "You two didn't have me fooled one bit. I was sure you were lawmen the minute I saw you."

Fishing tobacco and papers from his pocket, Pike eyed the girl thoughtfully while he rolled a cigarette. He sealed it with a sweep of his tongue and held it between his fingers a moment. "We ain't outlaws, and we ain't carrying badges, either. You're a bright lass, but you had us wrong on both counts. I work for the Pinkerton National Detective Agency. George Pratt's a rancher."

"It makes no difference to me," Polly retorted. "I'm not going to work for Pinkerton or the law. It would surely please me to see a mean-tempered man like Mitch taken off his high horse, but I'm not the one to see to that. I'm just a little eighteen-year-old girl with enough gall to be good at what I do, but I'm certainly not going to do anything to make Mitch mad enough to beat me up again—or kill me."

"Not even for money?" Scott asked. He had remained silent, trusting Pike's calm, deliberate approach to win the girl's trust and cooperation. But the conversation was not proceeding as he had hoped, and Scott sensed that the girl was about to walk away and leave them to deal with the Sadlers in their own way.

Scott's question revived Polly's interest. She gave him her full attention, her lips parted in anticipation. "You'll pay me to help you? How much?"

"How does five hundred dollars sound?"

"Gracious, it sounds like a fortune! I could go home like a queen and put my past behind me forever."

She kept her eyes on Scott's face until she was convinced of his sincerity. "Mitch must have done something terrible to you."

"To me and a lot of other people."

Joe Pike had not told the girl enough. She saw an opportunity to get the money she needed, and her expression told Scott the temptation of it was going to overcome her fear of harm. Before she made her decision, he wanted her to know the Sadlers were more vicious and ruthless than she had imagined. Omitting none of the details, he described the death of his father during the Blackwood Bank robbery, pointing out that Mitch had put an extra bullet in Frank Rawley's chest while he was dying on his feet. He told her about the killing of the Wells Fargo clerk in Sagemore and concluded with the slaying of the young Kansas girl named Kitty.

A whimpering cry of sympathy and shock escaped Polly's lips. She put her fingers against her eyes as if she were shutting out a horrible vision while Scott repeated the story Joe Pike had told him about the violence of Mitch's jealous rage when he slashed Kitty to death and killed the brother who was visiting her.

"For mercy's sake, you're scaring the living daylights out of me," Polly spoke in a choked whisper. "I'd dearly love to have five hundred dollars, but I don't want to go home in a casket. I'm guessing that you want me to trick Mitch into going after the money so you can follow him to it. He would want to take plenty of money with him if I can convince him he could be my lover and a prosperous planter in Mississippi. Isn't that your scheme?"

"You've got it," Joe Pike said hopefully. "You've seen right through the whole thing."

"I don't see through half of it," Polly corrected. "It wasn't hard to figure out what you wanted me to do, but I don't know what you two gentlemen are going to do. I'm certainly not going out in this wild country alone with Mitch Sadler. He could—"

"You won't have to go anywhere with him," Scott cut in. "We've got that worked out. We'll make sure you're safe."

Scott outlined the plan he and Joe Pike had agreed

upon. They were simple in concept but depended on Polly's skill as a siren and the lack of honor among thieves.

The girl had already guessed her assignment: If the Sadlers came back to the bordello, she was to persuade Mitch to go away with her—either to Mississippi or to a place of his choosing. They were to slip away from Big Betty's Place when Ned Sadler was too preoccupied to see them leave. When they were gone, Scott would plant the seeds of distrust by confiding to Ned that Mitch and Polly had eloped. Ned would guess immediately that his brother would not go away and leave the money behind. It would be a natural reaction for him to head for the hidden money himself, to make sure Mitch did not get away with it all.

Polly looked confused and worried. She wanted to know which of the Sadlers they were going to follow and how she was going to get away from Mitch before he discovered her deception.

Scott tried to dispel her worries. The plan would have to be put into effect at night so Scott and Joe Pike could operate under the cover of darkness, but he assured Polly she would be alone with the outlaw for only a few minutes. After leaving the bordello with Mitch Sadler, she was to tell him that her horse was picketed near the barn and ask him to help her saddle it. Mitch would be able to see a horse in the pasture—Betty Kelton's dun.

The barn was as far as Mitch would get. Joe Pike would be hiding there, ready to hold the outlaw at gunpoint and disarm him, or knock him senseless with a blow to the head. In either case, Pike would bind and gag

Mitch Sadler and wait for Scott. As soon as Ned left to pursue his brother, never knowing that Mitch had not gone anywhere, Scott would join Pike at the barn. Polly could run safely back to the house while Scott and the Pinkerton man followed Ned Sadler until he led them to the money.

"Thank goodness you'll go after Ned," Polly said. "I was afraid you wanted me to stay with Mitch until you caught him."

Pike dusted ashes from his cigarette. He took a deep draw from it, rubbed the fire out on his boot, and threw it away. "That wouldn't work. Mitch won't know we're going to egg Ned on, but he knows his brother will get suspicious as soon as he misses him. Mitch would be looking over his shoulder all the way. He'd spot us and give us the dodge for sure. Ned don't know we have any interest in him, and he'll be going hell-for-leather after Mitch and paying no mind to what's going on behind him."

It was the best plan they had been able to contrive, but it was not without flaws. Polly Wexler turned it over in her mind. Her smooth forehead, wrinkled in indecision while she weighed her need for money against the risks. Scott grew impatient with her silence and asked bluntly, "Are you going to do it or not?"

"I'm afraid I'll get killed. I—I keep thinking about that poor girl Kitty and what Mitch did to her." She shuddered and her voice assumed a hard edge. "They should have punished him more for such a dreadful crime. Are you sure this will work?"

"Depends mostly on you and whether the Sadlers ever

come back here again," Scott said. "If Mitch and Ned decide to leave this part of the country, or if you can't talk Mitch into running away with you, we'll all be losers."

The gloom of early evening did not hide the sudden brightness of Polly's eyes. Scott's comment was a challenge to her skills, and it strengthened her resolve. The tip of her tongue moved tantalizingly over her full lower lip. "I can put the kind of dreams in a man's mind that will make him crawl through a barrel of rattlesnakes to get to me. I can handle Mitch. If this is what it takes for me to see Mama and Daddy again, I'll do it. I—I've been through the longest three years of my life. Mitch will be back. I'll start warming his blood the minute I see him. I'm counting on you to keep your eyes on me when he shows up."

"We'll be here," Scott replied.

Polly rose quickly and went inside, walking with her head held high and her rounded hips undulating under her tight yellow skirt. It was the walk of a determined woman.

Feeling a small sense of relief, Scott was ready to leave. The activities inside the bordello were in full swing, but the Sadler brothers were not among the participants. Earl McKay was there to keep order and Scott saw no reason to stay longer.

He could not tell from Joe Pike's expression whether or not the Pinkerton man was satisfied with the outcome of their discussion with Polly Wexler. Earlier, Scott had sensed that Pike was not pleased that he had told Polly about the way Kitty Sadler died, although Pike had not tried to interrupt him.

"We might as well go back to the Elkhorn," Scott said. "Nothing's going to happen here tonight."

"You must be pretty worn out. I figured you spent your time in Hub before you came by the hotel for me. You're going to kill your horse if you keep that up every day."

"I'm going to keep it up," Scott asserted.

Pike stared into the night. "You going to eat with Millie?"

"Up to her," Scott replied. "I figured I'd eat with you."

"I'm going to stay a while. They've got food here, and I'll stir me up a meal directly."

Scott rode back to the hotel alone. His legs were stiff and his back ached. At dawn that morning he had ridden to Hub, spending the day much as he had before—walking the streets, watching incoming riders, and listening for the mention of any familiar name. Again, he spent the last hour at a table in the Running Iron Saloon, where he had a clear view of Cal Baylor and the town jail, but the time passed without incident.

Millie Adcock was too busy to have supper with Scott, but she was eager to hear about the results of his talk with Polly Wexler. She was watching the door when he entered the Elkhorn, and she left the desk to meet him. There was a worried look on her face when she saw that he was alone, and she was visibly relieved when Scott told her why Joe Pike was not with him.

"Since I've learned what you're trying to do, I worry about both of you all the time you're gone," Millie said. "I keep thinking this might be the day you finally had to fight those men, and I wonder if I'll ever see you alive again."

Scott's worry and frustration showed in his voice. "I wonder, too. I wonder if I'll be dead or if I'll have anything to live for if I'm alive."

The stockmen were still roaming around the lobby, and Millie led him to a quiet corner near the stairway, where they could talk without being overheard. She touched his arm and her coppery eyes were clouded with concern. "I hope things work out at Big Betty's Place, but what will you do if Polly Wexler can't get Mitch to fall for her?"

"There's another angle that might turn up something," Scott replied softly. "I've got a real knot in my belly about Cal Baylor. I don't know how it fits, but he's tied in with the Sadlers some way."

Like a ritual performed to appease unknown gods, Scott continued his daily trips to Hub. He followed the same routine each time with the same results, returning to the bordello in the evenings to join Joe Pike and wait for the Sadlers to return. It was about the only time he saw the Pinkerton man anymore. As the days passed, Scott avoided both Pike and Millie Adcock. He breakfasted early and delayed going to the dining room for supper until he was sure Pike and Millie had eaten. He grew increasingly quiet and irritable. He was poor company for anyone, and he kept to himself as much as possible.

When he stopped at the Running Iron Saloon each day, Corey Millsap tried to be friendly and cheerful, talking about trivial happenings and barroom gossip. Scott's curt replies soon conveyed the hint that he wanted to be left alone. A Sunday came and went, and then another, and Scott saw no end to his quest. Millie invited him to go to church services with her on both Sundays but he declined, and later he saw her and Pike going down the street together.

On some days Scott borrowed Betty Kelton's dun for his trip to spy on Cal Baylor, leaving his bay to rest and graze in the pasture behind the bordello, but the change of horses did not change his luck. With only five days left before the deadline for payment of his note, Scott's patience and persistence were at an end. Riding his own bay, he made his last trip to Hub.

It was the day he killed his first man.

CHAPTER TWENTY

TWO MEN STOOD AT THE BAR chatting with Corey Millsap while the bartender washed glasses, and at a table in the far corner of the room four other men were grumbling and cursing their way through a poker game. Otherwise, the atmosphere of the Running Iron Saloon was subdued, much like the rest of the world, which seemed to fall into a hush as daylight faded to dusk.

On other days, Scott had left the town in mid-afternoon so he could arrive at Big Betty's Place before the bordello's business reached its peak. For the past week, however, few men had patronized Big Betty's. So far Mitch and Ned Sadler had not returned, but Scott wanted to be sure he was there if—and when—they came back. It was hard for him to abandon the compelling hunch that had kept him walking the streets of Hub for days. He had made up his mind that this was his last trip and he meant to make the most of it. Twice he untied his horse from the hitching rail and prepared to leave, but each time he tethered it again. A premonition that something was going to happen on this day held him back, and he let the afternoon pass without returning to Bluestem.

The purple hues of early evening tinted the buildings along Main Street as Scott seated himself at the table near the front window of the saloon. He did not go to the bar and order his usual beer, but Corey Millsap brought a full mug to the table. The bartender waved Scott's offer of payment aside and studied the grim lines of the rancher's face.

The other customers at the Running Iron had seen him there so often they paid no attention to Scott's arrival. Nevertheless, Corey Millsap wanted to be sure he was not overheard. Resting his hands on the edge of the table, he leaned close to Scott and his voice was almost a whisper. "I know you're waiting for something to happen at the jail. I don't know what you're looking for, but I know you don't sit here every day and stare at it because you think it's pretty. You may think I'm meddling in your business, but I'm going to mention something anyway. When I was coming back from supper I saw a horseman turn into the alley behind the jail, and he didn't come back out. He must have tied up at the stall in the back."

"Is that strange?"

"To me it is. Most folks who have business with the law tie up in front, unless it's some friend or the deputy himself. I noticed this feller because he acted like he wanted to get off the street in a hurry, just whirled his horse between the buildings and disappeared. That was more than half an hour ago, and he hasn't showed since. There's a light in Cal Baylor's office, but I haven't seen him moving around over there since I've been back."

Scott's pulse quickened, but he kept his voice calm, almost indifferent. "Do you know what the rider looked like?"

"No. I just got a glimpse of his back."

"Thanks, Corey," Scott said. "Maybe I'll visit with the deputy before I leave."

Millsap nodded and went back to the bar. The ruddy-faced bartender wanted to be helpful, and Scott felt guilty because his response had been somewhat cool. Millsap was one of those who believed the Sadlers had friends in Hub, however, and Scott did not want it to become general knowledge that he was spending time in the town because he suspected the outlaws might try to contact Cal Baylor.

Despite the pretense of only a mild interest in the bartender's comments, Scott did not intend to wait long before going to the jail. He sipped at his beer and toyed with a deck of cards that someone had left lying on the table, eyeing the street from lowered eyelids. His nerves tightened with a sense of foreboding. His hunch about Cal Baylor was about to pay off.

The hours he had spent peering through the saloon window had allowed him to become familiar with Cal Baylor's habits. He studied the office, wondering why the deputy did not show up to work at his desk, to drink his customary cup of coffee, or to make his rounds along the street. The lamplight was bright enough to show Scott most of the office interior. There was something sinister in its silence and lack of activity. Apparently, Baylor was sticking to his living quarters on this night, but why?

Glancing toward the bar, Scott saw Corey Millsap engaged in a conversation with a customer. He chose the time to slip through the batwing doors and cross the street to the jail.

The building was not as quiet as it had appeared from a distance. The moment he stepped inside, Scott heard voices coming from the bedroom, which was in the back of the building.

"You owe me, Cal! There ain't going to be any skin left on your back if you don't write me out a bank draft. You promised to give me the money if I'd stop Frank Rawley from meeting his note. I got it done, and you can't welsh on me."

Scott had entered on his tiptoes, an inner sense warning him to be careful. He stood with his shoulder close to the hallway doorway, his breath sounding loud in his face. He recognized the voice from the bedroom. It belonged to Pat Logan, and there was a screeching, irrational tone in the ex-deputy's threats.

"Here goes! Maybe this'll change your mind!"

Whatever Logan did brought a yelp of pain from Cal Baylor. "Ow-w-w! You're out of your mind, Pat! I don't owe you any money, and I'm not getting mixed up in this. It was your crazy notion to bring in those killers."

"I'm not crazy," Logan raged. "I'm smart enough to

know a good deal when I see one, and I can buy the Texas Star Saloon with the down payment you promised me."

"Ouch! Cut it out, you damn fool!" Cal Baylor's voice was a wail of suffering.

"You wanted to help John Tripp get that stretch of open range and now he's going to get it. I done my part and—"

Sudden, shocking fury seized Scott's mind and boomed in his voice. His thoughts were out of control, and he dashed toward Cal Baylor's bedroom without considering caution or strategy. He screamed, "You had my pa killed, Logan, and I'm coming after you!"

He lunged into the hallway and rammed his shoulder against the closed door at the end of the passageway. His weight tore the lock loose and splinters flew around him. A door at the back of the room slammed shut as he stopped and stared at Cal Baylor. The deputy was sitting in a chair, his hands lashed behind him and his feet tied to the chair legs. His hat was off, his hair tousled, and his lean face was flushed with pain and fear. A coffeepot lay on the floor at his feet. The lid had popped open when Pat Logan threw it down, and steaming liquid was puddling around it.

"He's getting away!" Baylor yelled.

"I'll get to you later," Scott said grimly. He flung the door open and stepped into the darkness behind the jail. A bridle ring jingled nearby, and he saw Pat Logan fumbling with the leather harness. The big chestnut had struggled at the tie rail and the reins were knotted. Pat Logan could not get them free and Scott was only a dozen steps away from him.

Stray light from the street washed across the ex-deputy's short, compact form. Scott's vision adjusted quickly and he had a clear view of Logan's wild-eyed face.

Rage had dulled Scott's thinking and he had not drawn his gun when he ran down the hallway. His first thought was that he would leap upon Pat Logan, restrain him, and hold him captive. It was clear now that he would never be able to touch him.

Logan whirled and braced his back against the boards of the horse stall. "I knew it was you! You've hounded me from the first day we met and I hate your guts. You've ruined my name with everybody, and I'm going to blow your head off. I'm good with a gun, and there ain't no way you can beat me twice in a row!"

He was spitting out words one upon the other with such rapidity that he began to drool, and saliva ran from the corners of his mouth. Within a few days, Pat Logan's longing for riches had turned him mean and treacherous, or perhaps it had always been his nature. Scott had no time to consider the man's slide from respect to lawlessness. While he was still muttering threats, Pat Logan's hand stabbed at his holster.

He was better this time. Logan's gun came up so swiftly that Scott was startled to see it. There was no time for deliberation, no time to place a bullet in a spot that would disable the man and leave him alive.

Scott's Colt bucked in his fist. Exploding powder sent a spurt of flame toward Pat Logan. Two shots seemed to blend together and a slug buzzed close to Scott's head.

He saw Pat Logan's mouth fly open, and Scott stared incredulously at the red smudge on the man's forehead where a bullet had drilled into his brain. Logan wilted like a balloon losing air. He fell with his legs bent at the knees and they crumpled beneath him. Even as he fired his weapon, Logan was dying. Otherwise, Scott Rawley would be the one lying dead in the alley.

Scott could not take his eyes off Logan's body. He waited for the man to move, to straighten his legs and start cursing his bad luck. Finally, he accepted the fact that Pat Logan would never move again. Scott's tongue swelled in his throat and he gagged, sickened by the realization of what he had done. He held the Colt in his hand briefly, looking at it as though he had just discovered its deadly power. Finally, he took a deep breath, holstered his gun, and walked back toward the jail.

His first steps were unsteady, but a flood of anger renewed the strength in his legs as he recalled the exchange he had heard before Pat Logan fled the jail. He still had to settle with Cal Baylor.

By the time Scott returned to the bedroom, the deputy had bounced the chair around to face the rear door, in an effort to free himself. Baylor looked up expectantly. "I heard gunshots. Did Pat get away?"

Scott shook his head. "I killed him. He didn't give me a chance to do anything else."

Much of Scott's anger was gone. He looked at the floor, shaken by the episode at the horse stall, and he wondered how long it would be before the memory of it went away. He had spied on the jail in the hopes that he would be able to surprise Cal Baylor at a time when he was conferring with the outlaws about a payoff, driven by a hunch that such a meeting would reveal a clue to the place the Sadlers were hiding his money.

A shoot-out that ended in a man's death was the last thing Scott had expected, but the emotional impact of it did not diminish his hate for the men who had brought him so much grief. He looked at Baylor's pain-pinched face without sympathy. "You and Pat Logan set up that robbery to arrange the murder of my father. I won't kill you, but I'm going to hurt you some more before I turn you over to Wade Bandy. Maybe he can get you hanged."

"No, no, you're wrong!" Cal Baylor cried. "You saw what Pat was doing to me. He sneaked in through the back door and caught me off guard. He started off talking like we'd made a business deal and expected me to pay him without arguing. When I told him he misunderstood me, he went to pieces. Before I knew what he was doing, he put a gun on me and tied me up. He was pouring hot coffee on me, swearing he'd pour it in my eyes if I didn't give him money. My back hurts like hell!"

"I heard Logan say you promised him money if he'd keep us from paying the bank. Are you going to lie about that?"

Baylor jerked erect and the ropes rubbed his back. The pain brought tears to his eyes. "I'll tell you all I know, but I'd like to be untied first. While Pat was working at the Bar 40, he asked me to go into partnership with him to buy a saloon. I talked to Mr. Tripp about it and he vetoed the idea. Then Pat started hounding me for a loan.

I was laughing when I told him I'd be glad to give him a thousand dollars if he could find a way to keep Frank Rawley from buying up the open range. It was idle talk, just something you say like you're wishing for it."

Cal Baylor's shoulders sagged and he looked at Scott with pleading eyes. "Hell, man, I didn't want your pa to get killed. Anybody else wouldn't have paid any mind to what I said. Pat was crazy enough to think I was looking for a hired killer. It's been eating my guts out. That's why I wanted to come over here and see if I could help, try to make up for what happened. I found out what Pat had done. Right after Frank Rawley was shot, Pat tracked me down in town. He was proud of himself. He said he'd done a job for the Bar 40 and wanted to get paid. He was bragging about talking Mitch Sadler into killing your dad. He's been trying to find the Sadlers to see if they'd share the money with him. How was I to know Pat was going to turn bad?"

The deputy was too miserable and scared to lie. Scott said, "I guess it could happen that way. I'll believe you for now. I once told some friends I'd give a hundred dollars to get rid of a lady's husband. I meant for a few hours, not forever. I'm glad nobody ran out and killed him."

"I want to help you set things right. I was afraid Pat might try to make Mr. Tripp believe I was mixed up in that robbery. He would kick me off the Bar 40 if he thought I was."

Scott looked down the deputy's collar as he freed him from the chair. Baylor's shirt was stained with coffee, and there were patches of blisters on his back.

"Logan's body is still outside," Scott murmured. "You'll have to write up a report, but I don't want my name used where the Sadlers might hear it. Can you help with that?"

Baylor grimaced and tried to hold the shirt away from his skin as he rose. "I'll take care of it. I know you shot him in self-defense, and that's what I'll tell Sheriff Bandy."

The sound of gunfire was not unusual in a town such as Hub. More often than not it was someone scaring stray dogs away from their house or a cowboy celebrating the joys of a drinking spree. Scott was glad the shots behind the jail had not aroused enough curiosity to bring anyone to investigate.

He stayed at the jail long enough to listen to Cal Baylor explain how he was going to handle Pat Logan's burial. The deputy would get a wagon immediately and deliver the body to Logan's uncle in Sagemore. At this hour, his departure would not be noticed. His story of the man's death would be sketchy but sufficient to satisfy the relatives.

Scott wanted to get away from Hub as fast as he could. He shook hands with Cal Baylor and left, walking in the shadows as he crossed the street to reach his horse. He had made a friend of Cal, but their relationship would have no influence on John Tripp. The Bar 40 owner wanted land and he was going to get it any way he could.

He rode back to Bluestem with a troubled mind. His vigil at the Running Iron had verified his theory that someone in Blackwood had conspired with the Sadler

248

brothers to have his father killed, but the man who pulled the trigger was still alive. Scott's hunch that Cal Baylor and the Bar 40 Ranch were involved had been wrong. It had proved that Pat Logan helped the Sadlers plan the bank robbery, but Scott had learned nothing that would help him save the Crowfoot.

Lights blazed from every window of Big Betty's Place and the night was filled with raucous voices. Scott eased his bay in between the horses that were at the hitching rail, drew rein, and sat listening to the noise.

At one corner of the porch, where the shadows were deeper, he saw the glow of a cigarette. Joe Pike stepped into a patch of light and strode toward him.

"What's going on?" Scott asked. "What are you doing out here?"

"Waiting for you," Pike said, throwing away his cigarette. "I've been as nervous as a cat, wondering if you'd show up tonight. The Sadlers are back. They've been here thirty . . . forty minutes, and Polly Wexler is acting real sweet with Mitch. She's got him panting to jump her bones sure enough, but she's holding him off with little kisses and hugs now and then. If you ain't here at the right time, this whole scheme will fall apart. What kept you?"

"I killed a man tonight—Pat Logan."

A frown furrowed Pike's forehead. "First time for you?" Scott nodded and stepped to the ground. He told Pike about the gunfight and of his conversation with Cal Baylor.

"Baylor's probably been through some hell of his own, seeing how things turned out. I know how you're feeling. It'll wear off. You won't forget it, but you'll accept what had to be. You got no reason to mourn over Pat Logan."

Scott sucked cool air into his lungs and tried to force his pulse to return to normal. "My pa would be alive and I wouldn't be worrying about debts if Pat Logan had stayed away from the Sadlers. You can tell yourself a man like that needs killing, but you don't feel good after you do it."

Pike gave Scott a moment to dwell on his thoughts, then said, "Tie the reins and come on inside. We'll look after your horse later. I want Mitch and Ned to get used to seeing us around. Polly has told them we're running the place for Big Betty."

Scott walked slowly toward the porch. "I'm not sure I can look at those bastards without killing them."

CHAPTER TWENTY-ONE

LAUGHTER, happy voices, and the attention of pretty women could make a man forget the grueling labor and harsh environment of the frontier. Scott found such a world inside the bordello, and for a while he tried to be a part of it. Behaving like interested proprietors, he and Pike moved around the barroom, chatting and shaking hands with the customers. Rose Spring and Iris Blue circulated among the tables, delivering drinks and waiting for invitations to take the men to their bedrooms. Polly Wexler was devoting all her attention to the two men who sat with her at a table in the alcove between the bar and the stairway.

Scott saw Polly and her companions as soon as he came in, but he avoided going near the table. She was with Mitch and Ned Sadler, and Scott was not ready to meet the outlaws again. Rose and Iris paused in their rounds long enough to speak to him, but Polly remained where she was. Scott watched her from the edge of his vision. She had pulled her chair close enough to Mitch Sadler to let their shoulders touch. She was leaning against him, one slender arm resting on his shoulder while she looked into his eyes and spoke words that brought a smile to the outlaw's face. Ned Sadler sat across from them, his loose lips fixed in the half grin that was always a part of his expression.

In most bordellos, the sporting girls attracted attention by wearing bright colors—skirts of yellows, lavenders, reds, and greens, topped by frilly low-cut blouses. Rose and Iris were dressed in this fashion, but Polly Wexler was conspicuous by contrast. Her plain white blouse and long black skirt looked more appropriate for church. Her milk-white skin, round blue eyes, and finely chiseled features presented a picture of fragile beauty and girlish innocence.

Leaving Pike with the customers, Scott went to the bar. Earl McKay stood there with folded arms and a puzzled look on his freckled face. He nodded to Scott and said, "Wonder what Polly Wexler's up to. Last time that Mitch hombre was here she treated him like dirt, and now she's rubbing him up like a dog in heat."

"Beats me," said Scott. "Ain't a man alive who can figure out how a woman's mind works."

Joe Pike came over to stand beside Scott. He spoke

from the corner of his mouth. "Looks like Polly's doing her job, but you might have to give things a little push."

They moved toward the end of the bar, where Earl McKay could not overhear them. "What do you mean?" Scott asked.

"Show some interest in Polly yourself. Nothing makes a man do foolish things quicker than a bad case of jealousy."

Scott frowned and braced his back against the bar as he saw Polly and the Sadler brothers get up and come toward them. The hairs on the back of his neck crinkled and he felt his heart thump in his chest as the trio stopped in front of him.

"We meet again, George Pratt," Mitch Sadler said evenly. "I ought to thank you and Joe Pike for keeping this place going." He had his arm around Polly Wexler's waist, and he drew her closer to his side. "I was afraid Big Betty was going to close up and Polly would get away before I could see her again."

All Scott could do was nod. His first meeting with the outlaws had come so unexpectedly that he had only a vague memory of their appearance, but now he stamped their images in his mind.

Ned Sadler stood a pace behind Polly and his brother, his black eyes glittering in the lamplight. His white shirt and sharply creased gray wool pants made his swarthy skin appear even darker. He was not as tall as Mitch, but his big shoulders and slender waist hinted of strength and quickness. Scott studied them covertly. He was not sure which one might be the more dangerous.

Mitch was almost as tall as Scott, a lean, light-haired

man whose fair skin had been turned more pink than brown by sun and wind. His clothes looked expensive—tan pants of fine wool, a brown silk shirt, a black Stetson with only the edges of the brim slightly curled, and polished boots of intricately tooled leather. Scott recognized the design. He had seen the boots in the window of the California Emporium a week ago.

Joe Pike was right. The Sadlers had friends who would not betray them. They had been on a shopping spree in Hub.

Scott swore silently, but his face did not betray his feelings. He forced a smile and said, "Polly's quite a young lady. How're you two getting along?"

"Real good right now, but she wants to leave Texas. Maybe you can talk her out of that notion."

Remembering Joe Pike's suggestion, Scott said, "I'm not sure I want to change her mind. Polly wants to go back to Mississippi, and she thinks a Texas man would fit in all right with plantation life. I've given some thought about going with her."

A vein throbbed in Mitch Sadler's throat. His arm tightened around Polly's waist, and he yanked her roughly against him and looked down at her. "You'll take just any man who'll get you what you want. Is that it, Polly?"

The girl's eyes widened for an instant, fearing Mitch Sadler's temper. She pushed him gently to loosen his grasp and smiled sweetly. "That's a little bee buzzing in his own bonnet. I haven't invited Mr. Pratt to go with me."

Ned Sadler spoke between his teeth, his lips barely

moving. "Who're you going to believe, Mitch? Someday you'll learn not to take up with every woman you see."

"Shut up, Ned!" Mitch Sadler did a half turn to glare at his brother. Scott's breath hung in his throat and his hand slid toward his gun. As though it were accidental, Joe Pike suddenly shifted his stance and bumped Scott's shoulder, hooking his elbow so Scott could not get to his gun.

He saw the warning look in Pike's eyes and dropped his hand away, but his face remained dark and brooding. As Mitch turned, Scott had seen a watch fob with the outline of a star etched into the leather dangling from the man's vest pocket. Mitch Sadler was carrying Frank Rawley's watch—the watch the bank robber had snatched from the rancher's vest before fleeing Blackwood.

Stone-faced to hide his anger, Scott matched the defiant stare Mitch Sadler fixed on his face and said, "All's fair in love and war. I guess you've heard that."

"I decide for myself what's fair," Mitch snapped. "I told you once not to horn in when I'm with Polly. It might not be good for your health if I have to tell you again."

Shrugging, Scott said mildly, "Whatever you say," and Mitch whisked Polly away from the bar and went back to his table. Ned Sadler followed them, turning once to run his eyes up and down Scott Rawley's tall frame.

"You were going for your gun," Joe Pike murmured. "That would've messed up everything."

"I know," Scott conceded. "I wish Sheriff Bandy was

here. He's been wanting proof on the Sadlers, and he could get it tonight. Mitch is wearing Pa's watch, and I wanted to kill him when I saw it."

"Natural thing to do," Pike drawled, "but we have to wait."

For the remainder of the evening, Mitch and Ned Sadler stayed away from Scott and Joe Pike. Polly came to the bar once to get a fresh bottle, and while her back was turned she whispered to Scott, "You've got Mitch thinking. He doesn't like for anyone to take something he wants, and he's hinting that he wants to get me away somewhere to himself. It's just a matter of time before he'll agree to take me anywhere I want to go."

"I don't have much time," Scott said under his breath. "Three days from now I'll lose my ranch."

"Maybe it'll happen tomorrow," Polly said. "I'll try to make it happen tomorrow."

Scott rested his arms on the bar and held his head in his hands. He had used up his time and most of his confidence. For days he had believed he had two angles to pursue; now there was only one, and it was a gamble. Cal Baylor's relationship with the outlaws turned out to be insignificant, leaving the bordello as Scott's only hope of luring Mitch and Ned into a trap.

"How long do you want to stay around tonight?"

Until Pike spoke, Scott was so deep in thought he had momentarily forgotten where he was. He straightened and looked around the room. Ned Sadler had left Polly and his brother, and he was talking with Rose Spring.

"Ned's about to go to bed with Rose, and nothing's going to happen with Polly and Mitch tonight," Pike observed. "We can go back to the hotel and let Earl McKay close the place up. We've bet our hole card on this deal and we'll have to wait it out."

With hate glowing in his ice-blue eyes, Scott gave Mitch Sadler a final long look. "Something's going to happen before my deadline is up. If Polly can't get Mitch to leave with her, I'm not going to let him leave without her. Whether I get my money or not, he's going to pay for killing my pa."

In his room at the Elkhorn Hotel that night, Scott laid out the clean shirt he would wear in the morning. Days earlier he had put the tally sheet with a smear of his father's blood on it in the top dresser drawer. He took it out now and tucked it into the shirt pocket. Excitement coursed through him, and he went to bed with the hope that his mission would end before another sunset.

Scott slept late. He had a long day to kill before business hours began at the bordello. Despite their apparent boldness, Mitch and Ned Sadler exercised a measure of caution on their visits to Big Betty's Place. They came at dusk and left their horses behind the house, tying up at the small hitching rail Betty Kelton had built near the back door for her own use. Scott did not expect to see them before nightfall.

He ate breakfast alone. Millie Adcock was busy with her chores, and he assumed Joe Pike had dined earlier and gone his own way. For a while Scott sat in the lobby and read a week-old copy of the *Galveston News*, but the newspaper did not hold his interest for long. Afterward, he walked up and down the street, then finally got his horse from the livery and went for a ride. He explored a few trails around the edge of town, thinking he might stumble on the Sadlers' camp, but he found no sign of them.

Shortly before dusk he returned to the hotel. Joe Pike was waiting for him. When they went to the bordello, they left their horses saddled and hobbled them in the pasture behind the barn. They wanted to be ready to take up the trail quickly if Mitch Sadler left with Polly Wexler.

Mitch and Ned did not come to the bordello that night or the next. On the third evening, Scott sat alone at a table in a gloomy corner of the barroom. He sipped at a drink, his jaw clamped in a hard line while he drummed his knuckles on the table. Desperation put a chill in his bones. He watched the hands of the clock above the bar, and time that had passed so slowly in the mornings seemed to speed by. It was ten o'clock, and in slightly more than twenty-four hours Otis Potter would meet with his board at the Pioneer Bank and take the final action that would sacrifice the Crowfoot Ranch at auction.

Joe Pike mingled with the customers, glancing in Scott's direction occasionally but leaving him alone. Polly Wexler came down from her upstairs room, shooed a young cowboy toward the bar, and sat down across from Scott.

"I'm never going to get home," she said sadly. "I think Mitch got suspicious. There's something about Joe Pike that worries him, and he's not going to take any more chances."

"I'm sorry." Scott did not speak about his own regrets.

Polly Wexler could not help him.

The girl excused herself and walked through the narrow hallway that led past the kitchen and to the back door. She came back to Scott's table immediately.

"They're here!" she whispered breathlessly. "Mitch and Ned are tying up in back. For mercy's sake, keep your eyes on me. I'm going to get Mitch away from here, but don't let him kill me."

Polly hurried away. She moved around the room, smiling and acting like a normal sporting girl who was trying to generate business. Sliding his hand along one thigh that was stretched out beneath the table, Scott lifted his bone-handled Colt a few inches, then slid it back in place, making sure it was loose in the holster. He walked to the bar, catching Pike's glance on the way and signaling the Pinkerton man to join him.

Mitch and Ned Sadler entered through the front door, both clean shaven and well dressed. They came to the bar and asked Earl McKay to pour them a drink. Before he touched the whiskey, Mitch turned and looked at Scott and Pike.

"You hombres are never going to get rich here, you know." Mitch Sadler grinned as if he knew more about them than they suspected. "I thought George might have headed for Mississippi by now, but I guess Polly's not as man-crazy as I thought."

Scott forced a bland smile. "I'm going to will my share of Mississippi to you, Mitch."

"Maybe that's good. There must be more to life than Texas."

"Maybe, maybe not," Scott said.

Mitch chuckled and downed his drink. Ned Sadler touched his brother's arm and started to say something, but Polly Wexler interrupted him. She appeared at Mitch's side, slapped him playfully on the shoulder, and said, "So, you're here at last. I thought you'd found someone prettier than me."

Moving back a step, Mitch swept off his hat and held it at his side. His hair glistened like strands of platinum under the lamplight, showing a yellow tint where it lay in layers above his ears and at the back of his neck. His speech was educated, his face strong and handsome. He was courteous and soft-spoken, but the key to the outlaw's soul was reflected in his eyes—round gun-metal-gray eyes that were flat and lifeless, locking on one object at a time with a dull, emotionless stare.

"There's not a prettier woman in Texas," Mitch declared. He took her hand in his and ran his glance over the curves of her body. "A man would be a fool to give you up for anyone else."

Polly rewarded him with a smile. "You surely know how to make a girl feel good. Let's sit while you tell me more."

Mitch asked Earl McKay for a bottle of whiskey, then led Polly to the table in the alcove at the foot of the stairway. Ned fell in step behind them. Mitch gave his brother a mean stare and Ned drifted away to give his attention to Rose Spring.

"Looks like Polly's got him hooked," Pike drawled, gesturing to where Mitch sat with one elbow on the table while his other hand, partially hidden, caressed Polly Wexler's thigh. "We'd best stay ready."

Pressed by anxiety and doubt, Scott was unable to stand still. Without being obvious in his interest, he stole frequent glances at Mitch Sadler and Polly Wexler. They sat with their heads touching, cuddling and kissing and whispering to each other. They ignored everyone around them, and Scott began to think Polly was enjoying herself. Mitch had won the hearts of other women, and perhaps Polly was to be the next.

Telling Pike to alert him if the situation changed, Scott went out the back door and paced around the backyard. The horses left at the small hitching rail by Mitch and Ned stood with drooping heads, looking as doleful as Scott felt. Darkness had done little to push away the heat of the day, and beads of sweat dotted his face. He was not sure if the perspiration came from the heat or from nerves. Later, he stayed inside and mingled with the customers while Joe Pike took a break. For a while they both tried to ease their nerves by joking with the girls and their customers, but they soon grew tired of the effort, too edgy to carry on a pretense of gaiety.

The clock above the bar showed it was half-past eleven. Scott stared at it with clenched teeth, then swung his glance toward Polly Wexler and Mitch Sadler, feeling a futile anger for both of them.

Joe Pike was lounging against the bar beside him. He said, "Maybe we counted our chickens before they hatched. I don't think Mitch is going anywhere. I've got to do my job. We'll have to call a showdown right here in the next—"

He stopped talking when he saw Polly Wexler rise from the table. She brought the half-empty whiskey bottle to Earl McKay and handed him some money.

"You calling it a night, Miss Polly?" McKay asked.

"I'm calling it quits, Earl." She turned a nervous smile toward Scott and Joe Pike, moving closer to them. "Mitch and I are leaving in a few minutes. He said I could tell you goodbye and get a few personal things from my room. He thinks I'll send for my clothes later."

Mitch Sadler was watching her with hungry eyes. She glanced at him and wiggled her hand in a fluttering wave. She lowered her voice and looked from Scott to Pike, whispering, "Remember what you promised. You must protect me."

Scott's pulse quickened. "When you come back from your room, get Rose and Iris aside and tell them to keep Ned busy. I don't want him to notice when you leave."

"I'll head for the barn," Pike said. He put his hands on his hips, surveyed the barroom a moment, then strode down the hallway toward the back door.

A few minutes later, Polly and Mitch Sadler followed the same route. As they passed by Scott, Mitch winked arrogantly, as though he had competed for a prize and won.

Earl McKay rubbed a hand across his forehead, a puzzled expression on his face. "What the hell is going on?"

"Beats me," Scott said innocently, and began moving around the room. He stopped at a table to have a word with two range-dressed cowmen, but his eyes were on Rose Spring and Iris Blue. They were hovering around Ned Sadler and doing all they could to hold his attention. Iris was at the back of Ned's chair, leaning over with an arm draped on each side of his neck while her heavy breasts rested against his shoulders. Rose was playing a game with Ned's whiskey, sipping from it, then offering it to him, then sipping it again. The dark-skinned outlaw's frozen grin grew wider, and he pinched Rose's rump just as Scott stopped beside him.

Polly had coached them well. They suddenly remembered they were ignoring the other guests, excused themselves, and left Scott and Ned alone.

The interruption annoyed Ned Sadler. He turned surly eyes on Scott and growled, "You're always horning in on somebody. That's not the best way to run a whorehouse."

"I didn't mean to spoil your fun, but the girls will be around for a while if you want one of them," Scott said. "Maybe things will work out as good for you as they have for Mitch."

"What are you talking about?"

"Mitch and Polly," Scott said. "Maybe you'll learn to like Iris or Rose enough to marry one of them."

Ned's coal-black eyebrows lifted. "Married? Who the hell wants to get married!"

"Your brother for one. He dashed out of here with Polly Wexler a few minutes ago, and Polly said they're going to get married in Mississippi."

"Mitch is not going to marry her." Ned sounded as if he were about to laugh, but the serious look on Scott's face caused the sound to freeze in his throat. Sparks of light flashed in his eyes. "Are you joshing me?"

Scott shook his head. "I don't think so. They sounded mighty serious to me. Polly said her father would help Mitch buy some cotton land and that she was going to have a big house at Pearl River Landing. You know Mitch better than I do, though, so maybe they were pulling my leg about leaving Texas."

Ned kicked his chair back, shaking the table as he jumped to his feet. He tossed a bill on the table, mouthing curses in a guttural, growling monotone. "Sonofabitch! Yeah, I know Mitch too well. Do you know which way they went?"

"Afraid not," Scott replied. "I heard Mitch tell Polly he needed to pick up enough money to buy a big piece of land."

"Sonofabitch!" Ned snarled again, and rushed outside.

Scott moved equally fast, going down the hallway to the back door. While he listened for Ned to ride away from the hitching rail, Earl McKay came up beside him.

"I know who Mitch and Ned are now," the bartender said. "They're wanted men, and there's more going on here than you and Joe Pike have told me. Mitch and Polly took off somewhere, Joe Pike left, and now you're spying on Ned. If Polly's in danger, I want to help."

Scott was afraid everything would not go as planned. It was time to confide in someone in case both he and Pike ended up dead from the Sadlers' bullets. Speaking hurriedly without turning around, Scott told Earl McKay what he and Joe Pike were trying to accomplish, and the role Polly was playing in the scheme.

"Damn, that's risky," McKay said worriedly. "Polly ain't much more than a young'un, and I'd hate to see her get killed. If you're going after them killers, you'd better take me with you."

"Only as far as the barn," Scott said. "Just to make sure

263

Polly's all right. Joe Pike is supposed to waylay Mitch and tie him up before I get there. He'll go with me to trail Ned."

The jingle of a bridle and the sound of hoofbeats told of Ned Sadler's departure. Scott yanked the door open. Mitch's horse was also missing from the hitching rail. Scott ran toward the barn with Earl McKay trotting beside him.

Scott swore under his breath as he realized one phase of their plan had already gone awry. There was no one at the barn. As he and the bartender approached the open door, Scott called out Pike's name, then Polly's, but there was no response. They hurried inside, bumping into stalls and stumbling over hay as they scrambled around in the darkness. They went back outside, McKay going one way and Scott the other. A quarter moon had replaced the fingernail shape that had hung in the sky for days. The open areas were visible under its light, but shadows around the buildings were deep and foreboding.

Scott was halfway down one side of the barn when McKay yelled, "Over here! I've found Joe! I think he's dead!"

CHAPTER TWENTY-TWO

FLAT ON HIS BACK at the rear of the building, his hat crushed under his head, Joe Pike lay pale and still. Blood ran from a gash above his hairline, covering his forehead and streaming down his temples. His gun was on the ground near his right hand, and a short-handled shovel lay a foot beyond his shoulder. Scott saw a small leather case with Pinkerton cards spilling from it on the ground a few inches from Pike's limp left leg.

"Hit him with this," McKay said, tossing the shovel away. "It's got blood on it. Looks like Mitch Sadler spotted Joe and beat him to the punch. Polly didn't get away. Mitch has got her with him!"

"I'll find her," Scott said grimly.

He knelt beside Pike and felt his pulse. It was weak and Pike's breathing was so shallow Scott had to put his ear close to his lips to hear it.

"Joe's not dead, but he's bad off."

Seconds ticked away while Scott stayed on his knees. Fear was like a knife stabbing his belly. His head throbbed as he considered his obligations. He rose and grabbed McKay by the arm.

"Joe's cold as a rock. We need to get some blankets over him," he said. "Get one of those cowboys away from the girls long enough to help you take Joe to Betty Kelton's bedroom. If he doesn't regain consciousness in ten . . . fifteen minutes, ride to town and see if you can get a doctor to come out here. Close the place up and tell the girls to do what they can for Joe while you're gone. I can't let the Sadlers get away."

"I'm going with you. If Mitch catches on that Polly is part of a double cross, he'll kill her."

Scott's voice trembled with desperation. "You'll do what I say or I'll knock your teeth out! You've got to help Joe!"

A look at Scott's face convinced Earl McKay it was no

time to argue. He turned on his heel and raced toward the house.

Pike's horse was gone, but Scott's bay was grazing contentedly nearby. He swung into the saddle and circled the bay around the front of the bordello at a gallop. Ned Sadler was only minutes ahead of him, but he was out of sight and there was no sound to tell which way he had gone. Ned would not go toward town, Scott knew, so he headed for the crossroads. Valuable minutes slipped by while Scott dismounted and studied the ground at the turnoff that intersected with the stage road. If Ned had turned right, he would be going toward Sagemore; to the left was the town of Hub. Scott found what he was looking for—fresh tracks with particles of soil still sifting into the hoofprints. Ned Sadler was riding toward Hub.

Pushing the bay hard, Scott raced along the stage road in pursuit of Ned Sadler. He rode low in the saddle, his jaw set to keep his teeth from chattering from the panic that clutched his stomach. He had concealed his fears from Earl McKay, but he knew Polly's life was in danger. He thought of the young Kansas girl whom Mitch Sadler had cut to pieces in a jealous rage; of Billy Clyde Marcum lying in a brush pile with a bullet in his back; of Deputy Doyle Joyner, killed behind his own jail; and of Frank Rawley writhing in the dust in front of the Pioneer Bank.

Somewhere in the moonlit night, Polly Wexler was with a cold-blooded killer and Scott wondered if she was alive or dead. Mitch was no fool. Joe Pike's attempt to capture him at the barn was enough to warn him that he had fallen among enemies, but would he associate Polly with the plot?

Scott hoped not. He shuddered as he peered at the road ahead of him. Worry lines pinched deeper into his face. He was sorry he had depended on Mitch's weakness for women to trap him, sorry he had allowed Polly to participate in the scheme, sorry that Joe Pike was lying near death with a gash in his skull, and sorry that he had waited so long to force a show-down. It was a seven-hour ride to Blackwood, and he had to pay off the Crowfoot's note before the Pioneer Bank closed at three o'clock tomorrow. It was already past midnight, and his chances of beating the deadline were growing more unlikely.

Thirty minutes along the trail he spotted a horseman silhouetted against the silvery sky. It was Ned Sadler, moving at a canter to conserve his horse's strength. Scott had not anticipated a long ride. The Sadlers had arrived each time at Big Betty's Place without any dust on their clothes or lather on their horses. Scott knew their camp was nearby and had hoped they had secreted their loot close to it. Ned's pace indicated otherwise. Evidently, the outlaws had hidden the Crowfoot money somewhere near Hub and had camped far away from it.

Scott slowed the bay and reined it to the edge of the road, where he could ride in the shadows cast by brush and trees. He kept his distance, watching Ned's back. Mitch and Polly could not be too far ahead, and Scott wished Ned would move faster, but there was nothing he could do to hurry him.

A mile from the outskirts of Hub, Ned left the stage

road and turned northward on a route that looked like an old wagon road. It cut a fifty-foot swath between brush and trees. Waist-high saplings had pushed through the hard-packed ground to make travel tedious. Scott followed, tracking Ned by sound for a while rather than sight, as the outlaw's horse threshed through the undergrowth.

He crossed a small rise and spotted him again on the lower ground. Scott heard the sound of gushing water, then saw reflections from a rock-strewn stream. The trail curved westward, running parallel with the creek bank. Scott recognized the terrain that Corey Millsap had described to him on his first visit to the Running Iron Saloon. Ned was leading him along Sawmill Springs, heading toward his family's old mill site and former home.

Scott's anxiety was almost unbearable. He glanced at the sky. The moon was not far along on its downward slope toward the western hills, and he might yet be able to save his ranch if his money was hidden at the old sawmill. He had more than time to worry about, however. He had expected to face only Ned Sadler when it came time for a showdown, but Mitch would also be present if he had not already taken the money and fled. With or without his money, Scott would never go back to Blackwood alive unless he could outshoot both of the Sadler brothers.

Ned Sadler kept going, paying no attention to his back trail. Scott was two hundred yards behind him, but since Ned did not know of the confrontation between his brother and Joe Pike, he had no reason to suspect he was being followed. Ned believed Mitch was about to take a new bride and flee Texas, and he was determined to claim his share of the stolen money.

Luck was not with Scott. The money was not hidden at the old mill. Hillsides dotted with stumps, a massive mound of age-blackened sawdust, a three-room house with a sagging porch, and piles of bark slabs marked the area of the lumbering operation, but Ned Sadler passed them by.

The two ridges that sheltered the creek on either side most of the way spread apart to form a narrow valley, with Sawmill Springs slicing it in the middle. The land was almost flat, broken in places by grotesque monuments of red sandstone, and Scott had to drop farther behind to keep from being seen. Ned was following a pattern, guiding his horse along the wriggling course of the creek, and Scott was not afraid of losing him.

He heard voices before he knew he was at the end of the ride. The sounds echoed from a line of rock-faced bluffs at the headwaters of Sawmill Springs. Scott had paused in the shadow of one of the monuments and was closer to Ned than he thought.

"I see you over there, Mitch!" Ned yelled. "I see you and I know what you're doing."

"What the hell . . ." Mitch Sadler's voice was equally loud but ragged with alarm. "Don't come near me, Ned. I've got Polly with me. She wants me to take her back to her folks and I'm going to do it."

Scott breathed a sigh of relief. Polly had been quick-witted enough to play along and stall for time. She had convinced Mitch her affection was sincere.

"You're not leaving with my half of the money," Ned shouted.

"Don't push me, Ned! I need all the money I can get. I'm taking the rancher's satchel, but you've still got some left from what we took from the bank."

The brothers continued to exchange words, but Scott was only half listening. He was too far away to challenge them. Judging by the sound of their voices, the Sadlers were a hundred feet to his right. Easing out of the saddle, he went forward on foot, darting between rocks and brush. He raised his head above a boulder and took a quick peek toward the bluffs. Mitch Sadler was standing in a patch of moonlight, one hand clutching Frank Rawley's canvas money bag and the other resting on his holstered gun.

Movement caught Scott's eye. He saw Polly Wexler walk between two standing horses and grasp the bridle of one of them. It was Joe Pike's black mustang. He wanted to shout at her, urge her to run while Mitch was distracted, but he decided it was already in her mind and that she was waiting for the right moment.

A shot rang out suddenly and Scott flinched. A spurt of flame flashed thirty feet in front of Mitch. The bullet from Ned Sadler's gun ricocheted off a rock near Mitch's leg and whined away in the darkness. Ned was standing erect now, his gun in his hand and angry words pouring from his mouth.

"I whipped you a hundred times when we were growing up, Mitch, and I can do it again. I'm coming after my money."

"Don't do it!" Mitch warned. "You know how I am. I

don't give in to anyone who tries to take something I want."

Ned's laugh was loud and scornful. "Yeah, I know. That's why I'm going to take my part of the money and get away from you forever. I figured we might end up in jail sometime, but you're going to get us hung."

"What's that supposed to mean?"

"You kill too many people—too quick and too easy."

"I do my job," Mitch snapped. "I killed that rancher as a favor to a friend, and I killed Doyle Joyner as a favor to myself. That Billy Clyde Marcum feller couldn't be trusted. He was mad because we lied to him about moving horses, then he threatened to bring the law down on us because Frank Rawley was a friend of his. He tried to run out on us, and I had to stop him."

Ned did not laugh again. He said, "You kill because you like to outdo people, but you won't kill your own brother."

"Yes I will, Ned. Don't force me. I'll kill you before I'll give up the money."

"No you won't." Ned Sadler strode forward, his Colt in his hand.

Polly Wexler chose that moment to make her getaway. She leaped into the mustang's saddle, swung it around, and galloped toward the other side of the valley.

Mitch Sadler ignored her. His gun hand was hidden from Ned, but Scott saw his arm move as he reached for his gun. Mitch's .45 came level with his hips, spitting fire and lead. Ned staggered backward, his arms windmilling from the force of the bullet that thudded into his chest. For the space of a heartbeat, he regained his balance. His voice died in his throat as he wailed, "Mi—i—i—t—t—ch," then Ned fell on the ground in a lifeless heap.

"Damn you!" Scott screamed. "Damn you!"

He left his hiding place and sprinted across the open space that separated him from Mitch Sadler.

Horror numbed Scott's brain. He sprinted into the open, propelled by muscles that seemed to have a mind of their own and no regard for caution. In spite of Mitch Sadler's reputation, Scott would not have believed his cruelty ran deep enough to allow him to gun down the brother who had been a friend and comrade all his life. After watching him deliberately kill Frank Rawley, Scott should have been immune to the shock of Mitch Sadler's crimes. He was evil beyond belief, a man who pursued women to feed his insatiable desires and murdered to have his way.

Scott was hardly aware that he had drawn his gun until he felt the recoil from the three quick shots he fired in Mitch's direction, shooting as he raced toward him. His uneven gait spoiled his aim and the shots sailed harmlessly past the outlaw. Mitch Sadler remained calm. He whirled and fired in a single motion. Scott's ribs suddenly felt as if they had been rammed by a hot poker.

Only then did he realize his actions were reckless and ineffective. He dived into a clay-walled ditch that wet weather had eroded to a depth of two feet. Panting, he hugged the ground, cringing as a second slug from Mitch Sadler's gun dug into the rim of the ditch and showered him with dirt.

Rational thinking overcame his rage. He was determined to end Mitch Sadler's killing days, but his haste had left him at a disadvantage. The outlaw might keep him pinned down in the ditch for hours. If he was still there when the sky grew lighter, Mitch could climb the bluff and have a clear view of Scott's outstretched form.

Rolling to one side, Scott ran his hand gingerly over his ribs. His shirt was wet with blood, and the throbbing pain was worse. The bullet had torn into bone, but it glanced away without penetrating his body. He gritted his teeth and shifted his shoulders so his gun hand would be ready for a quick move. His hat had fallen off and rolled away when he dived into the ditch, and he could feel the night air blowing over the sweat that pasted strands of hair to his forehead. Except for the roaring of rapids where Sawmill Springs came to earth at the base of the bluff, the land was silent.

The stillness was nerve-racking. Scott searched his mind for a way to outsmart Mitch Sadler. Thirty feet away, the outlaw was watching and waiting for a chance to kill him. He raised his head cautiously to see if Mitch had taken cover among the giant boulders that had broken from the bluffs and rolled onto the valley floor over eons of time. A gunshot shattered the silence. Mitch's bullet came so close to Scott's head he could feel the warmth of the air left in its wake.

"That you, George Pratt?" Mitch yelled.

Scott's muscles tensed. "You don't have to call me that any more. My name's Scott Rawley—son of the man you killed in Blackwood."

"God!" The single word uttered by Mitch Sadler revealed his thoughts. He was the target of a man driven by vengeance, and he knew such men seldom gave up a chase.

"There's only one way you can leave here alive," Scott said, remembering the sickness he felt when he killed Pat Logan. "Throw your gun over here, come to me with your hands up, and I'll turn you over to the law. Maybe you can blow the sheriff apart and escape, or maybe he'll hang you."

"You're barking at the moon, cowboy! I thought you were some kind of lawman like Joe Pike. I bashed his brains out, and I'll do worse to you. Polly's waiting for me down the trail a ways, and we're going east. I'm going to start a new life, buy a plantation, and become a gentleman. I won't let you—"

Scott wanted to worry the man, rattle his thinking and slow his reflexes. He said, "Polly set you up, Mitch. She's not waiting for you. She's waiting for me."

"That's a lie!" Mitch's voice lost its level tone, rising in pitch. "She's in love with me. She wasn't surprised when I found those Pinkerton cards in Pike's pocket. Pike was trying to collect the price on my head, and Polly says she thinks you're a lawman, too. She doesn't like either of you, and she's tired of the work she's doing."

Boots crunched on rock as Mitch moved to another location, seeking cover in a spot closer to Scott. The outlaw was silent for only a few seconds. He said, "I hate a standoff. Let's see who's the best man. You've got thrcc shots left and I've got two. Stand up and we'll fire away until somebody falls."

Scott had a better idea, one inspired by the man's own

words. Mitch was too arrogant to consider reloading his gun as long as he had a bullet left. Scott had fired three times, and Mitch had counted the shots. He thought they were on an equal footing, but Scott was going to change those odds. Mitch waited for a reply, assuming that his reputation would keep a man from risking the few seconds his gun would be useless if he took time to replenish his ammunition.

"Have you got the guts for a shoot-out?" Mitch shouted.

"There's no reason for that," Scott said. "Earl McKay was trailing behind me. He'll be along any minute, and we'll get you in a cross fire. I'll wait on Earl."

A derisive laugh came from Mitch Sadler's throat. "That's another of your lies. It doesn't bother me, though. If Earl wants to throw in with you, I'll kill him, too. I'll wait you out."

Scott was busy while he kept the man talking. He flipped the three spent shells from the Colt's cylinder and replaced them with two cartridges from his gunbelt. One chamber remained empty. Scott carefully adjusted the cylinder so the vacant space would fall under the hammer on the fourth time he pulled the trigger.

"I don't see your helper anywhere," Mitch chided. Mitch's confidence was growing, and it suited Scott's purpose. Lying on his stomach, his elbows braced, he gathered a handful of dirt from the ditch and threw it over the top. It sounded like a heavy rain as it fell on the rocks and bushes.

Mitch Sadler laughed again. "If you're looking for me to give you a powder flash to fire at, you'll have to do better. That's an old trick."

Keeping his head low, Scott laid his wrist on the rim of the ditch and fired three shots in the direction of Mitch's voice. He let the echoes die, waited for silence to return, then squeezed the Colt's trigger again. The sharp click of the spring-loaded hammer was clearly audible in the stillness as it snapped against the empty chamber.

Again there was a crunch of boot heels in the rocky soil. Mitch Sadler was on the move.

"Tough luck, cowboy!" Mitch cried triumphantly. "Sounds like you're hitting on empty. I'm going to fill you full of lead like shooting fish in a pond!"

Mitch was running, counting on reaching the ditch before Scott could reload. Scott was already rising, thumbing the hammer back to let a live cartridge roll in place beneath it. Mitch Sadler was fifteen feet away, sprinting through the rocks with his gun hand waving up and down to help him keep his balance. He tried to stop, stunned by the sight of Scott's tall shadow looming in front of him. Sliding, half off balance, Mitch was still quick and deadly. He swung his gun around at arm's length, and the roar of two guns exploding simultaneously was like a thunderclap.

CHAPTER TWENTY-THREE

A BULLET plowed into the ground a yard from Scott's feet while his own gun was still vibrating in his hand. He saw part of Mitch Sadler's face fall apart. Scott's bullet struck the outlaw's left cheekbone, shattering it like an eggshell before it bored into his skull. Mitch made no sound. One leg remained extended momentarily, as if it were reaching for another step, and Mitch seemed to hang in midair before his body bent backward and lifeless weight pulled him down.

Scott's shoulders sagged. He holstered his gun and took a deep breath. The acrid odor of powder mingled with the earthy smell of wet moss from the creek banks. He walked slowly to Mitch Sadler's side. The outlaw lay on his back. His platinum hair was splattered with blood and his gunmetal eyes were open and staring, locked in death with much the same appearance they had when he was alive.

The leather fob of Frank Rawley's watch was visible in the moonlight. Scott lifted it out of Mitch's vest, glanced at the dial, and put it in his shirt pocket. His fingers touched the tally sheet that he had carried most of the time since his father's death. Sweat and wear had turned it limp and gray, and the smear of Frank Rawley's blood on the page had glued the folds together.

He turned the paper over in his hand, recalling the words he had spoken to Sheriff Wade Bandy. . . . "When I've settled with Pa's killer, I'll burn it."

Scott did not have a match, but it seemed important that he leave some symbol of his father's life where Mitch Sadler had died. He tore the tally sheet into strips and dropped them on the outlaw's chest. The money bag, which Mitch had been clawing out of the rocks when Ned caught up with him, lay on a slab of sandstone nearby. A burning pain raced through Scott's injured ribs as he clambered over boulders to get it.

He loosened the buckles and looked inside the bag. The bank notes appeared intact. He sighed with relief. He had guessed that the Sadlers would spend the small bills they had taken from the bank first, holding the large denomination bank notes until they could use them without attracting undue attention.

Taking a final look at the two bodies lying a few feet apart, Scott went back to his horse. He felt neither sad nor triumphant about the killing of Mitch Sadler. He had avenged his father's death, but unless he could find Polly Wexler quickly and get her safely back to Big Betty's Place, he could not reach Blackwood soon enough to stop the bank from selling his ranch.

It took him almost an hour to locate the girl. He rode through the brush and saplings of the valley floor calling her name, but there was no reply. Finally, he heard a horse nicker, and Scott followed the sound to a thicket where Polly was hiding. She was hunkered down on the ground, holding the reins of Joe Pike's mustang, too frightened to make a sound until she was sure it was him.

The white collar on Polly's dress caught Scott's attention and led him to her. He stepped from his saddle and said, "Come on out, Polly. Let's go home."

She ran toward him, flung her arms around him, and sobbed against his chest. "Oh, thank God! The way things echo here, I wasn't sure who was calling me. I heard the gunshots and thought you might be—"

"Not me," Scott cut in wearily. "The Sadlers are both dead. Mitch shot Ned—killed his brother for you and a bag of money. I killed Mitch."

Her hand touched the crusty surface of Scott's shirt

and she drew away from him, a worried look in her eyes. The blood had dried and his shirt was stuck to his ribs.

"You're hurt," Polly said. "Let's get some water and clean the wound so I can see how bad it is."

Scott shook his head. "It hurts, but it won't kill me. We need to get away from here."

"Can you still get to the bank in time?"

"I doubt it," said Scott, "but I'm going to try."

"You might save some time if you'd start to Blackwood when we get to the stage road. I can find my way back."

"My horse will be worn out by the time we get that far. I'll need to borrow Betty Kelton's dun to get me home. I'll send it back by my hired hand. I'm not leaving anyway until I find out if Joe Pike's alive or dead."

The sun was bright and hot by the time they reached the bordello. His eyes puffy from the lack of sleep, Earl McKay rushed to meet them when they stopped at the hitching rail. He had spent most of the night sitting on the porch, waiting to see if Scott and Polly would return safely.

Joe Pike had survived. The doctor McKay brought from town closed the gash in the Pinkerton man's head with a dozen stitches and stayed at his bedside until Pike regained consciousness shortly after dawn.

"He's had a good breakfast, lots of coffee, and is raising Cain because he has to stay in bed," McKay told Scott. "He's been worried about you." Pointing to Scott's shirt, he added, "Looks like you could use a doctor yourself."

"Wouldn't hurt," Scott conceded, "but I don't have time."

Leaving Polly to answer McKay's questions about the Sadler brothers, Scott went to the bedroom to talk with Joe Pike.

Propped up on pillows, his head covered with bandages, Pike had drawn himself to a sitting position on Betty Kelton's bed. Iris and Rose were at his side, offering wet cloths for his forehead, smoothing the bed, and trying to make him comfortable. They stepped back as Scott entered, greeted him in soft tones, and asked questions about the blood on his shirt.

In the midst of his replies, he saw their attention shift, and he heard footsteps behind him. He blinked in surprise when he looked over his shoulder and saw Millie Adcock. She had come from the kitchen with a fresh cup of coffee in her hands. Her hair was slightly mussed and she looked tired, but her eyes brightened when she saw Scott.

"I'm so glad you're safe!" Millie said. She put the cup on a table beside Pike's bed and took Scott's arm, pulling him around to look at his shirt. "I heard you telling the girls your wound wasn't bad, but you've lost a lot of blood. Men tell a lot of lies before they'll admit they're hurt. Are you sure you're all right?"

"Not the best," Scott admitted, "but I'm not off my feet. I didn't expect to see you here."

Millie told him how she learned of Joe Pike's injury. The doctor who treated him had returned to the Elkhorn for breakfast, and she overheard him talking about attending to a wounded man at Big Betty's Place.

"I got my horse from the livery and came right out, wondering all the way whether it was you or Joe."

"Looks like it's both," Scott said, chuckling.

Millie sat down on the edge of Joe Pike's bed. She ran her fingers along his hairline, then kissed him lightly on the cheek. Polly Wexler came in from the porch and the women flocked to her, exchanging hugs and smiles. Pike had been awake long enough to tell Rose and Iris about the arrangement he and Scott had made with the girl, and they showered Polly with compliments.

"I certainly wasn't acting out of bravery," Polly admitted wearily. "I did it for the reward. I'm going home at last!"

Everyone seemed to be talking at once for a few minutes, but the din gradually subsided and Polly turned her attention to Joe Pike. She patted his hand, inspected the bandage on his head, and wished him a speedy recovery.

Pike assured her he was feeling better, then the women went to the kitchen and left the two men alone.

Except for his boots, Pike was fully clothed and he appeared alert despite the ashen color of his face. He said, "Nobody's told me anything. I've been listening and guessing. You're here and the Sadlers ain't, so I reckon you got them. Looks like you picked up some lead."

Scott lifted his arm, wincing as his shirt tugged at the wound. "Mitch's first shot took some meat and bone off my ribs. I lost my head when I saw Mitch shoot Ned, and it's a wonder I'm not dead."

"Mitch killed his brother?"

Scott nodded, then gave Pike a brief account of the

fight at Sawmill Springs. "I got Mitch. I got my money, too."

"Figured you would. That means Pinkerton owes you some more pay, since you made sure the company can collect the rewards."

"To hell with that," Scott replied, shaking his head. "Can you believe a man would kill his blood-kin like that?"

Pike's voice was less vibrant than usual, but the drawl was the same. "I've heard of men like Mitch, but I never met one. He liked killing . . . liked the feeling of power it gave him. Brothers, friends, enemies, or dogs look the same to men like that when they fear they're about to lose that power."

Scott changed the subject. He felt pressed for time but hesitated to leave. His chest ached when he breathed, and he was not sure he had enough energy left to take him to Blackwood.

He gave Pike a searching look and asked, "Are you going to be all right?"

"Sure I am," Pike replied, and his behavior was reassuring. He complained about being bedfast and recited things which needed to be done that he could not do.

"That fool doctor said I had a concession, or concussion, or something like that. He said I'd best lay here all day if I didn't want to pass out. I'll have to send Earl McKay on my errands. Pinkerton headquarters needs to be notified the Sadlers are dead, and somebody needs to tell Deputy Cal Baylor where to find their bodies. It will take a few days, but I'll see that Polly gets her money. I won't be coming back to this place, but Rose Spring says she wants to talk to Betty Kelton about taking it over. If that works out—"

He left the words dangling and appeared embarrassed. "Hell, I'm keeping you, and I know time's about up for you."

Glancing through the window, measuring the shadows outside, Scott said, "It's already too late. I can't make it before the bank closes, but I'm going home. Maybe I can talk Otis Potter into breaking his rules and taking my money. If I can't, I might make him eat it."

"That's what I'd do," Pike said.

A dry wind blew out of the western hills, filling the air with swirling sand that chased most of Blackwood's foot traffic indoors. A few horses stood at the tie rails, heads drooping and tails tucked. Sitting astride Betty Kelton's dun horse, Scott Rawley came off the prairie with his head bowed and his hat tugged low to keep the dust out of his eyes.

He turned the corner at Arlie's Blacksmith Shop and headed down Main Street, a tall dark man with weariness in his bearing and a look of defeat in his ice-blue eyes. He looked at the drawn blinds of the Pioneer Bank and, without pausing, drew his father's watch from the pocket of his hide vest to check the time. It was half past four, too late for banking business.

A lump of muscle rumpled his jaw, drawing the skin tight beneath the day-old black stubble on his face. He had not been able to get away from Big Betty's Place as early as he had anticipated, but the time had not been wasted. He knew he could not make the ride home without renewing his strength, and Scott had not eaten in twelve hours. After a breakfast of steak and eggs, which Rose prepared while he was talking with Joe Pike, he went to the well at the back of the house to wash away the dust and blood.

His wound was more serious than he had admitted. Tiny slivers of bone poked through a spoon-shaped slash where Mitch Sadler had shot away part of his lower rib. He stripped to the waist, splashed water over his body, and tried to rub the sleepiness out of his eyes. With the caked blood removed, the wound started oozing blood again. He washed his shirt at the same time but carried it back to the house with him, deciding it was useless to wear it until he stopped the bleeding.

Millie met him at the kitchen door, gasped at the blood running down his bare torso, and ushered him to the bedroom. Joe Pike had seen many a bullet wound and was not as concerned about Scott's injury as the girl was. Scott watched him while Millie wrapped clean cloths around his chest and pinned them in place. The Pinkerton man's usually stoic face softened and his eyes followed the girl's every move. Joe Pike was in love with Millie Adcock, and Scott suspected he would soon be resigning his job with the Pinkerton National Detective Agency.

It was probable, Scott thought as he rode along Blackwood's Main Street, that Millie and Joe Pike would find more happiness than he ever would. He was not sure who he dreaded to face the most — the banker Otis Potter, or his father's old friend and employee, Hobe Calder.

The banker had to come first, and Scott knew where to find him. A widower with no children, Otis Potter had few interests in life except his business, and he was never in a hurry to get home after the bank closed. It was his custom to walk leisurely down the street to the Texas Star Saloon each day at three o'clock, take a table in a dark corner at the right of the bar, and spend two hours relaxing while he read a newspaper and consumed two drinks of bourbon—never more, never less.

Scott found him there. The sound of the money bag plopping on the table in front of him startled Otis Potter. He yanked the newspaper away from his face and rolled his hound-dog eyes when he saw Scott standing over him.

"There's enough cash there to pay Pa's note and have some left over," Scott said coldly. "I know you're stuck on rules, but you can't sell the Crowfoot because I'm an hour or so late. Take the money."

The banker's heavy jowls quivered. "I can't take it. That matter was settled this morning. The board met to start legal proceedings for the foreclosure and we—"

His explanation broke off, garbled by frightened, blubbering sounds in his throat. Scott had slipped into the chair opposite Otis Potter. The tip of his Colt's barrel was resting on the banker's knee as Scott said, "You're going to take the money and tear up the note, or I'm going to shoot a hole in your crotch."

"There's—there's no need for bad feelings," Otis Potter stammered. "Threats would never make me surrender my integrity, but you don't have a note at the bank. Our meeting ended when—"

"Damn you! Have you turned it over to John Tripp already?"

Slowly, Otis Potter regained his composure and there was a look akin to mischief in his eyes. "No, I mean you're out of debt. Milam Huff objected to the foreclosure. He paid off your note. Milam came here with money years ago, and he's done well with his livery. He said he owed you his life, and helping you out was the least he could do. Milam was sure you'd pay him back someday."

Scott's mouth fell open and he leaned limply back in his chair. He had complained many times to Milam Huff about the liveryman's excessive show of gratitude after Scott had rescued him from an attack by a bullying drifter. He would complain no more.

Shrugging sheepishly, too awed to speak above a whisper, Scott said, "Thank you, Mr. Potter. Thank you!"

He holstered his gun, picked up the money bag, and went back to his horse. The bartender yelled a greeting as he left, and several of the Texas Star patrons called his name. Scott raised his hand in a wave that included all of them, but he remembered only the face of Otis Potter.

The wind had died down, the dust was settling, and for the first time in three weeks, life looked bright and promising. The excitement that warmed his blood was born of happiness instead of fear and uncertainty. It would be good to go home again, to tell Hobe Calder the Crowfoot Ranch would remain in the family for another generation, but their reunion would have to wait until tomorrow.

Scott had other plans for the rest of the day. First he

would go to the livery and pay Milam Huff, then let a doctor give him something to ease the pain from the bullet wound. Later, he planned to rent a room at the Denver House, take a warm bath, and rest a while before he returned to the street. He had caught a glimpse of Della Grange through the windows of her father's store when he rode in, and memories of the day a gunshot interrupted their conversation flashed through his mind. Moments before Mitch Sadler shot down Frank Rawley at the Pioneer Bank, Scott was trying to tell Della he was leaving for the Big Muddy and a job on the riverboats. He was glad she had not heard him.

He would be waiting for Della when the store closed, and he planned to share with her his vision of the years to come, when their children would stand proudly on the home range of a cattle empire that he and his father had carved from the Texas grasslands. Before the night ended, he was sure he would have no regrets over his decision to live out his days with Della at the Crowfoot Ranch.

Center Point Publishing
600 Brooks Road ● PO Box 1
Thorndike ME 04986-0001 USA

(207) 568-3717

US & Canada:
1 800 929-9108